Praise for *Murder on the Rocks*
Book One in the Gray Whale Inn Mystery Series

"[An] appealing debut—this is a new cozy author worth investigating."—*Publishers Weekly*

"Sure to please cozy readers."—*Library Journal*

"…It may be old-fashioned to describe a book as charming, but MacInerney's writing is ~~~~~~ ~~~~~~~~~ htful,

co   wit.

                                                                    s.

                                                                    t

7/18/07

DEAD
and
BERRIED

OTHER BOOKS BY KAREN MACINERNEY

Murder on the Rocks

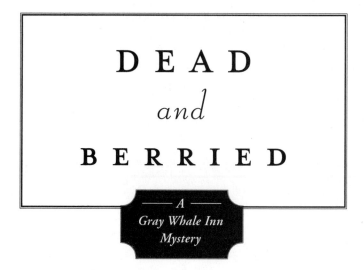

DEAD
and
BERRIED

A
Gray Whale Inn
Mystery

Karen MacInerney

MIDNIGHT INK
WOODBURY, MINNESOTA

First Edition
First Printing, 2007

Book design by Donna Burch
Cover design by Ellen Dahl
Cover illustration © 2006 Bob Dombrowski/Artworks
Editing by Connie Hill

Midnight Ink, an imprint of Llewellyn Publications

Library of Congress Cataloging-in-Publication Data
Dead and berried : a Gray Whale Inn mystery / Karen MacInerney. — 1st ed.
     p.   cm.
  ISBN 13: 978-0-7387-0914-7 (alk. paper)
  ISBN 10: 0-7387-0914-X (alk. paper)
  1. Hotelkeepers—Maine—Fiction. 2. Bed and breakfast accommodations—Maine—Fiction. 3. Murder—Investigation—Fiction. 4. Craberry Isles (Me. : Islands)—Fiction. I. Title

PS3613.A27254D43   2006
813'.6—dc22   2006046922

This is a work of fiction. Names, characters, places, and incidents are either the product of the author's imagination or are used fictitiously, and any resemblance to actual persons, living or dead, business establishments, events, or locales is entirely coincidental.

Midnight Ink
Llewellyn Publications
2143 Wooddale Drive, Dept. 0-7387-0914-X
Woodbury, MN 55125-2989, U.S.A.
www.midnightinkbooks.com

Printed in the United States of America

DEDICATION

For Eric, my partner in crime—and everything else.
I love you!

ACKNOWLEDGMENTS

I want to start by thanking my husband, Eric, and my children, Abby and Ian, for helping me find the time to do all this—and for volunteering their creative ideas for potential murder victims and methods. (Ian, I'm sorry I couldn't work in the fireballs; maybe next time.) Eric, thanks in particular for graciously executing all those little plot and design tasks I keep hitting you with—and for manning the fort while I'm out on the road. A writer couldn't ask for a better husband.

As always, Dorothy and Ed MacInerney, Carol and Dave Swartz, and my wonderful grandmother Marian Quinton deserve my unending gratitude for all their love and support. Thanks also to Jessica Faust, my fabulous agent, and Barbara Moore, Alison Aten, Connie Hill, Jerry Rogers, Brett Fechheimer, and the rest of the folks at Midnight Ink; I couldn't ask for a more supportive publishing team.

I want to thank Austin Mystery Writers, including Mark Bentsen, Andrew Butler, Dave Ciambrone, Judy Egner, Laney Henelley, Mary Jo Powell, Kimberly Sandman, Rie Sheridan, and Sylvia Dickey Smith, for their honest and thoughtful critique—and their friendship. I recommend you buy their published works immediately; if you can't find all of them yet, I have no doubt you'll be able to soon. Thanks also to my fellow mystery authors the Cozy Chicks for their humor, camaraderie, creativity, and support— Laura Durham, Diana Killian, Michele Scott, Maggie Sefton, J. B. Stanley, and Heather Webber. Their books are all fabulous and available at your local bookseller, and I recommend you read them all them the moment you put this book down. After you've finished it, that is.

Continuing thanks to Lindsey Schram, Melanie Williams, Debbie Pacitti, Mary Flanagan, Dana Lehman, and Bethann and Beau Eccles for their friendship and support—I'd be lost without you. My fellow author Candy Calvert also deserves special mention—she's made the road to publication (and beyond) a heck of a lot of fun. To Susan Wittig Albert, thanks for the words of wisdom; and to Barbara Burnett Smith, I miss you every day.

I particularly want to thank *Bed and Breakfast America Magazine*, the Maine Innkeepers' Association and Midnight Ink for their enthusiastic support of the Muffins are Murder contest, with special thanks to *Bed and Breakfast America* for publishing the Gray Whale Inn mystery stories in their terrific magazine. Thanks also to all the readers who sent in their recipes and spread the word about the contest—my judges gained five pounds each testing them, and I now have several new holiday favorites. (Barbara Hahn's Berried Medley Lemon Streusel Muffins was the winning recipe, in case you were wondering.)

And last but not least, thanks to all of the folks who have read *Murder on the Rocks* and taken the time to tell me what you thought—your wonderful e-mails have gotten me through many tough days at the keyboard!

ONE

I HAD GOTTEN USED to nighttime noises. When you live in a 150-year-old inn, you do. Guests bang around in their rooms, the pipes thump and clank in the walls, and the wind sometimes moans as it slithers past the eaves.

But I'd never heard anything from the attic before.

I sat bolt upright and glanced at the clock on the night table. 3:32. Biscuit hissed at the ceiling, her eyes glowing in the clock's greenish light. I fumbled for the bedside lamp and switched it on. The tabby's ginger-colored tail had puffed up to three times its normal size, and the fur on her back bristled.

Blood thundered in my ears as I sat motionless, listening. The waves slip-slapped against the rocks below the inn, and a stray breeze whispered past the window, but the ceiling above me lay silent. As the minutes stretched by, my body relaxed. It was probably just the wind.

I was reaching to turn off the light when it happened again. A soft thump, right over my head. I jerked my arm back and grabbed a fistful of down comforter, pulling it up to my chin. There had been nothing in the "How to Run a Bed and Breakfast" manual about dealing with freeloading guests in the attic. Or ghosts.

Several months ago, as we sat in the warm yellow kitchen downstairs, my friend Charlene had told me that the inn was supposed to be haunted. Since the only annoying manifestations to date had been demanding guests who didn't pay their bills, I had shrugged it off.

The whole ghost idea had a bit more credence alone in my bedroom on a moonless October night. My tongue felt thick in my mouth as I swallowed. A moment later, the thump was followed by a creak from the boards above my bed.

Biscuit bolted from the bed and scrabbled at the bedroom door. A creak answered from above, and she made a low sound deep in her throat before abandoning the door to scuttle under the white dust ruffle of my bed. I wanted to cram myself in beside her, but I didn't think I'd fit.

My eyes shot to the phone on the dresser. I could call my neighbor, John. He was the island's deputy. He would be here in five minutes, and I could join Biscuit under the bed and let him deal with the attic.

It was tempting, but I hesitated. John and I had started seeing each other recently, and I didn't want him to think I was pulling the damsel-in-distress routine. I glanced down at my faded flannel nightshirt. If John did come over, it would be pretty obvious that seduction wasn't my goal. Or that if it was, I wasn't very good at it.

I listened for a few moments more, but whatever was up there had fallen silent. Why had I tossed out my pepper spray? When I lived in Texas, I kept a small canister in my night table drawer.

While packing to move to Maine, though, I pitched it, along with several pairs of legwarmers and the paperback edition of *The Smart Woman's Guide to Finding Mr. Right.*

Tonight, as I slipped out from under the covers and eased myself onto the icy wood floor, I was wishing I hadn't been so thorough. Another board creaked overhead. Adrenaline shot through me. Pepper spray probably wasn't effective on ghosts anyway. If it *was* a ghost.

The cold air on the bare skin of my calves made my goose bumps grow a few sizes larger as I slid open the night table drawer and dug for the flashlight. Power outages on Cranberry Island were common enough that I kept a flashlight by the bed, and my hand quickly closed on the familiar plastic cylinder. I flicked the switch. Nothing.

Cursing, I rifled through the drawer again. My hand closed on a matchbox and I was fumbling for a candle when I spotted an old book light in the jumble. I grabbed it and flipped it open. A weak circle of watery light gleamed on the floor. It would have to do.

I crept to the bedroom door and turned the cold knob. The door squeaked as it swung open, and something brushed against my ankle. A scream froze in my throat when I glimpsed a flash of orange tearing down the hall.

I was headed toward the attic, but Biscuit wasn't about to join me. For the first time, I wished I had chosen a large dog, something in the Doberman family, instead of a chubby orange tabby cat as an animal companion.

As I tiptoed down the hallway toward the hatch in the ceiling, something clattered above me. *Ghost*, my mind whispered. *Poltergeist.* I hadn't thought about ghost stories for years, but now my mind churned up every spooky tale I had ever heard: the footsteps of small children, desperate to escape from phantom flames; the shades of women murdered by jealous husbands; tortured souls who had hanged themselves in a basement or an attic. *An attic.*

Nonsense. How could you walk across the attic if you were stuck hanging from the rafters? It was probably just a squirrel. A big squirrel.

As I reached for the pull cord, I reflected that I hadn't seen any squirrels around the Gray Whale Inn. The ceiling creaked again as my hand closed around the end of the string. If whatever was up there was a squirrel, it had been doing some major steroids.

I drew a ragged breath and jerked the hatch down toward me. The rusted hinges screeched in protest. I yanked the ladder open, and a black hole yawned above me. I thrust the book light up and played the feeble beam over the dusty rafters. Nothing. I fought the urge to run back to my room and bury myself under the covers. Instead, I forced one shaky foot onto the bottom rung.

You're a thirty-nine-year-old woman. Whatever's up there, you can handle it. I climbed the ladder cautiously, and my head was soon immersed in cold, empty darkness. I shone the pale light all around the attic. The wavering beam illuminated two broken ladder-back chairs, a rusted iron headboard, and a dilapidated hatbox. The air shuddered out of my chest. It must have been a squirrel, after all.

Then I ran the beam across the floorboards above my bedroom.

I knew I had heard footsteps. But the thin film of dust on the floor above my room lay undisturbed.

———

I woke the next morning with a start. It was 7:40; I had overslept by more than an hour. I hurled myself out of bed, wriggled into a pair of jeans and a sweatshirt, and sprinted down the stairs to the kitchen.

In the pale light of morning, last night's wild imaginings seemed far away. The early sun reflected off the antique pine floors, making the buttery yellow walls glow. As I filled the coffeemaker's glass carafe and glanced at the mound of sheets and towels peeking out from behind the laundry room door, I felt a twinge of misgiving. Polly Sarkes usually came and helped me with the laundry twice a week, but she hadn't shown up yesterday morning.

Polly had lived on the island her entire life. Her broad, cheerful face, surrounded by a halo of hair that frizzed up when it was humid, was a welcome sight in the mornings—and she was a housecleaning whiz. I'd hired her in July, when the number of dirty towels the inn produced started to give me nightmares about piles of soiled linens creeping up the stairs to smother me in my bed. Although the laundry had receded to a manageable level and I no longer needed help—in fact, I really couldn't afford it—I knew that Polly needed the work, and I couldn't bring myself to let her go.

In her early forties, Polly had never married, devoting her substantial warmth and affection to the cats she cared for. Polly was practical, cheerful, and very thorough. Which was why I was worried; it wasn't like Polly not to show up without calling, and she wasn't answering her phone.

My eyes lingered on the overflowing laundry baskets. If Polly didn't call this morning, I would go looking for her.

A few minutes later, the soothing aroma of freshly ground Moka Java and the reassuring gurgle of the coffeemaker filled the kitchen.

I reached into the refrigerator and pulled out eggs and butter for Peach Sunrise Coffee Cake, one of my favorite recipes. I glanced at the clock; it was already a quarter to eight. If I hurried, I could have the cake out of the oven just before nine. Breakfast officially started at 8:30, but with any luck, my guests would come down late.

The summer season at the Gray Whale Inn, the bed and breakfast I had started six months earlier, had been good, but the steady stream of guests had dried to a trickle after Labor Day. My stomach lurched when I thought of the unbooked months ahead. Between the heating bills and the mortgage, I needed at least a few guests over the winter if I wanted the inn to survive until spring. Maybe I would have to look for a part-time job. Doing what, I wondered? Knitting hats for the local gift shop? I didn't knit, but if the bookings didn't start coming, there might be plenty of time to learn.

I was searching for the sour cream when the kitchen door creaked behind me. I whirled around, heart thumping, but it was only Biscuit. She gazed up at me with wide green eyes and meowed as she sidled over to me, wrapping herself around my calves as if she hadn't abandoned me in my hour of need. "Traitor," I muttered as I bent down and rubbed her head.

As I filled a bowl with dry cat food and pushed the pantry door closed, the creak of the hinges sent a chill down my back. I thought what I'd heard last night had come from the attic, but could it have been something on the roof? I shivered slightly as I unwrapped the butter and plopped it into a large bowl. I didn't believe in ghosts, but last night had given me the creeps.

I glanced out the window. The rising sun had ignited the russet and gold of Mount Cadillac on the mainland, and the stretch of cold seawater beneath it was stippled with the pale peach of early morning. I tore my eyes from the window and rooted through the drawer for the beaters. There would be plenty of time to admire the view later. I had just located the beaters when the kitchen door creaked again.

I turned quickly, brandishing a wooden spoon, and stifled a groan. So much for late-rising guests. Candy Perkins stood at the door, a pink tee shirt stretched tight across her ample bosom. Her bright, cotton-candy smile and artificially rosy cheeks made her look like an overgrown Shirley Temple. My eyes drifted toward her chest. A well-developed, overgrown Shirley Temple.

"Good morning, Nat!" She spoke in a squeaky, bubbly voice I had always associated with teenaged girls. She walked over to the well-scrubbed pine farm table, pulled out a sparkly notepad and a purple pen, and sat down.

Her curly blonde hair was still wet from a shower and framed her round, pink face like a mass of corkscrews. My eyes strayed down to her tee shirt; today's slogan was "Girls Just Want to Have Funds."

"Hi, Candy." I tried to return her perky smile. "You're up early."

"I hope you don't mind," she chirped. "I thought I'd watch you go through your morning routine and take some notes." Candy had been staying at the inn for three days now. She was an aspiring bed-and-breakfast owner, and had decided to pick the Gray Whale Inn as a study subject. At first, I had been flattered. But after seventy-two hours of Candy watching my every move, I was feeling a bit stifled. "Mind if I have a cup of coffee?" she asked.

I nodded toward the coffee pot. "Help yourself. Mugs are up on the shelf. Cream is in the fridge, and the sugar bowl is next to the pot."

"Oh, no sugar and cream for me." She patted her flat belly lightly. "Carbs go right to my waistline." As she trotted past me toward the coffee, she peered at the mixing bowl with interest. "What are we making today?"

"Peach Sunrise Coffee Cake," I said, determined to be friendly. "It's one of my favorite recipes."

"Wow," she said, surveying the ingredients. "That's a lot of butter. And sour cream, too?"

"Uh-huh." I lowered the beaters into the bowl and grimaced. Nothing spoiled a good coffee cake like a skinny person looking over your shoulder and staging an impromptu lecture on the dangers of fat grams and carbohydrates. Candy hadn't reached her stride on the subject yet, but I knew it was imminent.

Candy poured herself a cup of coffee and minced back to the table as the beaters whirled, transforming the eggs and milk into a pale gold liquid. I turned the mixer off and reached for the flour, blotting all thoughts of calories from my mind and anticipating the flavor of the moist cake, drenched in butter and brown sugar and studded with peaches.

Candy's voice floated over my shoulder. "What else is on the menu?"

I glanced back at her. "Cheesy scrambled eggs, sausage patties, and broiled grapefruit."

Candy's eyes flitted to my waist, which I had to admit was a bit larger than it used to be. "Gosh. I don't know how I'm going to keep my figure in this business," she said.

I tugged down my sweatshirt and turned on the mixer again as I assembled the dry components. I was pleased to discover that the whir of the beaters made further conversation impossible. By the time I turned the mixer off, the eggs and milk were practically foam.

"Have you ever considered low-carb breakfasts?" Candy piped up as soon as the beaters stopped. She looked pointedly at my midriff. "It might help."

I smiled and turned the beaters back on again while I cut the butter into the flour mixture, letting them run until the last possible moment. The cake might be a tad chewy, but the silence was worth it.

Quickly, I assembled the layers of batter, peaches, and raspberry cream. I had just poured the last of the batter over the rows of sliced peaches and slid the pan into the oven when the phone rang. I said a small prayer of thanks—now that the mixer was off, I could see Candy preparing to launch into her favorite topic again—and grabbed for the receiver.

"Good afternoon, Gray Whale Inn."

"Afternoon? It's not even eight o'clock." I smiled at the bright voice of my best friend, Charlene Kean. In addition to her duties as postmistress and gossip queen, she also owned and ran the only grocery store in town. She wasn't what I had expected in a Mainer—her taste in clothes was more Neiman Marcus than L. L. Bean, and she regularly took large consignments of Mary Kay cosmetics—but we had become fast friends almost from the moment I set foot on the island.

"Sorry, Charlene. I'm a little short on sleep." I cracked an egg into a large mixing bowl as I spoke. I was about to tell Charlene about the noises in the attic, but glanced at Candy, whose blue eyes were still tracking me, and stopped myself. "What's up?" I asked instead.

"I didn't get a chance to call you yesterday, but I've got a special delivery down here for you," she said.

"A special delivery? What is it?"

"I don't know, but it's in a styrofoam cooler. Says it has to be frozen after forty-eight hours. I stuck it in the freezer. The return address is some town in Texas."

Texas? I had spent fifteen years working for the Texas Department of Parks and Wildlife in Austin, but I wasn't expecting any deliveries from that part of the world.

I emptied another egg and discarded the shell. "That's strange."

"Do you want me to bring it out to you?" Charlene asked. "Or are you coming down to the store later?"

I eyed the tub of home-baked toffee squares I had been planning to take down to Charlene's that afternoon. In addition to the coffee cakes and scones my kitchen produced for inn guests, I often made treats to sell at the store for a few extra dollars—and to entice people to stay at the inn. So far it hadn't worked out too well—usually Charlene ate them all and then complained about how her pants were fitting—but I was still trying.

"I'll probably be down as soon as breakfast is over," I said. "By the way, have you heard from Polly?"

"No, I haven't. Why?"

"I'm worried about her. She was supposed to come over and help with the laundry Monday, but she never showed. If she doesn't turn up today, I'm going down to check out her house."

"Weird. That's not like her. I'll ask around and see what I can find out."

"Thanks," I said, cracking the last egg and reaching for the milk. "How was your date with the good reverend last night?"

Charlene's voice perked up. "Richard? He took me to the lobster pound." To the envy of most of the women on Cranberry Island, Charlene had started seeing Reverend Richard McLaughlin, the charming Episcopal priest who had recently been assigned to the island. When he took up his post at St. James in August, women who hadn't been to church since they were baptized suddenly started finding religion.

"I didn't know clergy salaries were that good," I teased, grabbing a package of sausages from the freezer and plunking the frozen links into a cast-iron pan. "So how'd it go?"

"It was fabulous," Charlene breathed. "Just fabulous. Richard's such a wonderful guy—sincere, caring, compassionate . . ."

"And not too bad in the looks department either," I added. Richard McLaughlin's wavy black hair, deep brown eyes, and sonorous voice had done much to increase Sunday attendance at St. James. According to Charlene, sales of lipstick had tripled since he took up residence in the rectory.

"Tell me about it," Charlene said. "When I went to services last Sunday, he gave me a big hug instead of the usual handshake. I swear, half the women there looked like they wanted to skewer me alive."

I pried the sausages apart with a spatula and laughed. "I'll bet."

Charlene's sassy voice was dreamy. "You know, he *is* handsome, but what I like the most about him is that he has vision. He really sees the beauty of the island and what a wonderful community it is. He was telling me it would be a sin not to share it with the rest of the world."

I cleared my throat. I wasn't sure what she was talking about, but it didn't sound good. "What do you mean, share it with the rest of the world?"

She took a deep breath. "Well, I know we've been against bringing more people to the island in the past . . ."

"You mean Premier Resorts?" I was thinking of the developer who had almost managed to buy the land next to the inn. He had planned to replace the colony of endangered terns that nested there with a golf resort, and Charlene and I had both opposed the development. The developer had come to an unfortunate end, but the rest of the story had concluded happily. A conservation group bought the land, ensuring that both the terns and the rest of the island would remain unmolested by golfers in polyester shirts.

"No, no, no," she protested. "This would be completely different."

The sausages started to sizzle, and I pushed them around in the pan. "What would be different?"

"Weintroub Development's subdivision. The one on the old cranberry bog."

"You mean Cranberry Estates? Murray Selfridge's pet project?" Murray Selfridge was one of the island's three selectmen. He had bought a lot of land over the years, and had recently started courting developers in hopes of making a big profit on it. His bid to bring in the golf resort had failed, but he was encouraging the board to look for other projects that would "improve the quality of life on the island." I gazed out the window at a trio of seagulls wheeling in the breeze. How could it be possible to improve the quality of life on the island? Other than providing a subsidy for winter heating bills, that is.

"You're in favor of Murray's new money-making development scheme?" I said, glancing at Candy and wishing she would go somewhere else. She blinked her big blue Shirley Temple eyes at me. I turned to look out the window instead, entertaining a brief fantasy involving Candy, the Good Ship Lollipop, and a plank.

"It's not all about money," Charlene said tartly, pulling me back to reality. "Richard was saying that island communities have been diminishing for years. Look at what happened to Swan Island, and Isle au Haut. They're both deserted. The same thing could happen to Cranberry Island. There are hardly enough families here to keep the island alive."

"And building a subdivision of million-dollar summer homes will help remediate this?" I asked dryly.

"They'll all be winterized," she said quickly. "And besides, some of them are quite moderately priced."

"Moderately priced?" I shook my head in disbelief. "How do you support a $600,000 mortgage on Cranberry Island? The only thing I can think of is drug running." I knew Richard was a smooth talker, but I couldn't believe Charlene had succumbed to his honeyed tongue. Richard had come to the clergy late in life, after a long and very successful career selling bathroom fixtures. Evidently he had created quite an empire before he had a change of heart and entered the seminary. I had often wondered how he felt about being sent to Cranberry Island, which had a year-round population of just over a hundred people. I suspected his support for Murray Selfridge's plan might be his way of starting to build another empire.

Charlene continued. "The development's goal is to bring new families to the island, new kids to the school." I had to admit that the year-round population was an issue. Enrollment at the island's one-room school had peaked at seven a couple of years ago, but with the loss of another two families to the mainland, that number had dropped down to four.

"And to line Murray Selfridge's pockets," I reminded her.

"Progress and profit *can* go together," she said primly.

"My God, Charlene. You sound like a brochure."

"I knew you wouldn't understand," she sniffed. "Your package will be here when you get here." The phone clicked in my ear, and Charlene's voice was replaced by a dial tone. My best friend had just hung up on me.

TWO

CANDY CLEARED HER THROAT. "Everything all right?"

"Fine," I said, "just fine." I looked at the container of toffee squares and wondered if I should bake some of Charlene's favorite brownies as a peace offering. Then I remembered that she was on a diet—another benefit of Reverend McLaughlin's arrival on the island.

Candy had drawn a breath, presumably to ask another question, when I heard my niece's shoes clumping down the stairs.

Gwen was not a morning person, and had never been overly concerned about the early birds making off with all the worms. In fact, she often said she'd rather get up late and have pancakes, so I was a bit surprised to see her not just awake at eight o'clock, but coiffed and dressed. She had pulled her curly brown hair into a loose bun, and her ruby-red wraparound sweater and tight flared jeans accentuated her slender figure. I beamed at her. Gregarious Gwen would be able to keep Candy occupied while I finished making breakfast.

Her brown eyes shot to Candy, then flicked to me. Her mouth twitched in amusement.

"Good morning, Aunt Nat. Hi, Candy. My, you're up early."

"I didn't want to miss anything," Candy replied brightly.

"You're out of bed early yourself," I said to my niece. "What's the occasion?"

"I'm headed out to the lighthouse to do some studies."

"Are you sure you want to go this morning?" I glanced out the window at the two tiny wisps of cloud in the sky. "It looks kind of overcast to me."

"Sorry, Aunt Nat. I promised Fernand I'd be there." In addition to helping me out around the inn, Gwen studied art with Fernand LaChaise, Cranberry Island's artist-in-residence. She'd come to help out for the summer and take a few art lessons—she was a gifted painter—but decided to stay on. As talented as she was, though, I suspected that her desire to stay might have less to do with her love for art than with her feelings for Adam Thrackton, a young lobsterman she had met on the island.

I sighed and slumped against the counter. Gwen walked to the oven and peered in. "Mmm. Coffee cake."

"It'll be done in a half an hour," I said. "You could bring some to Fernand," I added hopefully.

"A half an hour?" She glanced at the clock. "I can't wait that long. Save some for me, okay?"

I sighed with resignation. "There are a few leftover scones in the breadbox."

"Thanks." She grabbed three scones and tucked them into the canvas bag that held her art supplies. No low-carb diets for her. I watched her with envy; despite her slender figure, she ate like a horse. Gwen filled a travel mug with coffee and was reaching for the sugar bowl when she spotted the tub of toffee squares. "Are those for Charlene?"

"Yeah. I was going to take them down later."

"I'll drop them by for you, if you want."

I hesitated. I should probably go down to the store myself and smooth things over with Charlene, but I wasn't up to it. Besides, if Polly didn't show up soon, I was going to have to ride my bike down to her house. I wasn't sure there'd be time to ride to the store, too. "That would be great," I said. "Also, there's some kind of special delivery there for me. Would you mind picking it up on your way back?"

"Sure." She twisted the lid onto her mug and headed for the door. "I'll be back in a few hours to take care of the rooms." As she pulled the door closed behind her, she paused, eyes twinkling, and tilted her head ever so slightly toward Candy. "Have a good morning!"

A gust of crisp autumn air swept through the kitchen as the door shut behind her.

"Your heating bills must be terrible," Candy said, rearranging her notebook. "Do you use gas, or electric?"

———

By 8:30, I had dislodged Candy from my kitchen table and installed her at one of the breakfast tables in the dining room.

She fingered the tablecloth and picked up her pen. "Who does your linens?"

"A local woman comes and helps out a few times a week," I said. "Now, can I get you some more coffee?"

I refilled her mug and headed for the kitchen, where the timer had begun to buzz. I turned it off and pulled a tray of broiled grapefruit halves from the top rack of the oven. Then I arranged the fruit on a serving platter and pushed through the swinging door.

Candy wasn't the only guest in the dining room. I lowered the grapefruit into the warmer and retrieved the coffee before heading over to greet my Missouri guests, Barbara and Ray Hahn, who had chosen a table near the window. They were accompanied by their dachshunds Elmo and Captain Pluto, and the little dogs had been a charming addition to the inn over the last week—despite Biscuit's frequent protests. It was the Hahns' last day at the inn, and I was sad to see them go, but fortunately Barbara had left me with her favorite muffin recipe, Berried Medley Lemon Streusel muffins. One of the best parts of being an innkeeper was meeting wonderful people—and being privy to their favorite recipes. I planned to try Barbara's soon.

"Good morning, Natalie!" Barbara's Texas accent—even after more than twenty years in Missouri, she still had it—brought a smile to my face, reminding me of my own roots in Austin. I hadn't heard too many Texas twangs since moving to Maine less than a year ago.

"Are the four of you off on the mail boat this morning?" I asked.

Ray nodded and reached down to stroke Elmo's silky head. The little dog scootched forward on his little walker; although his back legs were paralyzed, the Hahns had figured out a way to help him get around. The two of them loved animals as much as Polly, I thought, and my stomach wrenched again at the thought of my missing helper; I was beginning to think something might be seriously wrong.

"My son's expecting us back to help with the vineyard," Barbara said, adjusting the collar of her blouse. "We'll have one more lobster this afternoon before we head back."

"Maybe I should have gone into winemaking instead of innkeeping," I joked.

"You've got a gorgeous place here," she said. "Besides, the lobster's cheap!"

"I could go for cheap wine, too," I said as Russell Lidell walked into the dining room.

"Good morning," I said cheerily. Russell nodded in response. As I filled his mug with coffee, I noticed that he was wearing a suit instead of his normal khakis and wrinkled oxford shirt. A small lip of pink flesh protruded over the starched white collar of his shirt, and his charcoal suit jacket strained to cover his wide back. At least I wasn't the only one in the inn who appreciated the merits of high-calorie foods. "You look nice this morning," I said. "Early meeting?"

"Yup." He sugared his cup liberally and added a big dollop of cream. Russell worked for Weintroub Development Company, and had been staying at the inn for almost a week. Although he couldn't have been older than twenty-five, he had the stocky build and ruddy skin of a man at risk for coronary heart disease. "An engineer's coming out today to take a look at the drainage options down at the bog," he said.

"How are things going with the development?"

"Fine," he said, running a finger around the inside of his collar. His tie, which featured an assortment of red horseshoes, looked as if it might be cutting off circulation to his brain.

"Have you been with Weintroub Development for a long time?" I asked.

"Just started a year ago."

I leaned over and replenished his coffee, which was already half-gone. "Is this your first project, then?"

His fleshy lips tightened. "I've put together a couple of other deals." He gulped down another mouthful of coffee and his ruddy face flushed an even deeper red.

"Up here in Maine?"

"Yeah, in Maine."

"Anything I'd recognize?"

"Um . . . they never really got to the construction phase." He straightened his tie and lifted his chin. "But this one will." He fixed me with his brownish-green eyes. "I know you're not a big fan of development on the island—I heard about the golf resort—but this one's going to be a go."

"Yoo hoo." A sugary voice sounded from behind me. I turned to see Candy holding up her mug. "Could I have a smidge more coffee?"

I nodded at her and turned back to Russell, suddenly feeling a bit more optimistic about Cranberry Estates. If his other projects had stalled, then maybe this one would too. "Well, good luck with your meeting," I said. "Help yourself to the buffet."

———

By 10:00, the dining room was empty, but Polly still hadn't called or showed up. I was crouched in front of the refrigerator, trying to find room for leftovers, when Candy slipped through the kitchen door. She slid her denimed derriere into a chair and watched me wedge the last grapefruit half onto the bottom shelf. I stood up and wiped my hands on a dishtowel, then grabbed an empty coffee can from the pantry and flipped my jacket off of the hook by the door.

"Where are you off to?" Candy asked.

"I have some errands to do." Since Polly's house bordered the bog, I figured I'd pick a can of cranberries while I was down there. My mouth watered at the thought of the little gems, red and tangy, that waited for me. Fortunately, I didn't imagine Candy would think too much of squelching around in a bog.

"Inn business?" She licked her pink lips like a cat.

"No," I said. "Personal business." I smiled politely and slipped through the kitchen door before she could offer to join me.

As I walked around the side of the inn toward the shed where I kept the bikes, I took a deep breath of the brisk autumn air. The rose hips gleamed red against the weathered gray shingles of the inn, and a few dusty pink chrysanthemums bloomed bravely in the blue window boxes.

I paused at the sound of hammering from John's workshop. I glanced at the bike shed and decided it could wait a few minutes. My stomach fluttered as I headed down the hill toward the small gray building that hunched next to the inn's former carriage house. John had converted the carriage house to an apartment that he rented from me at a nominal rate. I hesitated at the door, thinking that perhaps I should go back and make myself a bit more presentable—a little lipstick, maybe, or at least a sweatshirt that didn't feature a constellation of bleach stains—but the thought of encountering Candy again prevented me from taking major reparative actions. Instead, I smoothed my hair down, brushed a bit of stray flour from my sweatshirt, and knocked twice. John opened the door, surprise and pleasure in his green eyes.

Before I could say anything, he pulled me into his arms. As always, the smell of wood on his skin and the warmth of his body under the red flannel shirt made me tingle "I was hoping you'd come by," he murmured into my ear. I leaned back and looked at his long face and tousled blonde hair. His lips curved into an easy smile that deepened the creases around his mouth, and my heart started thumping out an impromptu samba. I pulled my eyes from his face to survey the workshop behind him. The floor was covered with scraps of wood and sawdust, and a hunk of driftwood lay on his workbench.

"Starting a new project?" I asked.

"I will be in a few minutes. Got the last of the boats painted yesterday, and I'll deliver them today. I figured I'd take a month off and do my own thing."

John was a sculptor who specialized in transforming pieces of driftwood into gorgeous works of art. Although his work was beautiful, sales of it barely covered the heating bill, so John supported what he called his "art habit" by carving toy boats he sold at the Island Artists store on the pier. He further supplemented his income by serving as deputy for Cranberry Island, which had the added benefit of giving me a nice sense of security. I had read horror stories about guests preying on single women innkeepers. Having a deputy on the premises—particularly one as attractive and attentive as John—made it much easier to sleep at night.

"What are you doing for dinner tomorrow night?" he asked.

I made a wry face. "Reconstituted frozen clam chowder, probably."

"Why don't you come over? I'd say tonight, but I won't get a chance to go shopping till tomorrow."

"I'd love to. I'm headed over to the cranberry bog; do you want me to pick some berries for you?"

"No, thanks. I never get around to using them." His eyes twinkled. "But I wouldn't object to a few slices of cranberry bread, if you're baking any."

I laughed. "I'll bring a loaf when I come tomorrow." He folded me in his arms for another long hug, and my insides turned to jelly as his mouth brushed my lips in a hot, prickly kiss. Despite the financial implications, I was looking forward to a bit more downtime at the inn—and a lot more uptime with John.

"I've got to head down to Island Artists, but if you're around later, maybe we can have a cup of coffee," he said.

"Stop by anytime," I said. He kissed me again, hard, and I almost forgot about Polly and the cranberries. Finally he shooed me out toward the bike shed.

My lips were still warm as I wheeled a red touring bike from the shed and strapped the coffee can onto the back of it. As I huffed up the hill, I wondered what Candy would find to do in my absence. I hoped I had remembered to lock the front desk; it wouldn't surprise me if she decided to occupy herself by poking through my papers. At the top of the big hill, I paused, panting, and looked back at the inn.

The blue shutters of the gray-shingled cape were a shade paler than the deep blue sky, and the sparkling windowpanes threw back the lemon sunlight like polished mirrors. Behind the inn, a golden meadow that in early summer was awash with blue- and rose-colored lupines swept down to the rocky shoreline, where cobalt waves caressed the rocks.

23

The sight still took my breath away. As I gazed at the inn—*my* inn, I reminded myself with a flush of pride—my eyes lingered for a moment on the roof above my quarters. I felt a chill as I remembered the noises I had heard the night before. I wasn't too excited at the prospect of owning a haunted inn. On the plus side, maybe there was good business to be had hosting parapsychology conferences.

I turned away from the inn and pointed the bicycle down the other side of the steep hill. The deep green patches of blueberries flanking the road had turned to cinnamon, and the maples and birches blazed crimson and gold against the backdrop of spruce and pine. The wind whipped my hair as I picked up speed. Despite my concern for Polly, I was enjoying the temporary freedom from laundry and irritating guests, and I was excited at the prospect of picking cranberries. I felt a tug at my stomach when I remembered the development that was slated for the old bog.

When I first heard about Cranberry Estates, I headed to the Somesville Library on the mainland and read up on the subject of cranberry bogs. I hadn't realized it before, but the bog on Cranberry Island was one of the few natural bogs left on the East Coast—most of the rest had been drained or gobbled up by commercial cranberry operations.

It was unfortunate that Murray Selfridge had managed to buy most of it. The island itself held title to a wedge, and Polly owned the little bit of it that extended out behind her cottage, but Murray had the deeds to everything else. Charlene had told me that Murray had repeatedly offered to buy Polly out, but that she had always refused.

As I reached the bottom of the hill, instead of continuing straight down the road toward the pier and Charlene's store, I took a left on Cranberry Road, the narrow ribbon of blacktop that led to Polly's house.

The bike shuddered as it rolled over the corrugated asphalt, and I swerved just in time to avoid a pothole resembling a meteor strike. Polly didn't own a car, and it was a good thing; no car could survive this stretch of rutted pavement for long.

After several minutes coasting through a thick canopy of spruce and pine, dotted occasionally by houses and stacks of lobster traps, the trees fell away and I spotted Polly's small wood-framed house.

I crunched up the gravel walk and hopped off the bike, leaning it against the front porch railing, and climbed the three steps to the porch. The white paint on the railing was scrubbed clean, but peeling. I remembered Polly telling me she had asked her cousin Gary to help her paint it over the summer; evidently he hadn't gotten around to it. A calico kitty lazed on the well-swept boards of the front porch, and a large gray tom with only half an ear rubbed up against me as I stood at the front door and knocked. I reached down and tickled the tom's chin, then knocked again. No one answered.

I peered through the mullioned window. A brown tabby cat lazed on the threadbare couch in the front room, and the bit of kitchen counter I could see through the door from the living room was empty. The boards of the porch bowed beneath me as I walked down the stairs and followed the path to the back of the house. The back porch was where Polly kept the cats' food and water bowls. Polly always kept them filled, and with ten hungry feline mouths to provide for, I often wondered how she could afford to feed herself. Today, however, the line of bowls was empty. Something wasn't right.

A small contingent of cats emerged from the bushes as I opened the galvanized can by the door and scooped food into the plastic bowls. As I replaced the lid on the can, the brown tabby cat and a smaller, white cat popped through the cat door at the bottom of Polly's kitchen door. I looked for Pepper, a small gray kitten Polly had recently rescued, but she was nowhere to be seen. Had Polly taken her to the vet?

Vet trips don't last overnight, though. And Polly would have called. Where was she? I tried to remember who her relatives were—probably everyone on the island—but the only name I could think of was her cousin Gary's, and I didn't know how to reach him. I leaned against the railing and squinted out toward the bog. Red maples flamed up at intervals along the edge of the bog, and a seagull flashed white in the glare of the sun. I was about to turn and walk back around the house when something caught my eye.

Below one of the fiery maples a patch of blue peeked out from the faded grass. I walked down the back steps and started down the path that led through the bog, my boots squishing into the soft ground. As the blue patch grew closer, I craned to get a closer look. It was a jacket. A trickle of dread snaked down my spine, and I covered the last fifty yards in a clumsy sprint.

I stopped a few yards away from the maple, my rubber boots sinking into the loamy earth, and swallowed back a mouthful of bile. I knew that jacket. And I knew the person wearing it.

Her brown eyes gazed sightless at the deep blue sky. A red stain bloomed across her chest like a macabre flower, and a gun lay in her outstretched palm. I had found Polly Sarkes.

THREE

I STUMBLED BACKWARD AND closed my eyes, but the image of Polly's face was seared into my retinas. I swallowed back the bile that bubbled up in my throat and forced myself to look again. The gun gleamed in the sun, and the edges of the bloodstain had turned a rusty brown. I shuddered and turned away.

The broken body on the ground ripped at my heart. It was so awful . . . and such a terrible, terrible waste. Poor Polly. I remembered her soft voice, always with a hint of laughter, the stories she'd tell me about her cats, whom she'd loved like children. The pride she'd taken in her work.

What had been so awful that she felt she had to take her own life?

And how could I have missed the signs?

Polly had always been cheerful, and solidly practical. I had never glimpsed even a hint of the quiet desperation you would expect from a person considering suicide. As I turned back to the still form, a breeze lifted a strand of Polly's bushy brown hair, and the soft wisp settled across her pale cheek. As I looked closer, I noticed a purplish blotch, like a smudge, on the pale skin around her left eye. My eyes drifted to the gun resting in her limp hand. Such a violent way to die.

I needed to call the police.

I tripped over a tussock as I stumbled toward Polly's house and flailed to regain my balance. I had to get in touch with John. I leapt up the porch steps two at a time and prayed that Polly's house, like most houses on Cranberry Island, was unlocked.

Fortunately, the knob turned easily. The smell of cooking oil and lemon furniture polish enveloped me as I hurried through the front hall to the kitchen phone. I dialed John's number from memory, my fingers clumsy with the rotary dial. No answer: John must still be out in his workshop.

I glanced at the message board next to the phone, hoping to see a list of emergency numbers. Except for a hastily scrawled phone number with the word "Shelter" next to it, the board was blank.

Under the counter was a stack of slender phonebooks. I pulled out the top one and located the number for the police, wishing not for the first time that the island could afford 911 service.

A few moments later, I reeled off the details of Polly's death to the police dispatcher. My eyes roamed the room as I spoke. Knife marks crisscrossed the countertop, but the tan Formica gleamed in the light from the window, as did the olive vinyl floor. The cheery yellow walls were decorated with a cuckoo clock and a cat calendar, and white lace curtains framed the window. My fridge was plastered with notices and reminders to myself, but Polly's refrigerator was bare except for a cranberry scone recipe I had given her last week. I gave Polly's address to the dispatcher and agreed to stand guard over the body until the police arrived.

After hanging up, I walked over to the fridge and opened it on impulse. A brand new quart of milk and a freshly picked can of cranberries stood on the top shelf. The rest of the shelves were neatly organized. Polly had lined all of the jams and jellies in a row, and even the mustard squeeze bottle looked as if someone had wiped the crust off of it.

Closing the refrigerator door, I glanced around the spotless kitchen. Polly's death was so messy, yet everything in her house was almost compulsively clean—even with ten cats living in it. My stomach lurched again when I thought of Polly's body, alone in the bog. This didn't feel right. Not at all. Polly wouldn't have ended her life without at least providing instructions for the care of her cats; she loved them like children.

My eyes drifted to the porch, where the cats ringed the food bowls. I had forgotten to give them water. I retrieved two empty bowls and filled them in the sink, then walked back out and set them down beside the food. As the cats gulped down the dry food, I realized I still hadn't seen Pepper. Maybe she was hiding somewhere in the house.

I headed back inside to the living room, calling out to Pepper. Photos covered every available surface; not of people, but of Polly's furry charges. A line of porcelain cats marched across the mantel, and a small television set sat in the corner next to the fireplace. The couch looked comfortable, but well-worn; a hand-knitted afghan covered the back of it. It was obvious that everything in Polly's house had been in use for a long time, but she had taken good care of her belongings.

I climbed to the second story, still calling Pepper's name. The door to the bathroom was across from the head of the stairs. The white-tiled room smelled of shampoo and bleach, and despite the bright pink flowered bathmat, the green shower curtain gave the white walls a sickly cast. On a whim, I stepped to the sink and opened the mirrored medicine chest. If Polly suffered from depression, she might have a bottle of antidepressants hidden behind the over-the-counter medicines.

A quick sweep of the shelves revealed nothing but the usual array of antihistamines, antacids, and aspirin. A blue safety razor lay on the bottom shelf. I picked it up and turned it over, wrinkling my nose at the black hairs gumming the rusted double blade before returning it to the shelf. Then I stepped to the bathtub and pulled back the plastic curtain, revealing a pink razor and a can of shaving cream huddled together on the tub's porcelain rim. I took a quick look at the razor's safety blade—this one was clean—and rearranged the shower curtain before heading back into the hall.

To the left was a small bedroom/sewing room. My eyes skimmed over the furrowed double bed to the sewing machine pushed up against the far wall. A stack of folded fabric was the only splash of color in the room. I leaned down and peered under the bed, but it was empty.

The only other door led to another bedroom: Polly's room. The first thing I saw was an open suitcase sprawled across a neatly made double bed. I walked over and glanced at the case's jumbled contents: a few shirts, a couple of pairs of socks, and a green corduroy skirt I'd seen her wear to church. I fingered the corded fabric for a moment, thinking of the last time I'd seen her in that skirt. It was the church supper, at the end of September; I remembered the chicken potpie she had brought, the flowered green headband she'd used to corral her wayward hair. A pang shot through me as I tucked it back into the suitcase. Polly hadn't mentioned she was planning on taking a trip.

I turned my attention to the dresser. The dark wood gleamed from years of polishing, and Polly had decorated the marble top with a lace doily and a small crystal jar of dried lavender. The curved top drawer was ajar, enough for a kitten to have slipped inside, and I slid it the rest of the way open, exposing a line of balled socks and a basket of folded underwear. I caught a glimpse of a red cardboard box between the neatly rolled socks. I pushed the white cotton socks aside for a closer look and jerked my hand back when I realized it was a box of bullets.

I took a shaky breath, then called for Pepper again. When the kitten didn't appear, I hurried out of the empty bedroom and downstairs to the front door.

The crisp autumn breeze was a welcome change from the stagnant air inside, and I filled my lungs as the front door snicked shut behind me. As the gulls called and the wind rustled through the autumn grass, I set my shoulders and turned toward the bog— and Polly.

I had only taken a few steps down the path when the sound of a car engine floated to my ears. A burgundy Jaguar bumped down the pitted road, and I grimaced as I recognized Murray Selfridge's car. I hoped he had a good mechanic—preferably one who made house calls. I winced as the undercarriage scraped against a chunk of broken asphalt.

The car crunched to a stop in front of Polly's house, and three men unfolded themselves from its leather interior. Murray Selfridge was wearing his yacht club ensemble, and Russell Lidell was close behind him, looking redder than usual. I didn't recognize the third man, a gangly man in his mid-forties, but guessed he was probably a surveyor or engineer.

Murray's bushy eyebrows shot up when he spotted me on the narrow path. "What are you doing here?" he called down to me.

My throat closed up as I answered Murray. "I found Polly Sarkes in the bog." My voice was thick and unfamiliar. "She's dead. The police are on their way."

His eyebrows moved toward his receding hairline. "Dead? What happened to her?"

An image of the red stain on Polly's chest flashed before my eyes. I squeezed back tears. "Suicide," I choked. "Or murder."

Murray tripped, and his arms flailed as he regained his balance. "Murder? Are you sure she's dead?" The sun gleamed on his Brylcreamed hair as he closed the gap between us.

I nodded. "I'm sure."

"Where is she?" he huffed. "What happened to her?"

I pointed toward the red maple. "She's over there," I said. "I'm not supposed to say anything else about it. I'm keeping an eye on her until the police get here."

Murray hitched up his khakis and stepped off the path toward Polly, but I held up a hand. My voice was suddenly steady. "The police told me to keep everyone clear of the area." He paused. I glanced at Russell and the surveyor, who had started down the path behind Murray and had almost reached us. Russell peered at the soft ground anxiously, lifting his feet up in a strange, prancing gait, presumably to protect his polished black wingtips.

As he minced down the last few yards of the path, panting from the exertion, he said, "What happened?"

Murray answered him. "Polly Sarkes is dead." Then he stared at me. "Natalie won't say what happened to her."

Russell stood up straight. "Isn't Polly Sarkes the woman who owns this house?" He cast an appraising eye at the small wooden structure.

"That's right," Murray said.

"Huh."

The surveyor spoke for the first time. "I don't know when I'll be able to make it out again. Can we at least get a look at the place?" He turned to me. "We won't go near the body. I just need to take some measurements." He blinked at me in the sunlight.

A woman had just died, and he was concerned about measurements? "Fine," I said. "Just stay away from that maple tree."

I walked reluctantly over to where Polly lay and positioned myself about ten feet away, with my back to her crumpled body. Just being near her made the whole thing horribly real, and tears pricked my eyes again as I fixed my gaze on the gulls wheeling and diving in the blue air. After a minute, a scratchy sound rasped behind me. I turned, startled. It seemed to be coming from Polly.

I stepped a little closer, confused by the sound, and then it rasped again. This time I recognized it. The sound came from a skinny gray kitten that lay shivering at Polly's feet. It was Pepper. In my haste to get back to the house and call the police, I hadn't noticed her.

———

By the time the police arrived, Russell had abandoned all hope for his wingtips and was trudging along behind Murray and the engineer. I held Pepper in my arms and watched as they progressed across the bog, the engineer stopping every few minutes to squat down and look at something. Both Russell and Murray kept sneaking peeks at me and at Polly's house. I stood a few yards away from Polly, stroking the trembling kitten and glancing back at Polly every few minutes to make sure a marauding seagull didn't do her any further harm. It was surprising that the gulls hadn't found her already.

I had stood there for at least a half an hour when a rickety truck pulled up beside Murray's Jaguar, and three people got out. My heart sank as I recognized the slow swagger of Sergeant Grimes. His belly hung over his police belt, and his greasy hair was slicked back. I caught a breath of stale cigarette smoke on the wind as he tramped toward me, followed by two men I didn't recognize. They were carrying bulky equipment cases; I assumed they were the forensics team.

"Another body, Miss Barnes?" Grimes glanced at the crumpled form. His close-set eyes reminded me of a weasel's. "You've got a knack for finding corpses."

He was referring to the developer whose body I had discovered earlier in the year. For a long time, Grimes had been convinced that I was the murderer. I wasn't sure he had gotten over the disappointment of finding out that someone else had killed him. Grimes walked over to Polly and stared down at her. A camera flashed. I turned my head away.

"Classic case of suicide," he said.

I stared at Grimes. "Are you sure? She left her cats with no one to take care of them, and there's no note. Also, it looks like she was packing to take a trip."

Grimes' eyes narrowed. "Packing to take a trip? How do you know that?"

"I had to go into her house to call the police. I couldn't find Pepper, so I took a quick look around."

"Pepper?" Grimes looked confused. "What, were you eating a roast beef sandwich or something?"

I held up the small, furry body. "The kitten. I found her here." I shuddered, realizing that was probably why the gulls had left the body alone.

"So, you were tampering with evidence?"

"I didn't touch anything." I remembered the box of bullets. And the refrigerator door, and the medicine chest, and the suitcase. "Well, not much, anyway."

Grimes shifted his substantial weight from one foot to the other. "It doesn't look like it'll matter, anyway." He jerked his head toward Polly. "This here is an open-and-shut case if I've ever seen one."

"It doesn't feel right to me," I said. "I knew Polly. I can't believe she would go out to the middle of the bog and shoot herself. Not with her cats to take care of. Besides, why would you pack a suitcase if you were planning to kill yourself?"

Grimes shrugged. "Maybe she changed her mind. Maybe the tickets were more than she could afford, and she decided to take a one-way trip instead." He guffawed at his own joke. "Don't have to worry about the airlines losing your luggage that way, do you?"

"You *will* look into the possibility of homicide, won't you?"

Grimes dug a pack of Marlboros from his shirt pocket and tapped out a cigarette, flicking open a gold lighter. As he cupped his hand around the end of the cigarette, the wind swept a glowing ash toward where the forensics team leaned over Polly's body. The shorter of the two men looked up.

"Get that cigarette out of here. You're contaminating the scene."

Grimes grunted and moved a few steps further from the crouching men. His ears reddened, and he glared at me. "Just keep your nose out of things and leave the police work to the professionals, okay Miss Barnes?"

Heat rose to my face. If I'd left things to the professionals last time a body showed up on Cranberry Island, I would currently be serving thirty to forty years for a crime I didn't commit. I hugged Pepper to my chest. "You'll have to forgive me if I'm a bit reluctant to do that."

"Yeah, well, you don't have a choice." He leaned toward me and stabbed at his chest with his empty hand. "I'm the cop," he hissed. His blue eyes were ice cold. "If I decide it's suicide, then it's suicide. End of story." He took another drag from his cigarette and turned away. "Now go home. If I have any questions, I know where to find you."

FOUR

I was still hugging Pepper to my chest as I closed the kitchen door of the inn behind me. The warm pine floors and butcher-block counters were a nice change from Polly's olive vinyl and formica, but even the cinnamon smell in the air didn't do much to dispel my mood. I set Pepper down next to Biscuit's food bowl, and was relieved when she sniffed at it and then started eating. Fortunately, Biscuit was nowhere to be seen. I hated to think what would happen when she found out I'd let a strange cat—a kitten, no less—have a go at her food bowl.

I picked up the phone and dialed John, but he didn't answer. I glanced out the window toward the dock; John's skiff, *Mooncatcher*, was gone. He must have taken the last batch of toy boats down to Island Artists. I was trying to decide whether or not to call Charlene when I noticed a Styrofoam cooler on the counter. Gwen must have picked up my delivery for me.

I tipped over the foam cube and examined the address label. It was from Brenham, Texas, which was about two hours outside of

Austin. Who did I know who lived in Brenham? I grabbed a knife from the block and sliced through the packing tape, then pried up the lid.

Two half-gallon cartons of Bluebell Homemade Vanilla ice cream lay nestled in a bed of dry ice. My mouth watered as I extracted the containers from the cooler and set them on the counter. I had been devastated to discover that Bluebell wasn't available north of the Mason-Dixon line. It was my favorite ice cream, and I had missed it sorely since moving to Maine.

But who had sent it? I grabbed a potholder and pushed the dry ice to the side. After a few moments of digging, I excavated an envelope encased in a baggie. I tore it open and pulled out a card with a picture of bluebonnets and an ancient barn on the front of it. The inside bore two sentences in an unfamiliar hand. *Happy Birthday* was the first. *See you soon* was the second.

I flipped the card over, but the rest of it was blank. There was no signature.

I glanced at the yellow ice cream containers. Whoever had sent them knew not just my favorite flavor, but also my birthday; I had just celebrated my thirty-ninth last week. I stared at the card for a moment, trying to guess who had sent it. Then I gave up and tossed the card on the counter. Frankly, after the morning I'd had, I didn't really care who had sent the ice cream. I just wanted to eat it.

Grabbing a spoon, I tucked one half gallon into the freezer and pried open the second, closing my eyes as the lush confection dissolved on my tongue. Wow.

As I scooped up another spoonful, I decided that brownies would be a perfect foil to the cool, creamy vanilla. I couldn't do anything about Polly right now anyway, and baking always improved my mood. Carbohydrates be damned: I needed chocolate. I stole one more spoonful, then slid the second carton into the freezer and headed for the pantry.

As I pulled a package of baker's chocolate from the pantry shelf, I spied a box of dried cherries I'd picked up to make scones. Cherries and chocolate . . . I grabbed the box and tossed it onto the counter with the chocolate.

My mind flitted back to Polly as I unwrapped the dark squares and dropped them into the top of a double boiler. I still hadn't recovered from the horror of finding her. The image of the flat, cold steel of the gun against her pale fingers flashed into my mind. I remembered reading somewhere that men usually shot themselves; women were much more likely to take a less violent approach, like a drug overdose. Guns weren't the norm for women.

I stirred the chocolate with a wooden spoon, watching the hard squares dissolve into a thick, dark puddle. What was Polly doing with a gun, anyway? And if you were going to shoot yourself, why would you go outside and do it in the middle of a cranberry bog?

Unless it was a protest against the upcoming development, I ruminated. Maybe she'd seen killing herself in the bog as a statement about the pending subdivision. In that case, though, wouldn't she have left a note? I couldn't imagine her leaving her cats adrift. I glanced over at Pepper, who had finished eating and was heading toward the laundry room door. No, she wouldn't leave Pepper. Besides, Polly's refusal to sell her house was one of the only things standing in the way of Weintroub Development's project. If anything, Polly's death might make things easier; whoever inherited the house might be more inclined than Polly to sell it and take the cash. My eyes strayed to the empty can I had put on the counter, and I remembered the can of berries I had seen in her refrigerator. That was another thing that had bothered me. Why would Polly have bought fresh milk and picked cranberries for a new recipe if she was planning to kill herself? She had also started packing a suitcase, presumably for a trip. I gave the molten chocolate a final stir and reached into the refrigerator for eggs and butter. Nothing made sense.

If Polly hadn't killed herself, then who had? Murray Selfridge was an obvious possibility. He had almost killed me over the summer when he cut my bike's brake lines in an effort to scare me away from protesting the golf resort. It wasn't quite the same thing as shooting someone, but clearly the health and safety of others weren't overriding concerns for Murray, particularly when it came to making money.

As I plopped a stick of butter into the molten chocolate, my thoughts touched on the conversation I'd had with Russell Lidell at breakfast this morning. Russell also had a vested interest in Polly's death. He'd told me this morning that the Cranberry Estates development was going to go through, no matter what. He'd seemed surprised that Polly was dead, but he could have been acting. If his job was on the line, he might have been desperate enough to remove any potential obstacles.

I swirled the butter into the chocolate and turned off the burner. Who would inherit Polly's house? The only relative I knew of was Gary Sarkes, and Charlene would know where he lived. After I finished making the brownies, I resolved, I would call Charlene and smooth things over.

Then again, I thought, *she* had hung up on me. Shouldn't she be the one smoothing things over? I sighed and cracked an egg into the mixing bowl. Why did life have to be so complicated?

I was measuring out the sugar when the doorbell rang. I looked up with surprise; I was expecting a guest today, but not until late in the afternoon. It was probably a nosy islander who had heard about Polly. Or Sergeant Grimes, come to ask questions.

A wavy form moved behind the front door's antique glass as I walked through the parlor to the front hall. Whoever it was, I thought with relief, he or she was too tall to be Grimes.

As I fumbled with the brass knob and swung the door open, a wave of familiar cologne hit me full force. I took an involuntary step backward.

I stared at the tall man on my doorstep for a moment, taking in the lanky body, the tailored khakis and pressed chambray shirt, and the sensuous lips that, as usual, were curved into a wry smile. His blue eyes held mine for a moment. Then he stepped forward and engulfed me in his arms, crushing my face against his leather jacket.

It was my ex-fiancé.

Only it couldn't be. This was Maine. As far as I knew, Benjamin Portlock still lived in Texas.

"Natalie!" He spoke my name in a slow Texas drawl, his voice caressing the syllables.

I pulled away from him. "Benjamin . . . What are you doing here? This is Maine, not Texas."

He looked around, surprised. "Really? That would explain why it's so damned cold."

"It's fifty degrees, Benjamin."

"Exactly. It's only October."

"What are you doing here?"

"Why, I came to stay at your fine establishment." He peered past me at the living room. "Nice place you got here."

"But you don't have a reservation!" I don't know why that seemed relevant. The inn was practically empty.

He cocked a rakish eyebrow at me, and I remembered why I had gotten engaged to him in the first place. "Oh," he said, "but I do."

"No, you don't." I might be getting absent-minded, but I was pretty sure I'd recognize my former fiancé's name in the reservation book.

"If I remember correctly, a Mr. Bertram Pence is scheduled to arrive on the 4:00 mailboat. He'll be staying for a week."

I gaped. "You're Bertram Pence?"

He bowed slightly. "At your service. A little early, I'm afraid, but I hope you'll take me."

"Why didn't you use your real name?"

"Would you have accepted the reservation?"

I chewed on my bottom lip. He was probably right. I glanced at the leather suitcase by his loafered feet. "Come in, come in," I said. "I was just in the kitchen, making brownies." Benjamin bent down and scooped up his suitcase, then followed me through the door. "Do you want me to show you your room, or would you rather join me in the kitchen?"

"I think I'll join you in the kitchen, if you don't mind."

I glanced down at myself as Benjamin followed me through the parlor to the kitchen. I had kicked off my boots when I got home, exposing holey wool socks, and my faded sweatshirt bore several bleach stains and was frayed at the cuffs. Not the outfit I would have chosen for an encounter with my ex-fiancé. I pushed through the door to the kitchen with Benjamin close on my heels.

"I see you got my birthday present," he said. He picked the bluebonnet card up off the counter and flipped it open. Most men sent roses. Benjamin knew me well enough to know that food, not flowers, was the fastest route to my heart.

"Yes," I said. "Thank you. I didn't recognize the handwriting."

"That's because it wasn't mine. The woman on the phone wrote out the card for me."

Well, that was one mystery solved. "Actually," I said, "I was just making brownies to go with the ice cream." Benjamin put down his suitcase and settled himself at the table. "Can I get you a cup of coffee?" I asked.

"No, thanks. I'll just sit here and enjoy the view."

"Yeah, it is gorgeous, isn't it?" I looked at the blue ocean unfolding in front of the window and glanced back at Benjamin. He was staring at me.

Blood rushed to my face as I turned back to the counter and added a cup of sugar to the bowl. "So, what brings you to Maine?" I asked.

"You," he said.

I set down the measuring cup and leaned against the counter. Then I turned around and looked at Benjamin. His usually mischievous eyes burned with an unsettling intensity. "What do you mean?" I asked quietly.

He stood and walked over to me, placing his broad hands on my shoulders. His face was inches from mine, and memories rushed to the surface of my mind. Late breakfasts at Texas French

Bread, sipping hot coffee and laughing over the newspaper . . . flying through the Hill Country in his little blue Miata . . .

"I made the biggest mistake of my life when I let you go," he said softly. "I've come to ask you to marry me."

I stared at him with disbelief. "We've been through that," I sputtered. "You obviously weren't ready. Why should things be any different now?"

His blue eyes were liquid beneath long black lashes. "Losing you made me realize what you mean to me. How great we are together."

"Were," I interjected. "Besides, I have a different life now. Even if I could put everything behind me, my place is here. Yours is in Texas."

"I'm asking you to come back with me."

"What?" I croaked.

"You could sell the inn for a profit, and start one in Austin," he said. "We could pool our resources, do it together." He pulled me closer to him, and the heady scent of his cologne wafted over me. "Just imagine what we could do," he breathed, and I felt my knees buckle beneath me. His lips were centimeters from mine when the swinging door creaked.

I sprang back and smoothed down my sweatshirt. Candy Perkins stood at the door. She cast an appreciative eye over Benjamin, whose own eyes flicked up and down her curvy form involuntarily, lingering for a moment on her T-shirt. I didn't think it was because of the logo.

Candy blinked her blue eyes at me. "I hope I'm not interrupting," she said innocently. "I just wanted to know if I could watch you clean the rooms."

"My niece is taking care of them," I said gruffly. "If you can find her, she might let you tag along. She usually starts upstairs."

"Oh, well, I guess I'll go look for her then." Candy fluttered her eyelashes at Benjamin. "I hope I'll be seeing you around," she said. She shot him a smoldering look, then sashayed out of the kitchen, waggling her snugly clad bottom behind her.

Benjamin watched her go, then turned to me. He reached out to touch my arm, but the moment had gone. "I'm staying for a week, Natalie. You don't have to make any snap decisions. We can talk about it, decide what to do about the inn."

I gently withdrew my arm, trying to avoid contact with his dangerous blue eyes.

He sighed and walked over to the table. "Well," he said, "I guess I'd better go and unpack." As he reached for his suitcase, Pepper emerged from the laundry room with a scratchy meow. "Who's this little guy?"

"That's Pepper," I said. "I found her this morning. Her owner . . . died." A lump formed in my throat as I remembered Polly's body, crumpled in the bog.

Benjamin looked up, startled. "Died? How?" He quietly walked up beside me and put his hand on my shoulder.

Suddenly, the horror of what I'd seen came rushing back to me, and tears streaked down my face. "I found her, in the cranberry bog," I whispered. "She was shot. There was blood, and she was just lying there . . . It was horrible." The unfairness of it all—a life cut off early, violently—flooded over me, and my chest shuddered with a sob.

Benjamin gently turned my body toward him and wrapped his arms around me, rocking me back and forth. The smell of leather and cologne and his familiar musky scent was soothing, and I was tempted to sink into his chest.

Instead, I pulled away, wiping at my eyes. "I'll ruin your jacket," I said.

"Nonsense," he whispered. He pulled me toward him and drew my head to his chest. "It must have been awful," he said.

"It was. She was so pale, and the bog was so lonely . . ."

Benjamin stepped back and cradled my face in his hands. "What a terrible thing to find," he said. He leaned down, and before I knew it, his warm lips were pressed against mine. I yielded to the kiss for a moment, my whole body melting. Then my brain woke up and started yammering at me. *What are you doing?*

I pushed him away and wiped at my mouth. I was straightening my sweatshirt when a movement at the door caught my eye.

John stood outside, hand raised, about to knock. Our eyes locked for a moment. Then he turned and walked away.

FIVE

I RUSHED TO THE door, but John was already striding down the hill.

Benjamin came up behind me and put his hands on my shoulders as I watched John disappear into his workshop, slamming the door behind him.

"Who's that?" Benjamin asked.

"My neighbor."

"Why didn't he knock?"

"What do you think?" I shook Benjamin's hands off of my shoulders and marched over to the counter, where I retrieved the wooden spoon and thrust it into the bowl. Some days it feels like you're living in a badly directed B movie. Today was one of them.

"Oh, I see," Benjamin said.

I stirred the batter in stony silence.

"He's not just your neighbor, is he?"

"We've been seeing each other for a few months," I said tersely.

Benjamin laughed. "Well, no wonder he took off in a hurry, then." He walked up behind me and slid his hands around my waist, then bent down, his lips close to my ear. "Nothing serious?" he murmured.

I dropped the spoon and pried his hands off of my waist. "Why don't I show you to your room now?"

He raised his hands in surrender and stepped away. "Whatever you say, ma'am," he said with mock politeness. He retrieved his suitcase and followed as I led him out of the kitchen. As we climbed the stairs to his room, he kept his mouth shut and his hands to himself. But his eyes still tracked me like a pair of heat-seeking missiles.

———

By the time I got back to the kitchen, Pepper had curled up next to the heater and the chocolate had started to bubble on the stove. I rushed to turn off the burner. Then I stirred the chocolate—fortunately, it hadn't burned—and retrieved a brick of silky Valrhona chocolate from the pantry.

As I chopped the smooth dark chocolate into sweet shards, my eyes strayed to the window. The door to John's workshop, which often stood open on sunny days, remained shut, and I silently cursed Benjamin's forwardness as the knife came down on the cutting board again and again.

As soon as I got the brownies into the oven, I would go and talk with him. I needed to tell him about Polly, anyway. Surely he'd understand when I explained what had happened in the kitchen with Benjamin; I was pretty sure he'd seen me push him away.

My mind floated back to Benjamin, who would hopefully remain busy upstairs, unpacking, for the rest of the afternoon.

Ours had been a torrid affair. We'd met at a cocktail party, a benefit for the Battered Women's Shelter, and when he'd bumped into me and knocked my éclair onto my dress, a spark had arced between us as we tried in vain to clean the chocolate off the peach silk.

It had been that way the whole year we were together. After six months of courtship—evenings beneath the Congress Street Bridge, lying together on the soft green grass while the bats unfurled themselves in a long black banner, long lazy mornings in his downtown loft—he flew me to San Francisco and asked me to marry him on the Golden Gate Bridge.

I accepted immediately.

But as soon as that two-carat diamond slid onto my ring finger, things changed.

Benjamin's hours at the venture capital firm grew longer and longer, and our weekend trips to the Hill Country and Port Aransas were replaced by business trips to Vegas and L. A. New clients, he said. They needed lots of handholding.

I found out the truth on a Tuesday evening. My face burned with humiliation even now, and I brought the knife down hard, splintering the bar of chocolate.

Benjamin had been working late, again, and a friend of mine from work had convinced me to join her at Z Tejas, a little downtown restaurant that made her favorite fish tacos. I was always up for Mexican food, and I didn't want to spend the evening alone, so at seven o'clock we found ourselves at a small wooden table in the corner of the restaurant, enjoying the air-conditioned respite from the sultry July weather. I had just taken the first sip of my strawberry margarita and was reaching for a chip when a gorgeous woman with long, black hair walked into the restaurant, dressed in a black spandex skirt and three-inch stiletto heels.

The man behind her slid a proprietary hand around her narrow waist and guided her to a table in the middle of the room. I put down my margarita and swallowed hard.

He had gallantly pulled out her chair and was tucking her into it, his hand caressing her glossy black hair, when he saw me.

Panic flared for a moment in his blue eyes, but he mastered it quickly and replaced it with a look of pleasant surprise.

"Nat!" Benjamin strode over to the table where I sat, jaw clenched, tears threatening to spring from the corners of my eyes. "What a lovely coincidence!"

He came up behind me and kissed the top of my head lightly, like a butterfly alighting on a flower and then flitting away.

"I want you to meet a business associate of mine." He turned and beckoned to the woman in the stiletto heels. "Zhang? This is Natalie." He turned to me. "Zhang is consulting with us on the Trident deal. We were just meeting to discuss strategy."

Zhang's eyes flicked to the diamond on my hand, then to my face, fixing me with a cool, appraising look.

Benjamin nodded to my friend Janet, who sat across from me, speechless. "Won't you join us?" He laughed heartily. "We'll try not to talk too much shop."

I swallowed again, but the lump that had swelled to the size of a goose egg didn't budge from my throat.

"I imagine you won't," I said in a strangled voice. I stood up and retrieved my purse. I fumbled for my wallet and pulled out a twenty, then tossed it onto the table with a shaking hand.

"No thanks," I said. "I'm done."

Then I walked out of the restaurant.

———

I shook my head to dispel the memory, and slid the chocolate off the cutting board into the bowl. I had done a little digging after leaving the restaurant that night, and soon found out that Zhang wasn't the only "business associate" Benjamin had been seeing regularly. He had been meeting with two or three of them over the past six months. And he'd been doing a lot more than just handholding.

I set down the cutting board and sighed. Benjamin was part of the reason I had left Texas and come to Maine. I thought I had gotten over him. I was surprised to discover that he could still have this effect on me.

I measured out a half cup of glistening dried cherries and stirred them into the batter with the chocolate chunks before pouring it all into a pan. Then I slid the pan into the oven, set the timer, and squared my shoulders.

Benjamin had screwed up my life once.

I wasn't going to let him do it a second time.

I filled my lungs with the cool October air as I marched down the hill to John's workshop. A brisk wind rushed up from the water and ruffled my hair as I rapped on the door. John didn't answer. Maybe he had gone home.

As I crossed the narrow space between the workshop and the converted carriage house, I glanced down toward the dock.

John's skiff was gone again.

My chest tightened as I trudged back up to the inn. I had missed my opportunity. Well, I would have plenty of time to explain everything to John tomorrow night.

That is, if I was still invited.

———

When the timer went off forty minutes later, Pepper didn't twitch from her spot on the radiator—she was still recovering from the trauma—but I jumped up from my chair and peeked into the oven. The surface of the batter had crinkled, and the chunks of chocolate had melted into warm droplets on the shiny brown surface. I pulled the pan out of the oven and set it on a rack to cool while I made the frosting.

As I poured cream into the double boiler, I glanced at the phone again. Charlene and I might have had a tiff this morning, but she would kill me if I didn't give her the inside scoop on finding Polly—and on Benjamin's arrival.

The swinging door had remained blissfully closed since I'd led Benjamin upstairs, and as I picked up the phone and dialed the store's familiar number, I hoped both he and Candy would continue to stay out of my way, at least until I got done talking to Charlene.

The phone rang six times before Charlene picked up. "Cranberry Island Grocery Store."

"Charlene? It's Nat."

"Oh. Hi."

"I'm sorry about this morning," I said. "I've got some news for you."

"You mean Polly?"

"You heard?"

"Emmeline Hoyle told me. She lives one house up on Cranberry Road."

"Oh," I said. I should have called earlier.

"Is that all?" Charlene's voice was cool.

"Actually, no," I said. "I know who sent that cooler."

"Who?" Her tone was bland.

"My former fiancé. He's here, on the island." I paused for a moment, but Charlene didn't respond. "He's staying at the inn, and he says he wants to marry me," I blurted. "He kissed me in the kitchen, and John saw it."

"Well, that certainly complicates things for you, doesn't it?" Charlene said mildly.

I stood in silence for a moment, stirring the cream. This was not going as I had hoped it would. "I just baked a new recipe," I said desperately. "Chocolate cherry brownies. Would you like me to bring some down for you?"

"Oh, no thanks," she said. "I'm on a diet."

"Right. A diet." The phone line hummed between us for a moment, and I heard the murmur of voices in the background. "Well, then," I said. "I'd better let you go, I suppose."

"I suppose."

"Have a good day."

"Thanks," she said. And then she hung up.

Not good.

The swinging door opened as I replaced the receiver on the hook, and Candy poked her head into the kitchen.

"Baking again?" she asked.

"Yes."

"Who was that delicious man in here earlier?"

"You mean Benjamin?" I said. I was surprised to feel a flare of jealousy erupt in my chest. "He's my former fiancé."

"Former?" Her arched eyebrows rose, and she adjusted the sparkling pendant that nestled in her cleavage. "How interesting. I always thought Maine was a backwater, but you're just swimming in eligible men up here, aren't you?"

I shrugged.

"Anyway," she said, "I just wanted to see if there was anything else going on this afternoon."

"Not unless you like doing laundry," I said. "I'll probably set up the tables for tomorrow and do some paperwork a little later on, but that's about it."

"Good," she said, glancing at her jeweled watch. "I have an appointment in half an hour. I'd like to go over the daily paperwork with you sometime, though, if you don't mind."

"Sure," I said wearily.

She smiled, her freshly lipsticked lips setting off her even, white teeth. "Toodle-oo, then."

"Toodle-oo," I said to the door swinging in her wake.

I returned to the stove, glad that at least Candy would be out of my way for the rest of the afternoon. As I swirled chocolate into the cream on the stove, I turned my thoughts to Polly to distract myself from Benjamin, whose presence in the inn was making my stomach churn.

I replayed my conversation with Sgt. Grimes in my head and wondered when—and if—he would be coming to talk to me. He knew where I lived; he had spent a lot of time over the summer hanging around my inn and needling me with questions. I glanced at the clock. I had left Polly almost two hours ago. Last time I found a body, Grimes was on my doorstep within an hour of his arrival on the island.

I had a bad feeling that Grimes wasn't going to be asking any more questions about Polly's death. An image of Polly's face flashed into my mind, and I thought about the purple blotch I had seen. It almost looked as if she had blackened her eye. Could that have been a result of the blood settling?

I would have to ask John about the autopsy results tomorrow, I thought as I stirred the frosting briskly. I dipped my little finger into the chocolate and tasted it; it needed a touch of cherry liqueur, and then it would be done.

The brownies were still too warm to frost, but it wouldn't be long. Glancing at the laundry room door, I sighed. I was still tired from last night's attic antics, and a shot of caffeine was in order before facing the mountains of sheets and towels. If I didn't do something about the laundry soon, the piles might take over the first floor of the inn.

I put the kettle on and shivered, remembering the noises above my bedroom and thinking I needed to find out more about the Gray Whale Inn ghost. Unfortunately, Charlene didn't sound as if she was going to tell me any more ghost stories right now. I could always head to the town museum and ask, but I didn't want the whole world to know I thought the inn was haunted. Business was tough enough without the inn playing the starring role in the next issue of *Gruesome Ghosts and Goblins*.

Matilda Jenkins, the curator of the local museum, knew everything about the island, though; if the inn was supposed to be haunted, she would know about it. Maybe I'd tell Matilda I was researching the history of the inn, and she'd volunteer the information without any mention of strange noises in the attic.

My mind flitted back to Polly. I also needed to swing by Emmeline Hoyle's house. Grimes might think Polly had killed herself, but I wasn't so sure. It was a long shot, but if anyone had been down the road to visit Polly, Emmeline might know. Maybe she could tell me more about Polly's relatives, too. I was curious to find out who was in line to inherit her house.

The kettle whistled, and I fixed a pot of English Breakfast tea. By the time I had finished my first steaming cup, the brownies were cool enough to frost, and I was in a slightly better mood as I smoothed the rich chocolate frosting over the dark brownies. I cut myself a slab and sank my teeth into it. This recipe was definitely a keeper; the tartness of the cherries melding with the dark chocolate was heaven. Charlene didn't know what she was missing. I glanced out the window toward the dock—if John was back, I could bring him a plateful as an icebreaker—but the *Little Marian* still bobbed alone.

I sighed as I trudged toward the laundry room, and the mounds of linens that awaited me. I missed Polly in more ways than one.

SIX

THE SUN DIPPED LOW in the sky as I pumped the pedals of my bike down Cranberry Road. I had drunk two pots of tea and done six loads of laundry, but neither John nor Sgt. Grimes had turned up, and I was afraid Benjamin would corner me again if I hung around the inn.

Emmeline Hoyle's house huddled under the tall pine trees. The front yard was neatly kept and the house had recently been painted a bright mint green. I glanced down the road as I pulled up on my bike. The crusty blacktop was empty; the rusted truck the police had borrowed was gone, and Murray's Jaguar had either survived the trip back up the road or been towed. I left the bike leaning against a tree and wove through the garden gnomes that peopled Emmeline's front yard, wishing I'd shown a bit of restraint with the tea as I sloshed up the walk. When I stumbled over a cheery little fellow pushing a wheelbarrow, it felt as if the tides were shifting in my stomach.

Emmeline answered the door almost immediately, looking like a throwback to the 1950s in her pink housedress. A bright flowered apron was tied snugly around her ample middle, and her cheeks were as round and shiny as Parkerhouse rolls. The shrewd glint in her raisin-brown eyes, however, told me this was no June Cleaver.

"What can I do for you?" she asked, wiping her damp hands on her apron.

"I'm Natalie Barnes," I said. "I run the Gray Whale Inn. I'm the one who found your neighbor, Polly Sarkes, this morning."

She nodded. "She did some work for you, didn't she?"

"Yes, she did. I was hoping to talk to you about her, if you don't mind."

Emmeline clicked her tongue. "Terrible thing, isn't it? Quiet as a church mouse, Polly was. I never thought she'd come to an end like that." She shook her head. "But come in, come in." I followed her through the small but tidy living room into the kitchen. The window over the sink looked out onto the pitted road, and I could see Polly's lonely house in the distance.

"Please sit down," Emmeline said, and I pulled up a ladder-backed chair. My stomach gurgled as I sat down and watched her fill a kettle with water. "Can I get you some tea?"

I groaned silently, but said, "Thanks, that would be lovely." Between the caffeine and the constant trips to the bathroom, I was worried I'd never get to sleep that night. Then again, if tonight was anything like last night, the odds were that I'd be up anyway.

I surveyed the kitchen as she bustled around. Like Polly's house, the surfaces sparkled, but Emmeline was a bit more liberal in the decoration department; the pink walls were festooned with embroidered samplers of various shapes and sizes, and the window-sill was crammed with what looked like homemade pincushions shaped like vegetables. I felt like I'd wandered into the sewing section of a craft store.

"Did you do all of these samplers?" I asked.

Emmeline smiled proudly. "Yes, I did. Designed them, too. I've always had a knack for handwork."

I glanced around at the embroidered butterflies and flowers and focused on a particularly busy piece, loaded with roses and irises and at least six hummingbirds. "That one is so intricate," I said. "It's really beautiful."

Emmeline flushed. "Thank you. I've been thinking about going to some of the craft fairs on the mainland, but Henry always tells me it's not worth it."

"I think you should," I said. "I'll bet there's a market out there that would love your stuff."

Emmeline eyed me as she sliced a loaf of what looked like banana bread. "I could do one for your inn, if you'd like. With whales on it, maybe a few seagulls."

I cringed inwardly, but said, "That would be wonderful." I watched as Emmeline laid a plate of the brown bread on the yellow tablecloth. "Wow," I said with a touch of apprehension. "You cook, too?"

"It's not as good as the food up there at that inn of yours, I suppose, but yes."

"Oh, I wouldn't say that." I took a bite of the dense, sweet bread. The sweetness of banana mingled with a spice I didn't recognize, and my taste buds sang with pleasure. The cross-stitch might be a bit much for my taste, but this woman could cook. "I might need the recipe for this."

Emmeline tucked her lips into a small smile as she sat down. "I'd be happy to give it to you," she said. "But you didn't come down here to talk about banana bread and handwork, did you?"

I smiled sheepishly. "Not really, no."

Her voice was brisk. "Why do you want to know about Polly? The police said it was a suicide. No foul play."

I looked up. "They've been out asking questions?"

"No." Emmeline took a bite of banana bread. Her pink cheeks wobbled as she chewed a few times and swallowed. "That's what I heard down at the store."

I finished my bread, then dabbed at my mouth with an embroidered napkin and leaned back in my chair. "I don't know. Something about it just doesn't seem right to me. How well did you know Polly?"

"Well, we said hello and all, but she kept to herself, mostly."

"Do you think she seemed like the type of person who would commit suicide?"

Emmeline's brown eyes narrowed, and she glanced out the window toward Polly's vacant house. "I don't know," she said slowly. "It's pretty lonely out there, so maybe. But they said she shot herself." Her eyes were keen. "And that just doesn't seem like a woman's way to go, now, does it?"

"No," I agreed. "It doesn't."

The kettle whistled and Emmeline stood up. I watched as she poured hot water into a teapot shaped like a chubby rabbit, then plunked it onto the table with a sugar bowl and creamer shaped like cabbages. I waited until she had settled herself in the chair across from me before I asked the next question.

"Did anyone ever come down the road to visit her?"

"Not often. Like I said, she kept to herself." Her brow furrowed slightly. "Wait a minute. I did see that new priest headed down the road once or twice over the last few weeks."

I leaned forward. "Reverend McLaughlin?"

"That's his name. Good-looking young man, isn't he? Yes, he did come by."

"Anytime in the last couple of days?"

"Let me see . . . I was hanging out the wash, so it must have been Monday afternoon."

Monday afternoon. Four days ago.

"And he'd been down to see Polly before?"

"A couple of times, yes."

"But nobody else?" I asked.

"Well, Murray Selfridge has been down from time to time, of course, checking out that bog of his, but I don't know if he talked to Polly. And that development fellow, the chunky one with a face like a tomato, he was here earlier in the week. But I don't imagine he was down for a visit."

"No, I imagine not." Russell didn't seem the type to pay social calls to islanders. Unless, that is, he was trying to persuade Polly to sell her house.

"How about her cousin, Gary. Was he close to Polly?"

"Gary?" She swiped at the air with her hand. "He's a lazy one, that Gary Sarkes. Lives down by the dock, but he never comes down this way. He's a lobsterman, and a poor one at that."

"Is he Polly's only relative?"

"Only one I know of. Both of her parents died years ago, and she didn't have any sisters or brothers."

"Do you think Polly left the house to him?"

Emmeline shrugged. "I imagine so. Who else would she leave it to?"

I didn't know. "Not a bad deal for Gary, is it?" I wondered aloud.

Emmeline nodded sagely.

"So aside from the development folks and Reverend McLaughlin," I continued, "it's been pretty quiet down at Polly's lately?"

"We don't get much traffic on this part of the island. Every once in a while the day-trippers come down on their bikes, and I imagine I'll see a few more folks now that the cranberries are ripe, but it's pretty quiet down here." She poured tea into two cups festooned with carrots and slid one across the table to me. I picked it up and pretended to take a sip as she continued. "Of course, that will change once that development goes in. Maybe they'll do something about that road."

"That will really change things around here, won't it?"

She shrugged as she spooned sugar into her cup. "Probably so. Maybe Henry and I'll be able to sell up, though, turn a good profit on this place. Move into something fancier."

"Maybe," I said. "Have you lived here your whole life?"

"Mostly. Since I married Henry, anyway. I lived over in Somesville when I was a girl. Still have family over there."

"I'm pretty new here, myself. In fact, I was about to head over to the museum this afternoon and ask Matilda if she knew the history of the inn."

Emmeline gave me a sly look. "Been hearing things at night, have you?"

I started, spilling tea over the rim of my cup. I dabbed at it hastily with my napkin. "What do you mean?"

"That inn you've got is haunted. That's why it was empty for so long."

"Haunted?"

"Ayuh." She dipped her chin. "A young girl got herself murdered up there."

"Murdered?" I put down my cup. "What happened?"

"She was a cook. Pretty young thing, they say, and she's been haunting the place ever since. Moving around at night, bumping into things. Used to see lights in the windows, late at night, when the place was empty." She leaned over conspiratorially. "My Henry, he once did some work up there. Came home white as a sheet. Said he saw a lady on the stairs, wearing a big old-fashioned dress. In broad daylight, too."

A full-blown apparition? Bumps in the night were one thing, but dead people milling around on the stairs was something else entirely. A chill ran down my spine, but I kept my face neutral. "What was Henry doing at the inn?"

"Oh, he always does odd jobs for folks when the fishing's bad. He's pretty handy. Keeps the place up real nice, don't you think?" I looked around the gaudy kitchen and nodded.

"Anyway," she said, "He used to do some work for the lady who used to own the place. He was white as a sheet when he came home that day. I'll never forget it."

"When did the murder happen?"

She took a long sip of tea and settled back into her chair. "Oh, sometime in the 1850s, I think."

"Well, I'll keep my ears open, but so far it's been pretty quiet up there."

"Mmmm." Emmeline sipped her tea. "The museum's been closed since Labor Day, you know."

"You're kidding."

"Nope. Matilda lives right next door, though, in the yellow house. I'm sure she'd be happy to help you out."

"Thanks," I said. "You've been a huge help." I took a last fake swig out of my carroty cup and stood up, launching another series of waves in my midsection. "Well, I'd probably better head back home," I said. "It's getting late, and with Polly gone, I've got a lot to do." Emmeline pushed back her chair and stood. "Thank you for the tea, and for talking to me about Polly. If you think of anything else, please let me know."

"Why are you so curious about Polly?"

I looked at Emmeline's intelligent eyes. "Because I think she might have been murdered," I answered honestly. "And I don't think the police are going to do anything about it."

She was quiet for a moment. "Well," she said, "I don't know what good you'll be able to do, but I wish you luck. If I think of anything else, I'll call you." Her eyes twinkled for a moment. "And if you're interested in a sampler for the inn, you let me know."

"Why don't you work up a design for me, and let me know how much it'll cost? And if I could have a copy of that banana bread recipe, that would be great."

"I'll do that."

I was on my way out the door when I paused. "By the way, would you mind keeping an eye on Polly's cats? I fed them today, and I'll keep stopping by, but I don't think I'll be able to make it down every day."

"What do I have to do?"

"Just give them food and water. The food's in a can on the back porch. I just refilled the water in the kitchen."

I felt Emmeline's eyes follow me as my stomach and I sloshed back up the road. I felt strangely relieved when the trees obscured the small green house from view.

———

By the time I reached the main road, the red-gold light of evening had settled over the island and the temperature had started to drop. I shivered as I slowed the bike to a stop.

As much as I wanted to go straight to Matilda's house, it was getting close to dinnertime, and I still had a lot of things to do around the inn. Besides, I was in dire need of a bathroom. Benjamin's face flashed into my mind, and my distended stomach tightened. I hoped he had headed toward the pier for the evening. I hadn't even had a chance to talk with John yet; the last thing I needed right now was another confrontation with Benjamin.

I looked down the road toward the pier. The pine trees were wreathed in shadow, and a flurry of leaves skittered across the road as a chill wind blew up from the water. If I went into town now, I'd have to ride home in the dark. Cranberry Island didn't have streetlights, and there would be no moon to light the way. I sighed and pointed the bike toward the inn. Maybe John would be home. I needed to talk to him about Polly—and about Benjamin.

When I coasted down the other side of the hill toward the Gray Whale Inn ten minutes later, the inn's windows glowed a cheery yellow, but John's carriage house was dark. I rolled the bike into the shed and trotted to the kitchen door.

Pepper rose from her spot next to the radiator and trotted over to greet me. Her entire body vibrated with purring as I scooped her up and rubbed her chin. I glanced around the room, looking for Biscuit. She was nowhere to be seen, but a note lay on the table.

I tucked Pepper into the crook of my arm and picked up the piece of paper.

Nat –
Dinner tonight? I'm dying to see you. I'll wait for you in the parlor.
Love,
B

I folded the note in half and shoved it into my pocket, then put Pepper back down by the radiator. First, I ran upstairs to run a brush through my hair, and add just a touch of lipstick.

My heart started whacking out a wild rhythm as I pushed through the swinging door to the dining room a few minutes later. I held my breath as I turned the corner and walked into the parlor, anticipating Benjamin's long lean body stretched out nonchalantly on one of my flowered couches, already feeling the liquid blue heat of his eyes. I felt almost dizzy as I swept into the room, still unsure of what I would say.

I needn't have worried. Benjamin wasn't there.

My body felt deflated as I sank onto one of the couches. I had a sudden longing for a warm, feline body next to mine, but Pepper was still in the kitchen and Biscuit was nowhere to be seen.

"Biscuit!" I called. I listened, but I didn't hear her. The inn was silent—except for the steady drip, drip, drip of water.

I followed the sound to the staircase and sucked in my breath. A stream of water was flowing down the stairs, puddling on the carpet at my feet.

SEVEN

I TOOK THE STAIRS two at a time, following the water down the hall to its source. It was issuing from Candy's room. I knocked furiously, but no one answered, and the doorknob refused to turn; it was locked.

I raced back downstairs and grabbed the skeleton key, then rushed back up and threw open the door.

The pine floor was swamped.

I swore as I sloshed through what seemed like a foot of water to the bathroom. The faucet of the white pedestal sink was running, and a small waterfall cascaded over the oval rim to the lake on the floor below.

I waded over and turned the faucet off. The stopper was closed, and a wet washcloth was wedged into the overflow drain. I pulled the cloth from the overflow drain, opened the stopper, and turned to survey the damage.

The feet of the four-poster bed were submerged, dark water stains were seeping up the bed's pink and blue quilt, and the hand-hooked rug was sodden. I glanced toward the door; the water was still flowing into the hallway. I had some heavy-duty mopping to do— and I could only pray that would be the extent of it.

As I retrieved a giant stack of towels from the laundry room, Gwen breezed into the kitchen. Her smile faded when she saw me.

"Hey, Aunt Nat. What's wrong?" She drew in her breath when I told her what I had found in Candy's room, then grabbed another stack of towels and followed me upstairs.

"How the heck did she manage to stop up the overflow drain?" Gwen asked as we started swabbing down the soggy floorboards.

"She's not overly gifted in the brains department," I said.

"Is the downstairs room okay?" she asked as I wrung out a towel in the tub.

I froze. "The downstairs room?" I had forgotten about the room on the first floor. Had the water leaked through the ceiling? Panic welled in my chest as I tossed the towel into the tub and raced for the door. "Keep mopping. I'll go check."

As I let myself into the room beneath Candy's with the skeleton key, my heart plummeted. The ceiling sagged like a water balloon, and large chunks of plaster lay scattered across the floor. I slumped against the door for a moment, then pulled myself together and went to get more towels. At least this room was vacant. The last thing I needed was a lawsuit from a guest who had been hit by a slab of falling ceiling.

By the time I made it back upstairs, the water level in Candy's room had receded considerably. I stood in the bathroom doorway and watched as Gwen attempted to wring the rug out in the bathtub. She looked up.

"Is the room downstairs okay?"

"It's great if you want the *20,000 Leagues Under the Sea* look." I sighed. "I cleaned up as much as I could, but there's a lot of damage."

Gwen winced. "I hope these floors will be okay."

"Me too." I felt a stab of worry. Antique wood floors were difficult—and expensive—to replace. I grabbed a towel and got back to work.

"I heard about Polly," Gwen said quietly as I attacked a puddle. "What a shock."

"I know." I thought of Polly's sightless brown eyes and shivered. "I can't get over it. What did you hear?"

"That she shot herself in the bog near her house."

I snorted. "Well, that's what the police think, anyway."

Gwen paused as she squeezed the rug. "You don't think so?"

"Did she seem depressed to you?"

"Depressed? No, not depressed. Distracted, though."

I raised my eyebrows. "I hadn't noticed."

"She was helping me clean the rooms last week. Usually we talk, but this time she kept losing track of the conversation. When I asked her if something was wrong, she said something about a decision that she had to make."

"A decision?"

"She didn't say anything else about it," Gwen said. "She left a few minutes after that, and then yesterday . . ." Gwen trailed off. By yesterday, Polly had most likely been dead.

"Do you think she was considering selling her house to Murray?" I asked.

Gwen shook her mass of dark curls. "I wish I knew." She sighed. "I wish I'd asked."

71

"Well, there's no way to find out now," I said. "But don't blame yourself. You had no way of knowing what was going to happen."

Gwen pushed a stray curl behind her ear. "What does Charlene think? She knows everything about everyone."

I grimaced. "Charlene's mad at me because I gave her a hard time about her boyfriend."

Gwen laughed. "That explains it. She was awfully chilly today when I dropped those cookies off. She didn't even get off the phone to say hi."

"I guess I'd better get down there and apologize," I said.

"What was in that package, anyway?"

"I didn't tell you?" Gwen's brown eyes widened as I told her about Benjamin—and about John.

"Have you talked to John yet?"

"No, he's never home. I'm supposed to have dinner with him tomorrow night, but I don't even know if that's still on."

Gwen shook her head slowly. "Man, you *have* had a day. Why don't you let me finish this up and you go get some sleep?"

"Thanks, but I won't be able to sleep until I know this is taken care of." I glanced at Gwen. "By the way, have you been hearing any noises at night?"

"Noises?" Gwen looked perplexed. "No. Why?"

"Oh, nothing," I said. "I heard a couple of bumps last night. It was probably just the wind."

It was almost midnight when Gwen and I finished cleaning both rooms and the hallway the best we could. Despite the chill in the air, I opened the windows to help dry the place out. Candy hadn't gotten home yet, so I left her a note telling her to switch to another room down the hall. As I passed Benjamin's room, I couldn't help but notice that the gap beneath his door was dark as well. When we were together, Benjamin never turned out the lights before one. Maybe he was becoming an early bird in his old age.

Biscuit was still nowhere to be seen as I eased myself under the down comforter. I considered going downstairs to get Pepper, but decided against it. Life with Biscuit—particularly after a week with two dachshunds in the house—was going to be hard enough. No need to make it worse by inviting Pepper into my bed.

A quiver of apprehension passed through me as I glanced at the ceiling, but I reached over and turned the light off anyway. Soon I drifted off to sleep.

———

Either whatever was in the attic took the night off or I slept so hard it hadn't woken me up. By 8:30 the next morning I was feeling a little more in control of things; breakfast was laid out on the buffet, I had put in a call to the insurance company, and Candy was nowhere to be seen. To my relief, the insurance agent had promised to send out someone to assess and potentially start repairing the damage that afternoon. I walked out to greet my guests with a sense of having accomplished at least one thing that morning.

Benjamin sat alone in the dining room when I walked in with a fresh pot of coffee. He rose quickly as I walked to his table, and my personal percussion section started up a new number in my ribcage. His clothes, though casual—jeans and a green plaid shirt—were clearly expensive and had been pressed to within an inch of their lives. His familiar smile and the faint scent of his cologne sent tremors through me. I struggled to keep my hand steady as I filled his cup. Although I had sworn Benjamin off for life, I was glad I had put on a touch of lipstick that morning.

"I missed you last night," he said. "Did you get my note?"

"Yes, I did." I set down the coffeepot and Benjamin's hand closed on my wrist.

"Well, how about tonight?" he asked.

"I'm sorry. I already have other plans."

I glanced up at him, and his blue eyes bored into mine. "Lunch, then?"

I shook my head. Despite a shameful desire to say yes, I was pleased that my resolve was holding up at least as well as the Aqua Net I had spritzed on before coming downstairs. "Can't do it," I said firmly. "One of the rooms flooded last night. I have to wait for the insurance adjuster, and then I have some errands to do."

My errands, which included a visit to Matilda Jenkins and the museum, could wait. But Benjamin didn't need to know that. "So, where did you end up going last night?" I asked.

"Down to the lobster place," he said. "I ran into another one of your guests there."

"Oh?"

"Candy Perkins. We ended up having dinner together, since we were the only ones in the place."

"Oh." The percussion section slowed.

Benjamin ran his hand up and down my arm, then lowered his voice. "When can we talk?"

"I don't know, Benjamin. It's just . . ." At that moment, Candy walked in, dressed in a short pink skirt and a clinging spandex top. Benjamin released my arm and turned to her with a smile, which she returned with full wattage.

Her smile dimmed as she turned to me. "What happened to my room?"

"The sink overflowed."

"Overflowed?" Her blue eyes widened. "Oh," she laughed. "I must have forgotten to turn the water off. Silly me. I was giving myself a mini-facial—you know, with lots of hot water and steam?—and I must have gotten distracted."

I gritted my teeth.

"Well, on the plus side, my new room is even nicer than my old one," she said. Her eyes fell on the coffee pot. "Ooh, coffee." She giggled at Benjamin. "We got in so late last night, I'll need some caffeine to get going this morning. Your friend Ben here is quite a guy." She slid into the chair next to his and held up her mug. I pulled my lips into a strained smile and filled her mug with coffee.

"I'm glad you like your new room," I said. "I'm afraid both your old room and the one beneath it are pretty much a loss until next spring."

"Thank goodness for insurance, huh?" She took a big sip of coffee and closed her eyes. "Just what I needed." She opened them and studied the buffet. "Is there anything over there that I can eat this morning?" She ran a hand over her flat, spandexed tummy. "Got to watch my figure, you know. I think Natalie has done surprisingly well, considering. If I were eating all those starchy, fatty foods all the time I'm sure I'd be at least as heavy as she is."

I fixed a smile on my face, but I was beginning to understand how crimes of passion happened.

"I think Natalie looks great," Benjamin said heartily, but I couldn't help but notice that his eyes still lingered on Candy's concave stomach.

I retreated to the kitchen as they headed for the buffet. Benjamin's urgency to see me had evaporated awfully quickly. Candy whispered something to him, and his deep laugh followed me as I crossed the room. I gave the swinging door a hard push, and discovered a different kind of drama on the other side.

Biscuit had finally made an appearance. The big orange tabby stood in the middle of the kitchen hissing at Pepper, who was huddled in the corner, mewling pathetically. I scooped up the older cat, murmured a few soothing words, then filled up her food dish. She was mildly appeased, but when I took a second bowl from the cupboard and filled it for Pepper, Biscuit growled and looked at me as if I were something the dog had dragged in. Only after Biscuit had eaten and stalked off up the stairs did Pepper dare to emerge from her corner and approach her bowl. Candy and Benjamin were getting along famously, but Biscuit and Pepper could still use some work.

The next time I pushed through the door into the dining room, Candy and Benjamin were still chatting happily, and Russell Lidell had taken a seat near the buffet. He was more casually dressed today, in a polo shirt and jeans that were two sizes too small, but he looked quite pleased with himself.

"How are you this morning?" I asked as cheerfully as I could.

"Great," he said, giving me a boyish smile.

"Good news from the engineer?"

"It looks like everything is going to work out just fine."

It hadn't worked out too well for Polly, I thought. "I'm glad to hear that," I lied. I filled his cup and glanced over at Benjamin and Candy. They didn't even notice me.

The honeymooners came down a few minutes later, and I was conscious of Candy's trills of laughter as I filled their coffee cups and retreated once again to my kitchen. Everyone in the dining room was in high spirits, but I was sliding into Prozac territory. At least both Candy and Benjamin were out from underfoot, I told myself. I tried to be relieved when they exited the dining room together.

"Let me know when you have some time," Benjamin called to me over his shoulder as I picked up their dirty breakfast dishes. I could hear Candy inviting him to join her on the next mail boat as they climbed the stairs to their rooms.

As I carried a stack of dishes to the kitchen, an image of Candy and Benjamin snuggled up together on the boat flashed into my mind. I shook my head hard, trying to dislodge it. Benjamin and I were over, I reminded myself. If Candy wanted him, she could have him. I dumped the rest of the dishes into the sink and eyed the now-overflowing laundry room with dismay.

Then I rolled up my sleeves and got to work.

———

It was almost four o'clock by the time I rolled up outside the Cranberry Island Historical Museum. I had left the insurance adjuster and several loads of undone laundry behind at the inn, but I was curious enough about the inn's ghost that I didn't want to waste another day finding out about it. I also needed a break from the inn—and the people in it.

The Cranberry Island Historical Museum was a small brick building—the only brick building on the island, in fact. It squatted about a hundred yards south of the pier, and the smell of exhaust from a lobster boat loading up on bait wafted over me as I rode past it.

I'd never noticed it before, but a tiny wood-framed house was tucked up into the pine trees behind the museum, just as Emmeline had told me. I parked the bike next to the house's short white picket fence and made my way down the stone path to the front door. Matilda opened the cheery blue door almost as I knocked.

"Hi. I'm Natalie Barnes, the owner of the Gray Whale Inn."

"Hello, Natalie." Matilda adjusted the glasses at the end of her long nose. A blue shirtwaist dress hung on her thin form, and her white hair was cropped close to her head. She looked like the prototype for a librarian. "I'm Matilda Jenkins. What can I do for you?"

"I was talking with Emmeline Hoyle yesterday about doing some research on the inn. She told me that the museum is closed for the season, but that you might be able to help me out."

Her thin lips twisted into a smile. "I imagine summertime isn't the best time to do research for you, is it?"

I smiled back. "No, it's not. Too many pancakes to flip."

Matilda reached over and took a key from a hook on the wall next to the door. "Let's go. I know I've got some documents on the inn. They transferred a bunch from St. James, and Murray had some documents he copied for me, but I haven't had a chance to look through all of them. I know I've seen references to your building, though. It's had a colorful history."

As we passed through Matilda's white wooden gate, I remembered that the museum was a relatively new establishment. Murray had renovated the old brick building to fulfill a campaign promise. Once he funded it, however, I imagined he envisioned a blown-up exhibit dedicated to the Selfridge family. Charlene had told me the Selfridges were one of the oldest families on the island, and I was kind of surprised he hadn't insisted the museum be named after himself, or at least his family.

As Matilda fumbled with the key, I reflected that at least one good thing had come from Murray's presence on the island. Too many small towns and cities lost their history; the museum, if it actually contained information on families other than the Selfridges, might help prevent that from happening to Cranberry Island.

The inside of the small building smelled of dust and old books, and dozens of boxes lay stacked in the corners of the front room. "As you can see," Matilda said, "it's very much a work in progress. We've got three exhibits up"—she pointed to the Plexiglas cases, filled with old fishing implements and photos of a less-populated Cranberry Island, that stretched along the walls—"but once the season ended, I pulled out everything else that needs to be catalogued."

As I looked at the piles of battered boxes, some of which were stacked chest-high, I was grateful that all I had to deal with was dirty laundry. "You've got an amazing amount of stuff for such a small island," I said as I followed her through an arched doorway to the back room.

"Well, since all of the families are related—and most have been here for hundreds of years—lots of folks held onto everything about their ancestors. It's not like most places, where people move somewhere new every five years. People know their history here." She peered at me over her glasses. "And nobody forgets anything. Old grudges last a long, long time." She bent over and examined a line of boxes. "Ah, here it is," she said. She dusted off a box and heaved it up onto a table in the middle of the room.

"This is the box Murray gave me," she said as she flipped the top open. "I haven't had a chance to really go through it—I'm hoping to get that done this winter—but I know I saw a file on the house in here somewhere." She rifled through the papers, stirring up a good bit of dust. A large brown spider scuttled out of the box as she pulled out a yellowing manila folder. "Here it is."

She opened the folder to a black-and-white picture of the inn, now brown at the corners. The weathered shingled house looked very much as it did now, only with what looked like a small family grouped stiffly on the front porch. The man in the photo was short, and clad in a formal black suit. The dress of the woman beside him was tight at the bodice, but swelled into a huge, bell-shaped skirt. It was hard to make out their features; the people in the photo were squinting at the sun. I peered at the photograph, looking for differences. Instead of roses, delphiniums bloomed along the porch's painted railing, but other than that, the house looked eerily identical.

"When was this taken?"

Matilda flipped the photo over. "There's no date on it, but from the dresses and the people in it, I'm guessing sometime in the mid-1800s."

"Do you know who these people are?"

"That's Jonah Selfridge, and his wife, Myra. He built the house— I mean the inn—you're living in. Jonah was a prominent sea captain. Most folks built their houses near the pier, but not Jonah. His wife hated the smell of fish, so she convinced him to build out on the end of the island."

"The Selfridges? As in Murray Selfridge?"

"Oh, yes," she said. "They were a very important family on the island for a long time. They fell on hard times, of course, and had to sell the house, but Murray's done a good job of regaining lost ground."

I pointed to two young boys dressed in sailor suits, standing in front of their parents. They looked to be about five and eight years old. "These are their children?"

She peered at the photo. "Yes, yes. Jonah Jr. and William, I believe. William would be Murray's great-great-great-grandfather, or something like that." She gazed at the photo. "Small family, isn't it? For the times, anyway."

My eyes passed over the house, and stopped at one of the windows near the end. I looked closer. What looked like a white face, half in shadow, peered out of the kitchen window.

"Who's that?" I pointed at the face.

Matilda stooped over the photograph. "Well, well. I hadn't noticed that before. It looks like somebody's standing at the window, doesn't it?" She shrugged her bony shoulders. "They only had the two children, and they're in the photograph, of course. That's the kitchen, isn't it? I don't know. Maybe it's the cook."

The cook who had been murdered, I wondered? I decided to take the plunge. "Emmeline Hoyle told me there was a tragedy in the house."

Matilda looked up. "Oh, yes. People say that's part of the reason Murray didn't buy it back when it went on the market a few years ago. That the house is cursed for the Selfridges, or some nonsense like that. He told me once he just didn't like the maintenance of old houses, prefers something new. Quite sensible, if you ask me." She turned the photo over. "Of course, some folks say the old Selfridge place—your inn, nowadays—is haunted," she added nonchalantly.

"Haunted?"

"I don't believe a word of it. But lots of folks say they've seen lights out there, late at night, and people say they've heard strange noises. Bumping, and footsteps. Especially near the kitchen. That's supposed to be where she died, you know. She was stabbed to death in the servants' quarters, above the kitchen."

The hair prickled on the back of my neck. My bedroom was right above the kitchen.

She riffled through the pages. "I know I have the newspaper article about the murder here somewhere, but I don't think it's in this file." She walked across the room and rifled through a few more boxes before withdrawing another manila folder. "Here's the file on the ownership. Maybe it's in here somewhere." She flipped through the pages. "No, nothing but copies of old deeds. If you give me a few days, though, I know I can find it. They never found the murderer, you know."

I looked at the shadowy face in the photo again. "What was her name?"

"Oakes, I think. Anne, or Amy, or something. I can't recall. The name isn't an island name; she must have come over from the mainland."

I leafed through the rest of the file. It consisted largely of lists of boats and cargos. Based on the number of vessels listed, it appeared the Selfridges had once done very well for themselves, indeed.

"It looks like you've got a treasure trove of information here." I glanced at my watch: it was almost five. If I was going to have dinner with John at six, I needed to get back. "Maybe this winter, when business slows down, I can come down and help you go through the stuff on the inn. If you find anything else on it, would you mind putting it aside for me? I'd like to put together the building's history."

Matilda smiled. "That would be very nice. It's always good to have a bit of company."

As I pedaled away from the small brick museum, I felt a chill pass through me. Maybe the noises above my head had been made by the murdered cook. If so, I hoped she wouldn't be visiting me again soon.

EIGHT

I KNOCKED AT JOHN's door at exactly six o'clock, and stood picking pieces of lint off of my green sweater as I waited. Apparently it had been washed along with a wad of Kleenex. Although I had found most of the big chunks before I left the inn, there were still a few stragglers. I would have preferred to change into something that looked less like a flocked Christmas tree, but my wardrobe choices were limited; the laundry room was so bogged down in dirty towels, I hadn't had a chance to wash my own clothes.

Although John usually answered immediately—his apartment wasn't very large—nobody came to the door. I was pretty sure he was home; I had checked the dock first, and *Mooncatcher* was moored next to my own skiff, the *Little Marian*. Unless John had gone for a walk, he was here. I adjusted my blouse, rubbed my freshly lipsticked lips together, and knocked again. After a few moments, he opened the door slowly.

John's ready smile was nowhere in evidence, and when I saw the stillness in his normally mischievous eyes, I felt as if I had been punched. All thoughts of Benjamin dissolved instantly—except a desire to march back to the inn and send him packing.

"Hey," I said.

"Hey yourself." He stood leaning against the doorframe. He didn't invite me in.

"We need to talk."

"Do we?" He pushed himself back from the doorframe and walked into the small, dim living room, leaving the door ajar behind him. I stood on the front step for a moment, then followed him. My stomach rumbled as I closed the door behind me. I should have grabbed a snack; it looked like a pretty safe bet that dinner was off.

He sat down on the couch as I closed the distance between us, feeling as if I had a scarlet "A" on my chest and wishing I'd given a tad more thought to how I would handle this.

I leaned down and kissed him lightly on the head, inhaling the smell of his shampoo and the scent of freshly cut wood he always carried with him. Then I took a deep breath and dove in. "I'm sorry if what you saw yesterday upset you," I said. "It wasn't what it looked like."

"Oh, no?" I could feel the tension radiating from him.

I sighed. "I'll be right back." I walked past him to the kitchen. The sink, which was usually scrubbed clean, was filled with dirty dishes. Dinner was definitely off; it looked as if John had been subsisting on TV dinners and peanut butter sandwiches the last day or so. I opened the fridge and pulled out two Heinekens. Then I returned to the living room, set one down on the table next to the seal sculpture, and began twisting the lid off of the one in my hand. John watched as I struggled. After observing me strain and grunt for about thirty seconds, the corner of his mouth twitched upward.

I stopped twisting. "What?"

"They're not screw-top."

"Oh." So much for the take-charge, I've-got-everything-under-control approach.

He got up and disappeared into the kitchen. When he returned, he was armed with a church key.

"This might help," he said, and reached for my beer. I felt the heat from his fingertips as he took the cold bottle from my hand.

He handed it back to me and popped the top of his own beer. Then he sat back down on the couch, took a long swig, and proceeded to study the bottle's green and white label. I took a seat on the chair across from him and took a sip of my Heineken, feeling as if I were about to begin a chess tournament. I was never very good at chess.

"I know what you saw yesterday," I said slowly. I leaned forward and tried to catch his eye, but it was fixed on the bottle in his hand. "It's not what it looked like."

John turned the Heineken around in his hands and pulled at the corner of the label.

I plowed ahead. "I was once engaged to Benjamin." John's eyebrows rose a fraction. "But I was the one who broke it off."

After a heavy silence, John finally spoke. "You looked pretty connected yesterday afternoon."

"I had just gotten back from finding Polly," I said. "Benjamin showed up on my doorstep. I was upset. He took advantage of the situation." I glanced up at John. The expression on his long, tanned face was unreadable. "But everything is over between us. That's why I pushed him away. You saw that part too, didn't you?"

"I'm not sure what I saw." John's words were measured. He raised his green eyes from the bottle in his hands. "If it's over between you, then what is he doing up here?"

"I didn't know he was coming. He reserved a room under a false name. He knew that if he used his own name, I never would have accepted the reservation."

"That doesn't answer the question."

I sighed and leaned back in my chair. "He wants to get back together with me. I told him no." John sat motionless. "I told him there was someone else in my life now."

"Oh?"

"What do you mean, 'oh'?'"

"If you mean me, we've hardly spoken two words to each other the last several weeks."

"I know, I know," I said. "The inn sucks up all of my time. But the slow season's starting. That will change."

John took a swig of beer, then returned to studying it. "I'm sorry about Polly, by the way. That must have been terrible."

"Thanks. It was." We were making progress.

"I hear the funeral's tomorrow," he said.

"The autopsy's been done?"

John looked up sharply. "Yes. Why?"

"Grimes said it was suicide, but I don't believe him."

John shook his head. "I know he's not the best cop on the planet, and I know he was wrong last time. But Polly committed suicide. She wasn't murdered."

"Is that what the autopsy says?"

"Yes, that's what the autopsy says. I got a look at it this morning. She was killed by the gun she held in her hand. There were traces of gunpowder on her hands and around the wound. Everything is consistent with a suicide."

"Except for the fact that she was packing to take a trip. And she was about to try out a new recipe."

John narrowed his eyes at me. "How do you know that?"

"After I called the police, I looked around her house. I was trying to find the kitten she rescued a week or so ago. Pepper. Which is another thing that bothered me, actually. Her cats were hungry."

He shrugged. "Depressed people do crazy things. Maybe she didn't have the energy to feed them."

"But she had the energy to walk out into the bog and shoot herself?"

John let out another one of his long-suffering sighs.

"Any other injuries?" I asked. "Because it almost looked to me like she had a slight black eye."

"You're right. She had a few bruises. But they must have happened at least a few days before she died; they had a chance to heal."

"How many bullets were in the gun?"

"How many bullets were in the gun?" He looked at me incredulously. "What are you, Kinsey Millhone? How should I know how many bullets were in the gun?"

"Well, you are officially a cop. And you did see the autopsy."

"I don't know. If you really want to know, I can probably find out, but I can't see how it's relevant."

"Just because there was gunpowder on her hands doesn't mean she fired the shot that killed her."

"What are you suggesting? That she shot the gun once, and then someone else got the gun out of her hands and shot her? And nobody heard it?"

"You have to admit, it is a possibility."

He sighed. "Anything's a possibility with you."

"Will you at least look into it?"

He took another swig of his beer. "If you'll get your ex-fiancé out of your inn, I'll look into it."

It was my turn to sigh. "Believe me, I'm trying."

He ran his eyes over me. "You're wearing lipstick and you did your hair. Exactly how hard are you trying?"

He had hit closer to the mark than I liked, and I could feel myself flush. "We had a dinner date. Remember?"

"Oh, yeah. You'll have to forgive me if I assumed you had other plans."

"Well, I'll accept a rain check. Extenuating circumstances and all. In fact, why don't you come to my place for dinner? How about tomorrow night?"

"As soon as you've evicted the ex-boyfriend."

"He's only supposed to be here a few more days."

"I hear there's a nice inn on the mainland. About two hundred miles from here."

"What am I supposed to do, tell him to clear out of town?"

"I could do it for you."

"Actually, if you could give Candy Perkins the boot, I'd be almost as happy."

"Candy Perkins?"

"The bubble-headed woman who wants to open her own bed and breakfast. She's been following me everywhere. She stopped up her overflow drain last night and flooded her room, the room below her, and the entire upstairs hall."

John winced. "How much damage?"

"Well, the room below hers is missing about a third of its ceiling, and I'm not sure the wood floors are going to survive. Not to mention the furniture."

"You've got the windows open, I hope?"

"Yes. I've been hoping for a warm front, but it hasn't materialized."

He grinned. "You're not in Texas anymore."

I thought of Benjamin and shivered. "Thank God."

As I left a few minutes later, John gave me a tentative hug and a chaste, dry kiss on the cheek. I hugged him back as hard as I could. "Are you sure you won't come to dinner tomorrow?"

"Not until he's gone," he said. He released me, and I stepped out into the chilly evening. As I made my way up the path to the inn, he called after me. I turned to see him leaning against the doorframe of the carriage house. "By the way," he said, "I've been meaning to ask. Why do you have half a roll of toilet paper on the back of your sweater?"

———

Pepper sidled over to me as soon as I closed the kitchen door behind me, and I chucked her under the chin. At least she wasn't cowering in the corner. "Biscuit been treating you all right?" I asked. She purred and pushed her little back up against my hand. "Since it looks like you're going to be a regular around here, I'd better find out if you've had your shots." She rumbled like a miniature lawnmower, and I remembered the scrawled number on Polly's memo board. Maybe "shelter" was the animal shelter Pepper had come from. Next time I was down at Polly's, I'd have to remember to write down the number.

As I filled the cats' bowls, I reflected that the visit with John hadn't gone as badly as I had expected. His kiss had been brief, but it *had* been a kiss. I smiled, remembering his warm, woodsy scent. Now if only I could get Benjamin out of the inn . . .

I tidied up the kitchen a bit and pushed through the door into the dining room. I wasn't optimistic about how the floors were drying—I was hoping they wouldn't warp irreparably—but felt the need to check. As the door swung shut behind me, I heard a low voice.

"No, no, everything's fine. I dealt with it today." I paused in the darkened dining room, waiting for someone to respond. "I told you, it's taken care of," the same voice said, and I realized that someone was talking on the phone at the front desk. I had been meaning to have telephones installed in the rooms, but I didn't have the budget for it yet.

I tiptoed to the end of the dining room and peered around the corner. Russell Lidell stood at the front desk, cupping the receiver and glancing around nervously. I pulled my head back and stood with my back up against the wall.

There was silence for a moment, and then Russell spoke again. "What, did you think I'd write him a personal check? Of course I did it in cash." He was quiet for a moment, presumably listening. "All right. I'll let you know when it's finalized. Okay, okay. Fine. I'll talk to you later."

I shuffled backward toward the kitchen and ran into the sideboard, knocking two forks off of the edge. As they clattered to the wood floor, I winced.

I had turned on the light and was retrieving a fork from under one of the tables when Russell appeared in the door to the parlor. I glanced up at him and pretended to be surprised. "Oh, hi. I didn't realize you were out and about. Can I help you with something?"

His eyes narrowed as he studied me. "Were you in here the whole time?"

I furrowed my brow. "What do you mean?"

"While I was on the phone."

"Were you on the phone?"

"Yes," he said. "Just now."

I shrugged. "I don't know. I just got back from my neighbor's, and was coming to check on the floors. We had a flood last night, you know." I grimaced. "I'm afraid some of the hardwood floors will be ruined. I'm sorry if it's a bit chilly, but I need to leave some of the windows open to dry the place out."

His eyes were slits in his ruddy face as he studied me, trying to decide if I was lying. A shiver ran down my spine as I smiled back at him, suddenly aware that we were probably alone in the inn. And that there was still a murderer unaccounted for. "Well," I said, standing up, "if there's nothing you need, I'm just going to check on the floors and grab a bite of dinner in the kitchen." I smiled and brushed past him into the parlor. I could still feel his eyes on me as I climbed the stairs to Candy's room.

NINE

THE NEXT MORNING WAS exhausting. The timer on the oven broke, and I burned the first batch of muffins. Then the guests came down for breakfast. Russell spent an entire hour shooting me nasty looks, and Benjamin and Candy fed each other bites of muffin before deciding to go kayaking together. The afternoon was no better; I spent two hours arguing with the insurance adjuster over whether Candy's little "accident" was covered by my policy. When I got off the phone thirty minutes before Polly's funeral started, I realized I had forgotten to put the blueberry pie I planned to take with me into the oven.

I ducked into the sanctuary fifteen minutes late and slid into a rear pew, my hands hurting from the heat of the pie. After pulling out a hymnal and turning it into a makeshift trivet, I scanned the backs of the heads in front of me.

Most of the island had showed up for Polly's service. I recognized Murray Selfridge's balding head across the aisle, and when I leaned over for a better view of the front row, I wasn't surprised to see Charlene's caramel-colored locks right up close to the pulpit—and McLaughlin. Charlene was flanked, I noticed, by a number of other female heads. A few rows back sat John.

As I pulled the Book of Common Prayer out of the pew back, Rev. McLaughlin introduced Gary Sarkes and stepped down. A skinny man with a mustache and a shiny, ill-fitting suit jacket lurched up the center aisle and took his place behind the pulpit. He stood there for at least a minute, clearing his throat and pulling at his lapels.

After evicting what must have been an entire extended family of frogs from his throat, he pulled out a wrinkled sheet of notebook paper. His nasal voice wavered as he launched into perhaps the world's shortest eulogy.

"My cousin Polly," he began with a tremor, "was a real nice lady. Real nice. She was a great housecleaner, and took good care of those cats of hers." He coughed into his hand and wiped it on his pants. His audience recoiled slightly. "Real good care. We'll really miss old Polly, and hope she's happy wherever she is." He beamed at the room for a moment, as if expecting applause, or a request for an encore. Even from the back of the church, I could see the large gap between his front teeth, which were a revolting shade of brown. After a moment, Gary crumpled up the paper and stepped down, ducking his head as he returned to his pew.

"Lord knows *he's* happier now," the woman in front of me murmured to her husband. "He's already all but sold her house to Murray, I hear." The woman, a thickset middle-aged matron I recognized but didn't know, shook her head and leaned in toward her husband again. I strained to catch her words. "If I didn't know Gary doesn't have it in him, I'd a thought he'd done her in himself."

Richard McLaughlin took the pulpit again, and I found myself soothed by his deep, velvety voice as he moved effortlessly through the ceremony. It was only when my eyes drifted across Polly's shining wooden casket that I remembered with a guilty start why we were all here.

A half hour later, we followed Polly's coffin out the front doors of the church to the small cemetery next door. A rectangle of open earth yawned among the lichened tombstones and faded silk flowers. As Polly's casket descended into the cold ground, I felt more certain than ever that Polly hadn't taken her own life.

"I'll do my best to find out who did," I whispered to her casket. I stood a minute, letting the cold salt air push my hair back from my face, before following the throng back inside the church.

After retrieving my pie from the pew in the sanctuary, I headed for the fellowship hall. I added my offering to the assortment of desserts on the folding tables and wove through the crowd toward Charlene and Reverend McLaughlin. The local women were lined up to greet him, but McLaughlin was deep in conversation with Murray; at McLaughlin's elbow was Charlene, in a black scoop-necked dress that hugged her curvy figure. It looked as if her diet was working. I eased myself into the small crowd and put my hand on Charlene's arm.

"I need to talk to you," I said. "I'm sorry about the other day."

Charlene's eyes were cool, but I thought I detected a slight melt. She had opened her mouth to respond when her paramour noticed me.

McLaughlin broke off mid-sentence. "How about we continue our conversation later?" he said to Murray, who had traded in the yacht club ensemble for a sober blue suit and a tie with a huge gold pin in it.

Murray looked puzzled until his eyes flicked to me. Then he clapped McLaughlin on the back. "Good idea. I'll call you this evening." Then he turned to me. "Hello, Natalie."

I smiled tightly. Despite Murray's perpetual joviality, I hadn't forgotten that he had cut the brake lines of my bike earlier in the year. He winked at McLaughlin and drifted off.

McLaughlin engulfed my hand in his own and pumped it a few times. "Hello, Natalie. It's nice to see you, even on such a solemn occasion as this." He shook his head sadly, and his brown eyes looked at me soulfully from above his chiseled cheekbones. I looked closely. If I didn't know better, I would have sworn he was wearing blush. He delivered his next line as if he were auditioning for the lead in Hamlet. "Such a tragedy when a fine woman takes her own life."

"I understand you visited her a few times over the last couple of weeks," I said.

McLaughlin's eyes darted around the room, but he didn't answer. I pressed on. "Do you have any idea why she might have killed herself?"

He blinked twice. Charlene's sculpted eyebrows rose. "I was there to do my pastoral duties," he finally answered. "I had no idea it would . . . it would come to this."

"She didn't tell you that something was bothering her?"

McLaughlin had regained his composure, and his answer was silky smooth. "What passed between Polly and me is between God,

Polly, and me." He shrugged resignedly. "I had no idea she would take her own life." He arranged his features into a soulful look and rested his warm hand on my shoulder. "I know you feel terrible about Polly. If there's any way I can help you through your grief, you know I'm here for you."

"You can start by telling me why you were down at Polly's so much lately," I shot back. "And if you won't tell me, then tell the police."

McLaughlin glanced around and chuckled uncomfortably. Then he bent down and addressed me in a low voice. "Polly killed herself. A tragedy, to be sure. But I don't see how dredging up the sordid details of her life will do anything but destroy her memory."

Sordid details? "I'll tell you how you can help me," I said. "Tell the sordid details to the police."

He shook his head. "I'm afraid I can't do that."

He gave me a smile that had the wattage of a nightlight and turned away to greet one of his female admirers. "Such a sad occasion, isn't it?" He enfolded an octogenarian in a hug that, from the look in her watery blue eyes, gave her a thrill that was better than an entire month of *The Guiding Light*.

I glanced at Charlene. She gave me a nasty look and turned her head away. I gave up and walked over to the dessert table.

After loading up a plate with two brownies and a chocolate chip cookie, I scanned the room for a friendly face—okay, for John's face. I bit into the cookie, and the moist, buttery confection melted in my mouth. In fact, it was downright delicious. I reached for another one, and a familiar voice floated over my left shoulder.

"That's one of my favorite recipes."

I turned around, my mouth full of cookie. It was Emmeline Hoyle. No housedress today, but her blue and pink plaid dress looked like vintage 1950s Sears and Roebuck.

"These cookies are yours, too?" I mumbled through the crumbs.

Her brown eyes twinkled as she nodded. "You find out anything more about your ghost?"

"A little bit," I said. "I mean, a little bit about the inn. I haven't heard any ghosts."

"Mmmm."

"How are the cats?"

"They're doing just fine. That brown tabby is the sweetest little thing. Do you know, she followed me home the other day?"

"I'm sure Polly would be thrilled to know one of her cats had found a good home."

"I'll think about it," Emmeline said. "By the way, I forgot to tell you something. I remembered it while I was out picking berries yesterday." She paused dramatically. "The road isn't the only way down to the bog."

"No?"

"There are a couple of paths that cut through the woods to the main road."

"And?"

"Isn't it obvious?" I stared at her blankly, and she sighed with what might have been a hint of exasperation. "If people take the road, I see them. If they take the paths, I don't. So anyone could have been down at Polly's this week, and I wouldn't have known about it."

I chewed my cookie as I let this sink in. "Do you know who usually uses the paths?"

She shrugged. "Like I said, I can't see them from the house, so I don't know. Whoever doesn't feel like taking the road to the bog, I suppose."

Well, that sure narrowed it down. I shivered; just thinking about the bog brought the horror of finding Polly rushing back. I took another bite of cookie to comfort myself and tried not to think about it. Instead, I found myself focusing on the gun. "Hey, did you hear any gunshots last week?" I asked.

"Gunshots?" She shook her head and popped something that looked like silly putty from her ear. "No, but both Henry and I wear hearing aids. I think if someone blew up the house in the middle of the night, we'd both sleep through it."

Just my luck.

Emmeline looked up at me coyly. "By the way, I've been working up a design for that sampler we talked about."

I winced internally, imagining cavorting sea lions surrounded by mermaids, fluffy-tailed rabbits and hummingbirds. "Oh?" I said tentatively. "I'll have to stop by and see it sometime."

"While you're down, I'll show you those paths."

"Sure. I've been meaning to swing by and see if I could find any vet records on the cats anyway. Thanks for taking care of them, by the way."

"It's no trouble." Emmeline glanced at her watch. "Well, I'd better get back and put dinner on. Nice talking to you."

"You too," I said, grabbing another cookie.

"You might want to cut down on those," she said as she turned to go. "You're looking a little thick around the middle. Men don't

100

like that." She squinted at my face. "And you're not getting any younger, either. You might want to have Charlene order you some of that cream she uses."

I flushed and put the cookie back down. Granted, I had put on a few pounds, and my skin wasn't exactly Oil of Olay ad material; in fact, I had noticed the definite beginnings of jowls last time I studied myself in the mirror. Still, this was coming from a woman who looked like the Michelin Man's maiden aunt.

"I'll keep it in mind," I said as politely as I could. I watched Emmeline's plump form weave through the crowd and jammed the cookie into my mouth anyway. Then I strained to catch a glimpse of my profile in the plate glass window overlooking the cemetery. Between Candy and Emmeline, I was starting to get a complex.

I was sucking in my tummy and examining the results in the glass when I heard another voice behind me.

"Yeah, well, now that *she's* gone, I'll probably be picking up some new gigs." It was Marge O'Leary. I grabbed a few cookies and scooted a little further away. She must have been talking about Polly's housekeeping jobs. Polly might be gone, but even in the height of summer, I wouldn't be desperate enough to hire Marge. Charlene had told me the O'Learys' mobile home looked like a dumpster with windows, and Marge's penchant for nasty gossip made her one of the most unpleasant people on the island. Except, of course, for her husband, Eddie.

I glanced behind me. Marge looked just the same as ever. The same doughy, white skin, the same greasy reddish hair. Her beady eyes were set close to her wide nose, and her wrinkled muumuu looked as if it hadn't seen the inside of a washing machine in months. I ate another cookie, rationalizing that at least I had a ways to go until I reached Marge's proportions.

"I wonder what they'll do with all those strays?" I recognized the gruff voice of Marge's husband. "Damned nuisance. Probably cart 'em all off to the pound where they belong."

"This island is going to the dogs," Marge said. "It all comes from letting in outsiders. First there's that snooty southerner up at the inn, and now we've got these fancy houses going in."

I swallowed the rest of my cookie and turned around. "Oh, hello, Marge. I didn't see you." I smiled first at Marge, who swiped at her lank hair with sausage-like fingers, and then at her husband. He was a big, hairy man. His grease-stained jeans and plaid shirt looked cleaner than usual; he must have dressed up for the occasion. As I stepped toward him, I caught a whiff of fish. I wrinkled my nose. Whatever he'd been handling hadn't been sushi-grade.

"Terrible shame about Polly, isn't it?" I said. Both of them stared at me. It was Marge who found her voice first.

"If you're looking for help up there at the inn, I might be able to squeeze you in." Her small, dark eyes were calculating. "It might cost a few extra dollars, though, seeing as I've got so many people to take care of already," she said.

I choked on my cookie. She wanted me to pay her *extra*? I grabbed for a cup of lemonade and gulped it down, wheezing for breath. "Oh, no thanks," I finally managed. "I think my niece and I can handle it." Marge glowered.

I scanned the room and spotted John. Finally. "Oops. Gotta go. Nice seeing you." Soon I was weaving through the crowd toward John, glad to be free of the O'Learys. I felt a pang of regret for Emmeline's chocolate chip cookies, though. By the time Marge got through with them, even the crumbs would be gone.

I walked up behind John and touched his shoulder lightly. He jumped and whirled around.

I sucked in my tummy again and gave him what I hoped was a dazzling smile. "Boo."

He peered at my mouth. "Why are your teeth brown?"

So much for dazzling. I ran my tongue over my teeth. "Emmeline's chocolate chip cookies. If you want one, I recommend you go now. Marge has cornered the dessert section."

John glanced over his shoulder. I gave him a quick up-and-down; I'd never seen him dressed up before. As much as I liked him in jeans, the slacks and sport coat were a nice change. He turned back toward me and caught me looking him over. He didn't say anything, but his mouth twitched up slightly.

"I'm surprised she's here," he said. "Last I heard, Marge and Polly were squaring off over who would get to work for the summer people."

"Marge was just gloating over the cleaning jobs she'll pick up now that the competition's gone."

"Classy."

"Right out of Emily Post." I edged toward him slightly. He smelled good. Very good. I'd never thought of sawdust as sexy before, but I was starting to consider dabbing it on my own pulse points. "So, any word from the medical examiner?"

"I have a call in, but I haven't heard back. Any word on when your friend from Texas is headed back to cowboy land?" he added nonchalantly.

I grimaced. "No. His reservation goes through next Thursday." Then I fixed him with my best steely eye. "And there's more to Texas than cowboys, mister."

"Oh, yeah. I forgot about the cactuses."

I rolled my eyes. "Someday, if you play your cards right, I'll give you a grand tour and introduce you to barbecue. And Tex-Mex."

"Just as long as it's not in the summer." He looked over toward where Charlene and McLaughlin stood. "Hey, have you smoothed things over with Charlene yet?"

"How did you know we were arguing?"

"Nat, Cranberry Island covers less than a square mile. When something happens, even the seagulls talk about it."

Oh, yeah. I wasn't in Austin anymore. "I tried to talk to her a few minutes ago, but McLaughlin interrupted me."

"Why don't you see if you can catch her when she's by herself?"

I glanced over at Charlene, whose arm was still wrapped around McLaughlin's left bicep. "I don't know. That might require surgical intervention."

John glanced at his watch. "I've got to go. Good luck with Charlene." He reached out and brushed a few crumbs off of my shirt. "Gosh, did you eat a plateful or something? You're covered in chocolate."

Now I really was starting to get a complex.

———

I milled around for about twenty minutes, steering myself away from the dessert table and looking for an opportunity to talk to Charlene without McLaughlin hovering over her. She had dropped a good bit of weight recently; last time I'd seen her in that black dress, the seams had been about to pop. Tonight, however, the silky fabric curved in and out in all the right places. I sucked my stomach in again. Maybe I did need to cut down on the cookies.

It was only when the ladies started shuttling the empty plates to the kitchen that a brief window of opportunity appeared. Charlene reluctantly detached herself from McLaughlin's arm and started carting casserole dishes. Fortunately for me, McLaughlin stayed at his post near the door. Apparently his pastoral duties did not extend to kitchen patrol.

I grabbed an empty plate and hustled through the kitchen door. Charlene stood at the sink. Before she could move out of the kitchen and back into McLaughlin's orbit, I cornered her.

"We've got to talk."

She rolled her expertly made-up eyes. "You already tried that line."

"I miss you."

"Do you?" She wiped her hands on a dishtowel. "If I didn't know better, I'd say you were jealous."

"Jealous?"

"Yes," she said. "Jealous. Why else would you be attacking Richard?"

"I haven't been *attacking* anybody. I think someone killed Polly, and I think Richard knows something about it. All I want him to do is go to the police and tell them what Polly told him."

"Yeah, right."

"I'm serious, Charlene. I have Polly's interests at heart."

"Just like you have everybody else's interests at heart. The terns, the sanctity of the island, and all that stuff. Give me a break." She tossed the dishtowel onto the counter. "And that's not the only thing."

"Oh, boy. I can't wait to hear what's next."

She narrowed her blue eyes at me. "For all your talk about 'saving the island,' and how Murray's a money-grabber, sometimes I think the only reason you don't want other people to build things is that you're protecting your own investment." She tapped her plum-painted fingernails on the countertop. "I mean, why do you care if Murray builds a few houses? Unless you're worried that the inn won't be quite as popular if it's got a subdivision down the road."

"That's not the point."

"Isn't it?" She smoothed down her dress and flounced toward the door. "I'm not sure I believe you." By the time I came up with a response, she was gone.

TEN

I WAS STILL STEWING over Charlene when I got back to the inn half an hour later. My mood did not improve when I opened the door to find the kitchen filled with smoke. Benjamin stood at the stove, wearing a grease-spattered yellow apron. What looked like every pot, pan, and dish I owned were scattered haphazardly around the room. My nose wrinkled at the reek of charred food.

"Natalie!" Benjamin stopped stirring a smoking pot and rushed to greet me. "You're here!"

"What's all this?" I slid a greasy pan aside and deposited the empty pie plate on the countertop. My kitchen looked as if it had been the subject of a terrorist attack. From the heaps of blackened foodstuffs arranged on trays, I was guessing biological warfare.

I was suddenly glad I had stuffed myself with Emmeline's cookies. It was a good excuse not to choke down any more culinary offerings.

Benjamin took my elbow and escorted me to the dining room, where he had laid an elaborate table. A candle flickered. The centerpiece was a dozen huge red roses.

"Where's Candy?" I asked.

"Oh, after the kayaking, she decided to take a nap."

"Benjamin," I said. "This is too much."

"Nonsense." He pulled a chair and guided me to it, his hand caressing my back. I remembered the night at Z Tejas with a stab. "I'll be right back with your champagne."

"Champagne?" I turned in my chair. "But Benjamin . . ."

He had already disappeared into the kitchen, leaving me alone with Frank Sinatra, who was giving it his all from the stereo in the parlor.

Benjamin backed through the door a moment later carrying two flutes of champagne. "Dom Perignon," he beamed. "Only the best for you."

I took a small sip, and an image of John's face popped into my head. "The lady is a tramp," crooned Frank in the background. If I didn't make a stand now, Frank could be right.

I set the flute down on the table. "This is all wrong."

Benjamin glided over to me, hurt in his blue eyes, and reached for my hand. At that moment, the door to the kitchen opened, and John poked his head through.

"Natalie? Your kitchen is smoking . . ." His eyes took in the roses, the candles, and Benjamin, who hung onto my hand as if it was a life preserver. "Oh. Sorry to interrupt."

I yanked my hand out of Benjamin's and jumped up, bumping the table with my knee. My champagne flute toppled over, spilling about $50 worth of champagne onto the floor. "John! Just the person I wanted to see!"

I turned to Benjamin. "Benjamin, this is my neighbor John. John, this is Benjamin." They shook hands like prizefighters about to enter the ring.

I smiled at John, hoping the champagne had washed any remaining chocolate off of my teeth. "Benjamin just surprised me by cooking dinner. It looks like he made a *ton* of food. Won't you join us?"

John took a step back. Whether it was a reaction to the prospect of spending an hour in Benjamin's company or to the possibility of having to eat what he'd just seen in the kitchen, I wasn't sure. "Oh, no," he said. "I couldn't." He turned to me. "I just came by to tell you that the medical examiner called. You were right. There were four bullets in the gun, not six."

"How many bullets did they recover during the autopsy?"

"Only one."

"Then where's the other bullet?"

He shrugged. "It was a semi-automatic, and they only retrieved one casing. Maybe the gun wasn't fully loaded."

"There was a box of bullets in her dresser drawer. Did anyone count them?"

"It's considered a suicide, Nat. They hardly looked at the house."

"Won't they now?"

"I wouldn't count on it."

Well, the police hadn't, but I would.

Benjamin stepped forward. I had forgotten he was there. "Are you in law enforcement?" he asked John.

"Among other things."

"How interesting. I've always wondered. Is it lucrative, being a policeman?"

John stiffened. "Why do you ask?"

"Oh, I once considered it, but decided that business was a far better bet. So far," he chuckled, "it's worked out pretty well." Benjamin turned to me. "Now, darling, are you ready for the first course?"

"I don't know," I said, watching John's face. "I had an awful lot of cookies at the church."

"Well, I'd better be going," John said. His eyes were on me. "Have a nice evening."

"Are you sure you won't stay?"

"Positive. Bon appetit. Sorry to interrupt." He wheeled around and disappeared through the kitchen door.

As I stared at the door, Benjamin clapped his hands together and beamed at me. He pulled out my chair, tipped my glass upright, and refilled it. "Why don't you sit down and I'll be back in a moment with the first course?" Then he vanished into the kitchen. While he was gone, I took a few long sips of bubbly. After what I'd smelled in the kitchen, I needed all the courage I could get—even if it did come in liquid form.

By the time Benjamin backed through the door a few minutes later, Sinatra had moved onto *Dinner at Eight*. "Blackened shrimp scampi," my former fiancé announced with a flourish, and produced a platter of what looked like charcoal briquettes swimming in a pool of aged automotive oil.

I poked at one with a tentative fork. "I've never heard of blackened scampi."

"It's a brand-new recipe," he said. "It kind of developed during the cooking process."

I steeled myself and took a small bite. Then I reached for the champagne.

"Wait till you see what's next. I've prepared you a full three-course meal."

I smiled weakly and drained my glass.

———

Two hours later, I crept up the stairs and downed a handful of Tums and some aspirin. Benjamin had lobbied hard to join me, but after "blackened" shrimp scampi followed by hockey-puck-style filet mignon and ending with a baked Alaska that looked and tasted like burnt Styrofoam, it had been easy to say no.

My stomach gurgled threateningly as I climbed into bed. I lay down and almost crushed Biscuit, who shot me an irritated look and rearranged herself in the small of my back. I eased my head onto the pillow and hoped the Tums would do their magic soon. I didn't want to think about anything—Polly, the flooded rooms, Benjamin, Charlene, my kitchen. . . .

I groaned. I had forgotten about the kitchen. Thanks to Benjamin's culinary fireworks, I needed time to sandblast the place before I started making breakfast. The room spun around me as I reached to set the alarm clock for an hour earlier. Then I groaned a second time and fell back into the pillow.

Whether because of the champagne or the charred cuisine, I quickly fell into a set of lurid dreams. One moment I was stuck on a rotisserie, with Benjamin, John, Candy, and Charlene roasting marshmallows and poking at me with a meat thermometer. Then they all morphed into trees, and I was at the bog again, staring down at Polly. A cat mewed urgently, but I couldn't find it. As I stood transfixed, Polly's brown eyes faded to gray, and the contours of her face melted into features I didn't recognize. I tried to back away, but my limbs were frozen. I watched with horror as the bloodless lips began to move. "Natalie," the dead woman whispered. "Help me . . ."

I sat up panting, my nightshirt clinging to my sweaty body. I wiped my hair out of my eyes and tried to slow my breathing. Biscuit mewed in protest and burrowed further under the covers. I lay back down, resolving never again to eat anything that Benjamin had cooked, and closed my eyes.

I had just drifted off when the ceiling creaked.

My eyes flew open. Biscuit uttered a low growl and dug her claws into my back.

I heard a slithery sound, like something being dragged, from the ceiling above the window. Then a creak. Biscuit hissed as I pulled her off of me. My mouth was sour with fear and stale alcohol as I cowered under the covers, listening as the slithering sound moved closer. I held my breath until it had almost reached the ceiling above my bed. Then, before I knew what I was doing, I yelled.

"STOP IT!"

The dragging ceased instantly. Biscuit leaped from the covers and scrambled under the bed. Footsteps rushed down the hall.

Gwen burst through the door and flipped on the light. Biscuit shot past her legs and bounded down the stairs.

"What's going on? Are you okay?"

"Did you hear anything just now?" My throat was raw, and the words came out as gasps.

"Just you. Are you okay?"

"You didn't hear anything?"

"No. Why? What's wrong?"

I sagged back against the pillow. Was I suffering from hallucinations? "Nothing. It must have been a dream. I had too much champagne with dinner."

Gwen peered at me. "Maybe you need to cut down on the drinks. You don't look so good."

I scowled at her. "Are you going to tell me I should stop eating sweets and start an exercise program, too?"

"Might not be a bad idea," she said. "Adam's getting me hooked on running."

I lay back and pulled the pillow over my head. "I can't think about running right now."

"Maybe you could come with us some afternoon."

Maybe I could stick hot skewers under my fingernails, too. "I'm too old to run."

"You should give it a try sometime. It's fun."

"Yeah. Like getting a skin graft."

"Good night, Aunt Nat." She flipped off the light and closed the door behind her. I pressed the pillow to my head. Had it been the champagne? Or had it been something else? I remembered the woman in the dream and shuddered. Maybe the inn *was* haunted. I squeezed my eyes shut. Soon, sleep crept up on me, and I slipped back into queasy dreams.

———

My stomach still hadn't recovered when I shuffled down the stairs at 6:00 the next morning. The kitchen was at least as bad as I had remembered it. Filthy pots and pans littered the countertops, and the whole room smelled like the aftermath of a grease fire. I made an extra-large pot of coffee and filled the sink with soapy water.

Then I started scraping something that looked and smelled like tar out of my best omelet pan. As if dinner last night wasn't bad enough, I thought sourly, now I had to clean it, too.

Two cups of coffee and a half a container of dish soap later, the place was beginning to look recognizable. I was doing better, too; the pounding in my skull had diminished to a more manageable roar, and my stomach had stopped gurgling ominously. I glanced at the clock; breakfast started in less than an hour. I hadn't succeeded in chiseling off the stovetop yet, but that would have to wait.

Before long, the grease-fire aroma was, if not completely eliminated, at least masked by the smell of bacon sizzling on the stovetop and lemon-raspberry muffins browning in the oven. As I pulled a few wizened apples and a bag of grapes from the refrigerator, I realized with a sinking feeling that it was time to place another grocery order. I'd put off going down to Charlene's store as long as possible, but I had to pick up the mail and restock the fridge eventually.

As I chopped the apples and dropped them into the bowl with the grapes, the dream I'd had the night before flashed into my mind. A chill crept down my back. I wanted to believe that what had happened in my bedroom was the product of an alcohol-steeped imagination, but Biscuit's reaction suggested that I wasn't the only one who had experienced something weird. I still hadn't seen her this morning. If the nocturnal noises continued, I might have to follow her lead and start sleeping on the couch.

I tossed a few orange segments and banana chunks into the bowl and topped the whole thing with paper-thin slices of the lone, wrinkly kiwifruit I had found in the back of the drawer. It wasn't the most beautiful fruit salad I had ever made, but it would do.

When I pushed through the door to the dining room a few minutes later, Benjamin sat alone at his usual table.

I deposited the fruit salad on the buffet table and retrieved the coffeepot. "Where's Candy?" I asked.

"I think she had an early morning appointment," he said.

"On the island?"

"I didn't ask." He grimaced. "Sorry about the kitchen, by the way. I meant to get up early and clean, but I overslept."

"It's okay," I said with a tight smile. "I took care of it."

As I filled his coffee cup, he reached for my free hand. "We still haven't really talked, you know."

"About what?"

"About us."

I sighed. "Benjamin, I've already told you. There's nothing to talk about."

He squeezed my hand and released it. "I've got something to show you." He reached down and retrieved a sheaf of papers from the chair next to him. "Take a look at these."

I set the coffeepot down and picked up the stack of papers. It was a list of properties in Austin.

"What is this?"

"I ran a search on everything for sale in Austin. Some of these are already bed-and-breakfasts, but I included the ones that had potential, too. I tried to talk to you about it last night, but you kept changing the subject."

I leafed through page after page of stunning Victorian homes. "You're serious about this, aren't you?"

"I know you're pretty heavily mortgaged here. I've got some investment capital kicking around, and I think real estate is the place to put it. You could start a new inn, mortgage-free," he said. "We could leave town for a month in the summer. Come back here to visit, if you wanted to."

I leafed through the pages of properties, pausing at a grand two-story Queen Anne Victorian, right in the heart of Austin. I eyed the sweeping front porch, the leaded glass windows, the red roses ablaze under the white painted railings. No monthly mortgage payments to dread. No more sleepless nights, wondering if I'd have enough bookings to make it through the winter. I put down the stack of papers and sank into a chair.

Then Benjamin reached into his pocket and pulled out the diamond ring I had returned to him eighteen months ago.

"Oh, God."

His deep blue eyes were liquid. A lock of his dark hair fell over one eye as he leaned toward me. "I know I screwed it up last time," he said softly. "I know I hurt you terribly. I don't know if you can forgive me, but it's what I want, more than anything." He caressed my fingers lightly. "Say the word, and we can start over. Just the two of us."

Benjamin dropped to his knees on the floor at my feet and folded my hand in his own. His familiar smell, leather and cologne and a faint spiciness, wafted over me. I closed my eyes. This couldn't be happening. His next words floated toward me as if from a long distance away.

"I'm asking you for the second time, Natalie. Will you marry me?"

ELEVEN

I WAS SAVED FROM answering by a delicate throat-clearing from the doorway. Benjamin leaped to his feet and slipped the ring back into his pocket as Candy entered the dining room. She wore a skin-tight blue miniskirt, and the slogan on today's clingy rhinestone-studded top was "I Kiss Better Than I Cook."

Her corkscrew curls bounced as she sashayed over to the buffet table. "Is it time for breakfast?"

Benjamin raked his hair back from his face. "I thought you had an appointment this morning."

"It got delayed." She cast a doubtful eye at my bottom-of-the-fruit-drawer salad. "Is this all there is?"

"No, there's plenty more," I said. "I'll go get it." I pushed through the door to the kitchen, grateful for the reprieve. I was happy for any excuse to avoid giving Benjamin an answer. On the other hand, it would have been nice to get through an entire morning without seeing Candy.

The door swung closed behind me, and I sagged against the kitchen wall. Until now, I had thought Benjamin was toying with me. I was staggered by his offer of marriage . . . and of a new inn, debt-free. I walked over to the sink and looked out the window. A lobster boat chugged along the water, trailed by a few seagulls, and the mountains rose like craggy beasts in the background. Did I really want to leave Cranberry Island and go back to Texas?

I loved my life on the island, but there were no guarantees that the Gray Whale Inn would succeed. In fact, now that the insurance company was threatening to stick me with the bill for Candy's flood, I was worried about making it to spring. A major outlay could bankrupt me.

I sighed. Despite my problems, I had dreamed of moving to the coast and starting my own inn for years. That dream was finally a reality. Did I want to give it all up now? I squinted at the boat on the water, but my mind floated back to the beautiful Queen Anne Victorian with the bright red roses. And long drives through the Texas countryside, with Benjamin's hand warm on my leg.

Did I trust Benjamin?

My eyes drifted to John's carriage house. Did I even want to try?

I turned away from the window. Decisions or no decisions, at least two hungry guests were waiting for me.

A minute later, I backed through the door holding a basket of muffins and a platter of bacon. I set them down next to the fruit salad and headed toward Candy, who had slid into her customary chair next to Benjamin. "You have your own boat?" she cooed at Benjamin. "Oooh, how lovely."

"If you're ever in Texas, let me know," Benjamin said cheerfully. "I'll take you out on the lake sometime." While Candy gazed starry-eyed at Benjamin, I retrieved the coffeepot and filled her cup. Benjamin winked at me.

"Eggs are to order this morning," I said briskly. "Would you like them scrambled, poached, or fried?"

Candy tore her eyes away from Benjamin and peered at the buffet table. "What else is there?"

"Lemon-raspberry muffins, bacon, and fruit salad."

She frowned. "I'd like one egg, poached, and a slice of wheat toast, dry."

"Two eggs over-easy will do it for me," Benjamin said.

I glanced at Candy, who was checking to see that her curls were in place. "Don't worry, Benjamin," I said. "I remember how you like them." Candy gave me a dirty look and scootched her chair closer to Benjamin's.

When I brought the eggs and dry toast in, Russell glowered at me from the corner table. I strolled over and filled his cup. "Good morning!"

He grunted in response. I took his order—three eggs, scrambled—and walked back to the kitchen. The developer had never been overly friendly, but since I had overheard his phone conversation, he was positively frosty. I could feel his eyes boring into my back as I reached the kitchen door. So much for my fantasies of relaxing mornings with charming guests.

After an hour of Benjamin's secretive winks, Candy's high-pitched giggles, and Russell's suspicious glances, it was a relief when everybody filtered out of the dining room. I cleaned up the breakfast dishes and left a message for the insurance adjustor, then headed for my bike. I needed to get out of the inn for a while. I also needed to talk with McLaughlin about the number of bullets in Polly's gun.

The blue sky sparkled overhead as the touring bike coasted down the hill toward the rectory. It was a beautiful afternoon, and truth be told, it was a pleasure being away from the inn—and the people in it. The island was ablaze in autumn glory. Beneath the wheels of the bike, the blacktop was dotted with bright red and yellow leaves, and the apple trees that appeared from time to time along the edge of the road were laden with ripe fruit. Riding past the brightly painted houses clustered near the church, I smelled the faint tang of wood smoke.

The rectory was a small white house tucked in across the street from St. James. As I pulled up outside of it, I saw for the first time the extent of the renovations that McLaughlin had undertaken. Charlene had told me he was doing some work on the rectory, but I hadn't realized just how much. When it was finished, the skeletal structure attached to the back of the tiny house would triple the size of the building.

I almost tripped over a foil-covered Pyrex dish on my way to the rectory door. My nose wrinkled as I bent down to retrieve it—it smelled decidedly fishy—and knocked at the door twice.

McLaughlin answered a moment later, dressed in slacks and a red button-down shirt that skimmed over his flat stomach and accented his dark good looks. He greeted me with a lukewarm smile. I didn't miss the flash of irritation that preceded it.

I handed him the dish. "It looks like this is for you."

He flipped back a corner of the foil and sighed. "Another tuna-fish casserole."

I grimaced. "Does this happen often?"

"Almost every day, I'm afraid. Since I moved here, I've had a steady diet of tuna casserole, lasagna, and some concoction that involves green peas and hamburger meat." I shuddered. There were more challenges to life in the ministry than I had realized. "The big problem, though," he continued, "is trying to figure out who to return the dishes to." He gave me a wry grin, and for a moment I could understand what Charlene saw in him.

Then he seemed to remember who he was talking to. The grin disappeared, replaced by the more usual solicitous smile. "What can I do for you, Natalie?" he said briskly. "I hope you haven't come to hound me about Polly again?"

"Mind if I come in for a moment?"

"Oh, of course. Forgive me."

I followed him into the front room. I had always imagined that a priest's living room would be furnished entirely with tatty, hand-me-down couches and mismatched chairs. Not this living room. Two vast leather couches flanked the fireplace, and my feet sank into the deep pile of an obviously expensive oriental rug.

"Please, sit down," he said. He lifted the Pyrex dish. "I'm just going to take this to the kitchen. Can I get you something to drink?"

"Oh, no thanks." McLaughlin disappeared into the kitchen, and I settled myself into the buttery leather of one of the couches and glanced around. At the far end of the room, a number of com-memorative plaques hung. I was too far away to read the text, but from the brass toilets adorning them, I guessed they harked back to his former life in plumbing. The walls were lined with book-shelves. The books' heavy leather bindings looked a little pricier than the run-of-the-mill Reader's Digest condensed books. McLaughlin soon reappeared and arranged himself on the couch across from me.

"I noticed you're doing some major renovations," I said.

"Oh, yes. It's a nuisance, but it'll be nice when it's done."

"I didn't realize the work was so extensive."

"Well, this place has been pretty much untouched since it was built. It was time to do a little upgrading, bring it into the twenty-first century."

"Yeah, most of the island is a little behind the times." I leaned back against the leather couch. "You're such a talented minister," I said. "I'm kind of surprised you're posted here. Is this your first church?" I asked.

"Thank you for the kind words," he said. His smile was saccharine. "I think part of the reason God called me here was to breathe life back into some of the smaller ministries."

"So this is your first posting?"

"I've done some good work with other churches before," he said, shifting in his seat. "But Cranberry Island is really something special. I can see why you chose to open an inn here."

"I've heard you had a very successful life in the business world before you came to the church." I nodded toward the row of commemorative toilets. "What made you switch gears?"

"I did have some success in the plumbing fixtures industry," he said. "But I always felt there was something missing from my life."

He leaned forward in his chair. "That's ancient history, though. And we still haven't talked about why you're here. I'd like to believe you're looking for my support in this time of crisis, but I'm afraid that's not why you came here today."

"No, it's not," I admitted. "I'm here because I found out some new information last night. I was hoping it might change your mind about talking to the police."

His dark eyebrows arched. "Oh?"

"The gun that killed Polly Sarkes had only four bullets in it."

His tanned brow wrinkled. "And the significance of that is?"

"The significance," I said slowly, "is that one bullet is unaccounted for." I studied his face as I continued. "And I don't think that even an inexperienced markswoman would need two shots to hit herself in the chest."

Although McLaughlin's face remained expressionless, I thought I caught a flicker of something behind his dark eyes. Then he shrugged. "How do you know a bullet is missing? Maybe the gun wasn't fully loaded."

"I'm planning to confirm that this afternoon."

"How do you intend to do that?"

"I know where the box of bullets is." If I had a metal detector, I'd check the bog, too. I was sure that casing was out there somewhere.

He blinked twice. Then he sighed. "Natalie, I have to tell you I am very concerned about you. Charlene is, too. Your obsession with the development, and with Polly . . . it's worrisome."

The development? I hadn't said a word about the development.

"Are you sure the inn isn't too much of a strain?" he asked.

"Thanks for your concern," I said shortly, "but the inn is doing just fine." Except for the fracas with the insurance company. But he didn't have to know that. "What I'm more worried about is that somebody got away with murdering Polly."

He looked to the ceiling and sighed.

I forged ahead anyway. "I know she talked to you about her personal life. I know that she felt she had some kind of decision to make. I think you may know something that will help bring Polly's killer to justice." I paused, but he continued to study the ceiling. "Please. Even if you don't think it's relevant, she might have told you some bit of information the police can use."

His eyes dropped back to me. He raised his hands in a help-less gesture. "According to the police, there is no murderer. Polly was depressed. She killed herself. Natalie, bullets or no bullets, I'm afraid you're jousting at windmills here."

"The police aren't always right," I said. As a former murder suspect, I felt more than qualified to make that statement.

He shook his head sadly. "I'm sorry, Natalie. Until you come to terms with your . . . obsession . . . there's nothing I or anybody else can do to help you." He stood up and swiped imaginary lint from his khakis. I fought to contain my frustration and rage. Then I stood and followed him to the door.

"If you change your mind, or just need someone to talk to, I'm always here," he said.

"Gee, thanks," I said. "I'll keep that in mind."

I was still fuming as I pumped the bike's pedals toward the Cranberry Island store. I couldn't avoid it any longer; I had to drop off my grocery list. Although the little wooden store with the big front porch was usually one of my favorite places on the island, today I felt as if I were approaching Medusa's cave.

I parked the bike, walked past the store's painted wooden rockers, and sucked in my breath as I pushed through the door. I cringed as the bell jangled above my head and steeled myself for Charlene's icy green gaze. To my relief, the green eyes that greeted me from behind the register belonged not to Charlene, but to her niece.

Tania smiled at me, exposing a line of silver braces. "Hey, Nat."

I walked over to the counter and sagged onto one of the barstools. "Thank God you're the one manning the store. I was terrified Charlene would be here."

"Aunt Char?" She waved a hand. "Oh, don't worry about her. She gets into snits sometimes. It'll pass."

I sighed. "How long does it usually last?"

"Depends," she said. "Chocolate usually helps, but she's dieting." Tania made a face. "What's with that preacher guy, anyway? All the women on this island are just bonkers for him."

I grinned. At least McLaughlin's charm didn't extend to the under-twenty set. "Well, this woman's not."

Tania leaned forward across the counter. "I know Aunt Charlene said no more cookies, but would you mind sneaking us a few brownies from time to time?"

"Any time you have a need for chocolate, just swing by the inn."

Her face lit up. "Really?"

"You bet." I pulled out the grocery list. "Could you fill this order for me?"

She picked it up and studied it. "I'll have it for you tomorrow," she said. "Are you going to come pick it up? Or do you want me to deliver it?"

I thought about that for a moment. Charlene usually drove the groceries up in her truck in exchange for dinner—I didn't have a car on the island—but I wasn't sure she'd be willing to do that now. "You can drive your dad's truck, can't you?" She nodded. "If you could deliver it, that would be great. I tip in chocolate."

She grinned. "Count me in."

I was about to leave—I didn't want to risk a run-in with Charlene—when an idea popped into my head. "By the way," I said. "At Polly's funeral, Reverend McLaughlin was talking to Murray about something, some sort of business, I think. I was just curious; has Charlene said anything about Murray?"

She squinched up her face. "Only that he's been really good for the church," she said.

"Good for the church?"

She shrugged. "That's all she said."

"Thanks, Tania. And if you have a chance to put in a good word for me . . ."

"Don't worry. I will. We miss you."

I walked out of the store feeling marginally better. If Tania thought Charlene would get over it, maybe she would.

Twenty minutes later, the wind bit at my cheeks as I hurtled down the pitted pavement of Cranberry Road. I coasted into Gnomeland and knocked on Emmeline's door, but her small, well-kept house was empty. The brown tabby Emmeline had told me about lazed on the front porch, and I gave her chin a quick rub before I hopped back onto the bike. The sampler Emmeline had designed for the inn would have to wait for another day.

I pumped the rest of the way down the pitted road to Polly's house. The small house had an empty, lonely air, and I felt a stab of sadness for Polly as I parked my bike against the front railing and walked around to the back. The cats' bowls were full almost to overflowing, and the water in their bowls was clear. Emmeline had already been here today.

The back door opened easily, and the smell of lemon furniture polish greeted me as I stepped inside. The kitchen looked no different than it had the day I found Polly, and my eyes fell on the memo board next to the phone. I took a moment to copy the shelter number onto a slip of paper and then headed upstairs to Polly's bedroom.

The wind moaned through the eaves as I slid open the top drawer of the dresser and extracted the red cardboard box. "Fifty Cartridges" was printed on the side in bold black letters. I cleared a spot on Polly's disordered bed and set the box down. Then I began counting.

The wind continued its eerie moan as the cold metal clinked on the flowered comforter. The pile grew quickly. If Polly had loaded the gun with only five bullets, there should be 45 left.

I counted 44.

I was about to count them a second time when a door creaked open downstairs. *Emmeline*, I thought, and a greeting was on the tip of my tongue before I remembered that Emmeline had already been here today. Heavy footsteps crossed the hardwood floors below, and a ripple of fear coursed through me. I didn't know who was downstairs, but suddenly I was afraid to find out.

I shoveled the bullets into the box and crammed it back into the dresser drawer as the steps creaked. I had just scuttled into the closet and pulled Polly's wool winter coat in front of me when the footsteps entered Polly's bedroom.

TWELVE

I crouched in the corner of the closet and sucked in my breath, my stomach churning at the smell of old wool, mothballs, and fear. The heavy footsteps came closer, and I curled myself into a small ball, wishing I had something other than Polly's coat to defend myself with. The next time I made it to the mainland, I was stocking up on pepper spray.

Then they stopped.

I held my breath, waiting for the closet door to open, the thumping of my heart as loud as a snare drum. Just when my lungs were about to burst, the footsteps began again, this time moving away from my hiding place. I clutched at Polly's coat and gasped for air.

The rough wool chafed against my cheek as I listened to the thunk of drawers being yanked open on the other side of the closet door. The drawers slammed shut one by one, and my chest tightened again. I tried to remember the Tae Kwon Do I had learned twenty-five years ago. For the next few minutes, while the intruder rifled through Polly's belongings, I occupied myself by experimenting with different ways to arrange my fists and wishing I had taken more than five days of classes.

Another drawer opened, and I heard the clink of metal. A moment later, the drawer thudded shut. Again, the footsteps moved toward me. I balled up my fists and crouched behind Polly's long black coat, preparing myself to explode out of the folds of wool. The wind moaned around the eaves. The doorknob turned. I sucked in my breath and tightened my fists.

Then the knob slipped back and was still.

The footsteps crossed Polly's bedroom, away from my hiding place. I dropped my fists and sagged into the corner of the closet, sweating.

A moment later, the intruder clumped down the stairs and across the floor beneath me. I let out a long, slow breath as somewhere below a door creaked open and shut with a bang.

I waited a few minutes, just in case whoever it was decided to come back for a second look, before creeping out of the closet and peering out Polly's bedroom window at the road. The pitted blacktop was empty. I walked to the dresser and pulled out the top drawer.

The box of bullets was gone.

I sank down onto the bed, the bitterness of disappointment stealing in to replace the cold tang of fear. Unless I could somehow find that casing, the evidence that Polly was murdered had disappeared from under my nose.

But who had taken the bullets? The only person who knew about them was McLaughlin. Had he come back and removed the evidence? Whoever had been here knew where to find them; he or she had made a beeline to Polly's dresser. My stomach clenched as I realized how narrowly I might just have escaped joining Polly in the small graveyard next to the church.

I heaved myself from the bed and crept downstairs, clutching the banister to support my still-wobbly knees.

A few moments later, the cool breeze greeted me as I stepped outside and headed for the bike. *The bike.* It was as good as an announcement that someone in the house. Why hadn't the intruder seen it?

I looked up, and my eyes fell on Emmeline's house in the distance. She had mentioned paths to town. Anyone coming down the road would have seen the bike. That meant that the intruder had probably used the paths. And if the intruder was also the murderer, he or she had probably also used them the day Polly was killed. As I climbed into the saddle, a chill crept down my back, and it wasn't because of the wind off the water.

———

When I walked through my own kitchen door a half hour later, Gwen sat at the kitchen table eating a peanut butter sandwich.

"Hey, Aunt Nat. Where have you been?"

"Just about everywhere," I said. I was about to tell her about the intruder at Polly's house, but for some reason I hesitated. "I had to run down to the store. Tania was there, thank God, so Charlene couldn't give me the ice-queen routine. What's up here?"

"The insurance company called."

I cut myself a large piece of brownie and groaned. "More good news?"

"They didn't say. But I found out what Candy Perkins has been up to."

"What do you mean?" I grabbed a plate and pulled up a chair across from Gwen.

"Adam told me she was up at Cliffside with a real estate agent this morning."

I paused with the brownie halfway to my mouth. "Cliffside?" Cliffside was the second-largest building on the island, a regal three-story house with a stunning view of the harbor. "You don't think she's planning on turning it into a bed-and-breakfast, do you?"

Gwen took a bite of her sandwich and shrugged. "That would explain why she *accidentally* stopped up the sink."

"You think she's trying to put me out of business?"

"Maybe. Oh—and Benjamin's looking for you." She squinted at me. "What's the story with him?"

"Ex-fiancé."

"He's a good-looking guy, Aunt Nat. I'm impressed. What does John think?"

"Don't ask." I took a big bite of brownie and let the chocolate flood my mouth. "I can't believe Candy's looking at Cliffside." Competition on Cranberry Island was going to make running the Gray Whale Inn even harder. I hated to admit it, but that Queen Anne in Austin was looking better and better. "How's Adam, by the way?"

"Oh, he's all right. Eddie O'Leary's causing all sorts of trouble at the co-op, though." Every lobsterman on the island belonged to the Cranberry Island Lobster Co-op. The group sold lobsters to area restaurants and shipping companies; they also worked together to defend the island's traditional fishing grounds from other lobstermen.

"What kind of trouble?" I asked.

"He's complaining that we need to expand our fishing territory."

I groaned. "How's he planning to do that?"

"Three guesses." I had learned since moving to the island that the waters off the coast of Maine were divided into zealously guarded territories. Since the dividing lines were unofficial, some lobstermen guarded—or expanded—their fishing grounds by moving other lobstermen's traps and replacing them with their own traps. Or, if they were less kind, by cutting the ropes that connected the surface buoys to the traps far below, making them unretrievable.

"Don't tell me he wants to start a gear war," I said.

"Wants to? I think he already has."

I sighed. "What does Adam think?" Gwen's boyfriend had been known to do some gear cutting of his own.

"That we should stay out of it. Unfortunately, O'Leary's got a lot of the guys on board."

I sucked my teeth. "I hope it doesn't escalate beyond cutting gear."

Gwen looked up, her eyes dark. "So do I."

We sat for a moment, munching on our respective snacks and ruminating on what might happen if the lobstermen started a gear war. It had been a lean year for lobsters, and with money short and tempers high, I was afraid the cutting might not stop at trap lines.

I had gotten up to put the kettle on when John burst through the kitchen door, his face taut and his eyes filled with urgency.

"Natalie!"

"What's wrong?" My throat tightened with fear.

"Can you get hold of Charlene?"

"Is Tania okay? Did something happen?"

He twisted his mouth into a grimace. "Richard McLaughlin is dead."

I felt like a brick had slammed into my chest. "Dead? I just saw him this morning."

"Then it's a recent development," John said.

"What happened?" My mind flipped through the alternatives. Heart attack, stroke, accident . . .

"He was murdered."

My hand shook as it pushed a strand of hair from my eyes. Richard McLaughlin and I had had a conversation just two hours ago. Now he was dead. Murdered. An image of Polly's body, her jacket stained with rust-colored blood, reeled through my mind. Had Murray been shot too?

"How was he killed?"

"Somebody stabbed him to death. Emmeline Hoyle found him. She was dropping off a casserole, and found him on the front step." He sighed. "Grimes is on his way back to the island."

An image of Charlene popped into my head, from last Sunday, when she was snuggled up with McLaughlin at church. My stomach clenched.

"Does Charlene know?" I asked.

"I was hoping you'd break the news to her."

I closed my eyes for a moment. Then I turned to my niece. "Can you hold down the fort for a while?"

Gwen's brown eyes were solemn. "As long as you need me to, Aunt Nat."

"I'm on my way to the scene," said John, heading for the door. As his hand touched the knob, he stopped and turned back toward us. "Whatever you do, don't let Charlene go to the rectory."

I cringed. "That bad?"

"According to Emmeline, yes."

My mind recoiled at the thought of McLaughlin's body on the freshly painted wood porch. I'd do my best.

THIRTEEN

TWENTY MINUTES LATER I stood on Charlene's front doorstep, inhaling the chill autumn air and dreading the upcoming encounter. As my hand hovered over the doorbell, a cold breeze lifted a few dead leaves, sending them skittering along the front walk. *Like bones rattling*, my mind whispered.

My finger had barely pressed the glowing button when Charlene opened the door, and a wave of *Beautiful* washed over me.

Her smile faded when she registered me. "What are you doing here?"

"Can I come in?"

She wavered for a moment, then nodded shortly. I followed her across the dark hardwood floor of the entry hall to the living room and sat down on the edge of her chambray couch. She perched on a loveseat across from me, and a pang of sadness shot through me—both for the loss of Richard and for the distance he had created between us.

"I don't have long," she said, crossing her jean-clad legs. The beaded fringe at the hem rattled as she swung a foot in irritation. "I'm meeting Richard in half an hour."

"Charlene." I swallowed hard. "I'm afraid I have some bad news."

"What?" She tossed her head. "Cranberry Estates is going through?"

"No."

Something in my voice caught Charlene's attention.

"What is it?" Her voice broke on the last syllable.

"It's Richard." The words sounded as if they were coming from another planet. "He's dead."

Charlene stared at me. "Dead? He can't be dead. I talked with him this morning."

"I'm sorry, Charlene."

She sprang up from the couch and lunged for the phone, her fingers shaking as she dialed. A shaft of late afternoon sunlight glanced across her caramel-colored hair as she clutched the handset to her ear, her eyes wide with fear. I don't know who answered—if anyone did—but suddenly her face crumpled. I crossed the gap between us and caught her as she sank toward the floor.

"Richard," Charlene keened, rocking back and forth. Tears streaked down her face, and her body shuddered in my arms.

"Come on," I said gently. "Let's get you to the couch."

"What happened?" she whispered as I guided her to the blue sofa.

I squeezed her shoulders. Why did I have to be the one to tell her? "Somebody stabbed him."

She blinked. "Stabbed him?" Her hands rose to her mouth, and her face turned gray. "Oh, God. God, no. He was such a good man, a wonderful man . . . Why?"

"I don't know, sweetheart," I crooned, rocking my weeping friend. "I just don't know."

"He was so alive, so *vibrant*. We were going out to dinner. He can't be dead. He just *can't* be."

"I'm so sorry," I whispered, hugging her tight.

———

I stepped out of Charlene's house into a brisk, cold breeze a half hour later. Tania and her mother Clarice had come over to help Charlene pack and escort her to the inn; I'd invited her to stay with me for a few days, so she wouldn't be alone, and after some persuading, she'd agreed.

Once the initial shock wore off, Charlene's first impulse was to drive to the rectory. We managed to dissuade her, but only after I promised I would do anything I could to find out who the killer was. "You figured out who killed Katz," she said. "Please. Help me find out what happened to Richard." Her voice faltered, and the tears streamed down her face again. "I thought he was the one," she whispered.

I squeezed her tight and promised I'd do anything I could to help. Which was why I was now headed to the scene of the crime.

As the bicycle rolled up the little driveway past the church, it didn't seem possible that I had been to the rectory just that morning. A cluster of policemen crowded the front door. Only when one of them stepped down to retrieve something from his bag, revealing the crumpled form on the porch, did the reality sink in.

Where the tuna-fish casserole had sat a few hours ago, Richard McLaughlin lay, one arm stretched toward the steps, his dark eyes vacant, his tanned skin pale. The collar of his red shirt was still crisp, but the fabric was stained almost black, and a river of blood extended almost to the front of the porch. My stomach heaved, and tears pricked my eyes.

No wonder John wanted me to keep Charlene away.

I parked the bike and walked over to the small group of bystanders—mostly women—that had collected on the driveway. Emmeline Hoyle, still clutching a foil-topped casserole, walked over to me as I approached.

"Another tragedy," she said, shaking her head.

"I heard you were the one who found him," I said.

"Ayuh." She clucked her tongue. "Some people think being handsome is a blessing, but it can also be a curse."

"What do you mean?"

She jerked her head toward the cluster of women. "I wouldn't be surprised if it was one of them done him in. Spurned love, and all."

"You think?"

She nodded sagely. "Crime of passion."

I glanced at the body on the porch. Maybe she was right. It was so haphazard, unplanned; no attempt even to hide the body. I forced my eyes away from the red shirt, the pale skin. Poor Richard. And Charlene. My heart ached for my friend. "When did you find him?" I asked.

"Oh, 'round about one o'clock," she said.

An hour after I left the rectory.

"Did you see anyone?"

She shook her head. "Whoever did it was long gone," she said. "Although I would have thought poison, for a woman. Maybe it was a cuckolded husband."

"Maybe," I said, trying to remember if I'd seen anyone when I left the rectory. I glanced around, looking for John, and asked Emmeline if she'd seen him.

"He was here a few minutes ago, but I don't know where he's got to."

A familiar voice called to me from the porch. "Miz Barnes!"

I turned to see Grimes sauntering down the steps. "Figured I'd see you here before long," he said.

He trundled up next to me, hitching his belt up over his belly. My nose wrinkled involuntarily at the smell of stale smoke.

"Can't keep away from dead bodies, can you?" he said.

I straightened my spine. "What can I help you with?"

He whipped out a notebook. "I hear the dead guy was close with one of your friends."

"He was dating Charlene Kean, yes."

"Know if they had any lovers' spats lately?"

I shook my head. "Not that she mentioned, no."

"Scuttlebutt is, you and she kind of fell out over her new boyfriend."

"Oh?"

He glanced at the group of island women. "He seemed to be kind of a ladies' man. Good-looking guy."

"I suppose so."

"Where were you today?" Grimes asked, fixing me with close-set eyes.

What was he getting at? "I was at the inn, of course. And later on, I stopped by Polly's house to check on the cats." I swallowed hard. "I also swung by the rectory for a few minutes."

"The rectory."

"Yes."

"What time was that?"

"I guess around eleven thirty." Which I knew was less than an hour before Emmeline found him. Which meant, I now realized, that I was probably the last person—other than his murderer—to see him alive.

Slow as he was, Grimes looked like he'd picked up on that fact, too. "And why did you pick this particular morning to visit Rev. McLaughlin?"

"I wanted to talk to him about Polly."

"Polly. The suicide out in the bog, right?"

"He had been out to visit her a few times, and I thought he knew more than he was telling."

"Mmmm. So you came to talk about Polly. Did you happen to bring any cutlery with you?"

"Cutlery?"

He smirked. "I'd ask to take your prints, but we already got 'em on file. Don't have your friend's, though. Where does she live?"

"She lives down by the store, but she's going to spend a few days at the inn."

"You two seem to be getting a little friendly again," he said.

"Her boyfriend was just murdered," I said tartly.

"And now you two are all buddy-buddy again. Isn't that nice?"

"Where's John?"

"Your boyfriend? Oh, he's around somewhere. What kind of knives do you use, Miz Barnes?"

"Henkels," I said. I remembered because they'd cost me a small fortune.

He nodded. "I'll send someone down to take a look at them."

"What?"

"I think we'll be doing a lot more talking in the near future, Miz Barnes. So if I were you, I wouldn't plan any vacations. Or your friend, either."

"Are you saying I'm—I mean, Charlene and I—that we're murder suspects?"

He smiled like a Cheshire Cat. "Too soon to tell, Miz Barnes. But I hope you and your friend got some good lawyers."

Before I could come up with a response, John walked up behind him. "Is there a problem?"

"I'll let your girlfriend fill you in," Grimes said. Then he hitched up his belt and swaggered back to the crime-scene team.

John swept a hand through his sandy hair, and the crease between his eyes deepened. "Nat. What's going on?"

"Charlene and I are suspects."

His bushy eyebrows shot up. "What?"

"I was the last person to see him alive, probably. Grimes thinks it was a crime of passion, and figures I lost my temper with him."

"I don't get it. If it's a crime of passion, where do you come in?" He arched an eyebrow. "Unless you and Richard . . ."

I rolled my eyes. "Yeah, right. Apparently Grimes heard that Charlene and I had a falling-out over McLaughlin. I got the impression he thinks I killed McLaughlin to smooth things over with Charlene."

John shook his head. "That's ridiculous!"

"Try telling Grimes that," I said. "Was it a Henkels knife that killed him?"

He nodded. "How did you know?"

"Something Grimes said. Just my luck. Charlene and I both use Henkels, and they're sending someone over to check out my kitchen. Probably Charlene's, too." My throat closed up. "Oh, no."

"What?"

"Charlene told me one of her knives was missing. God, what if it's the same one?"

"I'm sure it's not," John said soothingly. But I wasn't. I glanced over at the group of islanders, who were staring at John and me. Emmeline smiled and nodded, her brown eyes glinting. "We should probably talk about this when we don't have an audience," I murmured. "Besides, Charlene's headed over to the inn to stay a few days, and I need to get back and check on her."

"Probably not a bad idea. How's she doing?"

"As well as can be expected, under the circumstances," I said. "How long are you going to have to stay here?"

"I don't know. As long as they need me." He leaned forward and planted a quick kiss on the top of my head, and a swell of murmurs rose from the gaggle of islanders.

"Why don't you stop by when you're finished here?" I said. "I'll microwave some clam chowder."

"It's better than another TV dinner."

I laughed. "Charlene made it, so you know it's good."

He headed back toward the rectory, and I walked past the group of islanders to my bike. "He's a handsome young man," Emmeline said as I passed her.

"I suppose you're right," I said, blushing.

"Stop by sometime soon," she said. "I've got a sampler design ready for you, and I copied out that banana bread recipe." Her eyes glinted. I knew she was also anxious to show me the paths she had discovered.

"Maybe I'll swing by tomorrow morning, after breakfast."

"I'll look for you. We'll have a pot of tea!"

The woman next to Emmeline tugged at her sleeve; the men on the porch were lifting McLaughlin into a black body bag. I turned my head away as his arm fell, dangling lifelessly, and caught a glimpse of a young girl in the undergrowth beyond the house. I saw a flash of blonde hair and a pink, tear-stained face. Then, with a rustle of leaves, she was gone.

———

Charlene's truck was in the driveway when I rode up to the inn a few minutes later. The sun was setting over the mainland, painting the hills crimson and gold. It was hard to believe a life had been cut short with such violence today, when everything around me was so beautiful, so serene.

A gust of wind sent a shiver through me as I stowed the bike in the shed and hurried to the kitchen door. I glanced to the east, where a bank of gray clouds was rolling in from the water. Things were about to get a lot less serene; I hoped the investigators had time to gather all the evidence before the storm hit.

Gwen and Charlene sat at the table, their hands cradling mugs of tea, as I closed the door behind me. Mascara streaked my best friend's face, and her shoulders were slumped in her cashmere sweater.

I slipped off my shoes and walked over to squeeze her shoulder.

"How bad was it?" she croaked.

"He's at peace now," I said gently. She burst into tears again, and I wrapped my arms around her as she sobbed. After a few minutes, she straightened.

"I've got to get myself together," she said, wiping her eyes.

"Take all the time you need," I said. "Did you get yourself situated?"

"We put her in the Lupine suite," Gwen said, sipping her tea.

"One of my favorites. By the way, anything I need to deal with?" I asked my niece.

"Candy was looking for you. And Benjamin."

I sighed. "What did they want?"

"Candy just wanted to ask you more questions, I think. And Benjamin said something about dinner."

"In other words, nothing I need to deal with now." I walked over to the freezer and pulled out a container of clam chowder. "Benjamin will have to figure out dinner on his own," I said. "I invited John to come over for chowder after he's finished . . ." I glanced at Charlene and trailed off, realizing the conversation John and I had postponed earlier would have to wait until Charlene had gone to bed. I pulled a package of rolls from the freezer and opened the fridge to search for salad fixings. The shelves overflowed with fresh fruit and eggs. I turned to Charlene. "You brought the groceries?"

She smiled weakly. "It was Tania's idea. She said you tip in chocolate." For a second, I saw a glimpse of my jovial friend.

"Thank God. Otherwise I'd have to serve pine mulch and tern eggs for breakfast."

"So does that mean you've terminated your membership with *Save our Terns*?" Charlene said with a faint grin.

"If we didn't get back on good terms, I was afraid I'd have to," I said.

The grin suddenly faltered, and her face crumpled again. I hurried to her side. It was going to be a tough night for all of us.

FOURTEEN

THE SKY HAD DARKENED to lead, rain lashed the windows, and the wind was howling through the eaves when John pounded at the kitchen door an hour later. Thunder cracked overhead as I ran to let him in.

"Did the investigators get everything taken care of before the storm blew in?" I asked as he closed the door behind him and began peeling off his raincoat.

"I think so," he said, nodding at Charlene, who huddled next to the radiator wrapped in a blanket, sipping a mug of tea. She'd been staring out the window at the storm for the last half hour, clutching Pepper to her chest, while I tried to make conversation and attempted to make a dent in the mountain of laundry.

John hung his coat on the hook and pulled off his boots. "I'm glad I checked the weather this morning and grabbed my raincoat," he said. "Otherwise I'd be a drowned rat."

"Now that you're here, I'll heat up the chowder," I said. "Can I get you a cup of tea?"

His green eyes crinkled in a tired smile that sent tendrils of warmth through me. "That would be great."

"Do they know who did it yet?" Charlene croaked from next to the radiator.

John's eyes flicked to me. "No," he said quietly. "Not yet. But they're working on it."

I nodded at him. Charlene didn't need to know that she—and I—were suspects. Not yet, anyway.

"Who do you think it was?" she asked, hugging the kitten to her chest.

"Honestly," John told her, "I was hoping you might be able to help the police figure that out."

"Me?"

He pulled up a chair across from Charlene and leaned toward her, his hands clasped between his knees. "Do you know anyone who argued with him recently? Or anyone he talked about, even from his past?"

Charlene shook her head slowly. "Everyone loves . . . loved . . . Richard." Her voice caught, and she stifled a sob.

"I know it's hard," John said. "But if you remember anything—even a sharp word, or an unusual phone call, it would help if you told the police about it."

She pulled the blanket closer around her. My heart ached at her tear-streaked face. "There was one unusual thing," she said slowly, "but I doubt it means anything."

John leaned forward in his chair. "What was it?"

"Richard . . . Richard said he found something during the renovation. A diary, I think. He hadn't decided what to do about it yet, though."

"You mean whether he was going to take it to the museum?" I asked.

Charlene sniffled and pushed her hair behind her ears. I was so used to seeing her made up; her raw face looked so vulnerable now. "No," she said. "I don't think that's what it was about. He was going to talk to someone about it."

"Whose diary was it?" I asked.

"I'm not even sure it was a diary. I think it must have belonged to one of the priests."

My mind turned back to something Matilda had said. *Old grudges last a long, long time.* Could someone have killed Richard over an old diary?

"Do you know where he kept it?" I asked.

She shook her head.

I turned to John. "Could you find out if the police turned anything up?"

He nodded. "I'll call tomorrow."

My stomach gurgled, and I remembered the chowder. "Anyone hungry?" I asked.

Charlene didn't answer, but John said, "I'm starving."

"I'll get dinner started, then."

"Can I help with something?" John asked, standing up and pushing his chair in.

"How are you with salad?"

He winked at me. "My specialty."

A few minutes later, the smell of browning rolls and clam chowder filled the kitchen. Despite the day's tragic circumstances, the kitchen felt more comfortable than it had in days, with Charlene by the window and John tearing up romaine lettuce beside me. I'd missed John, I realized.

I was just giving the chowder a final stir when the door to the inn swung open, and Candy popped in. Her eyes quickly took in Charlene, then focused on John.

"Can I help you?" I asked, not trying to keep the chill from my voice.

"I was just wondering if you'd seen Ben," she said brightly. Despite the weather outside, she looked like she was ready for a beach party in a tiny red Hawaiian-print dress and strappy high-heeled sandals. "We were supposed to go to dinner."

I shrugged. "Sorry."

She gave John one last lingering glance. "If you see him, tell him I'm looking for him."

I nodded sharply as the door swung shut behind her.

"I can't believe her," I said.

John's eyebrows rose. "What do you mean? Because she's wearing a sundress in October?"

"No," I said, stomping across the kitchen to the oven. "First she follows me around the inn for days, claiming to do 'research' for an inn she's planning to open over on the mainland. Then she 'accidentally' lets the water overflow in her room, causing me thousands of dollars in damage." I opened the oven door to check on the rolls, then slammed it shut.

"Easy now, Nat. You don't need a broken oven, too."

"But I haven't even gotten to the best part yet," I said. "I just found out she's putting in a bid on Cliffside. She's trying to steal my secrets and put me out of business so she can start her own inn right down the street."

Even Charlene looked up. "What?"

"Gwen told me this morning."

Charlene blinked. "I knew a real estate agent was showing Cliff-side, but I thought it was to someone looking for a vacation home. Are you sure that's what she has in mind?"

"Charlene," I said. "That woman has been dogging my footsteps, taking notes on everything I do—from my suppliers to my cleaning products—for almost a week now."

"What are you going to do?" John asked.

I sighed and sank into a kitchen chair. "I don't know. Guard my guest list, for starters. Other than that, though . . ." I shrugged. "It's a free country."

———

Dinner went relatively well, considering the circumstances. Gwen came down and joined us, and between the three of us, we managed to keep Charlene's mind from dwelling too much on what had happened at the rectory.

After Gwen, John and I had finished bowls of chocolate ice cream—Charlene barely touched hers—my friend turned to me, her face pale. "I need you to find out who did this to Richard," she said.

I pushed my bowl away. "I know," I said. "And I'll do whatever I can."

"We have to go to the rectory tomorrow."

I started, "I don't know if we're allowed . . ."

"I don't care. I have the key. If this diary is the reason he died, I need to look at it, see if I can figure out the connection."

John nodded. "That makes sense. But I'm sure the police have it by now, and are doing everything they can to piece things together."

"You mean Grimes?" She shook her head. "He's an idiot."

I had to agree with her there.

"No," she continued. "I need to see the rectory myself."

"I know Grimes isn't the ideal investigator, and that it wouldn't hurt to do what we can to help. But the rectory may be closed off for a few days. It's a crime scene," John said.

"Then as soon as it isn't closed off anymore," she said, shooting me a look that made it eminently clear she wasn't planning on waiting. I stifled a sigh.

"What do you know about Richard's past?" I said, hoping to change the subject. "Maybe his death had something to do with his life before he came to the island."

"It's worth looking into, anyway," John said.

"All I know is that he had a post in Boston for a few years before he was called to Cranberry Island."

I leaned forward. "Boston to Cranberry Island is a big switch. Did he ever say why he moved?"

"He never really talked about it much," Charlene said.

John's green eyes flicked to mine, and I knew we were thinking the same thing. Priests don't get reassigned from major metropolitan areas to backwaters like tiny Maine islands as a reward for good behavior. It might not be a bad idea to get in touch with the Boston diocese and find out a little bit more about McLaughlin's history—and why he was reassigned.

"Was he ever married?" John asked.

"I don't think so," Charlene said. "Although I got the impression he had had a relationship that ended badly." Tears leaked from her eyes again. "That's why what we had was so . . . Oh, God . . ." Her chest started heaving again.

"It's okay," I murmured, reaching out to squeeze Charlene's arm as Gwen handed her a Kleenex. Rain pounded against the window and thunder rumbled ominously overhead as we waited for Charlene to collect herself.

She blew her nose and looked up. "I don't think I can talk about this anymore tonight. It's too . . . too . . ."

"I know," I said softly. "Why don't I go and run you a bath? That always relaxes me. Maybe a candle, and some bubble bath?"

"Thank you," she said in a small voice as I headed through the swinging door to the Lupine suite.

Fifteen minutes later, when Charlene was ensconced in a tub full of warm, scented bubbles, I rejoined John. Gwen had headed upstairs, so it was just the two of us in the yellow kitchen.

"This is going to be tough on her," I said.

John's green eyes were tired. "And she doesn't even know she's a suspect yet."

I grimaced. "I know." I pulled up a chair next to John, thinking of how comfortable it was to have him in my kitchen. With Benjamin, it was like living with a tropical storm—he was hot, unpredictable. John was more of a steady warm front . . . comforting, stable, with a slow-burning heat. I found myself staring at his brown, weathered face, the crinkles around his green eyes. I forced myself to look away, focusing instead on the rain running down the windowpanes. "I never told you what happened when I went to Polly's today," I said.

"You were at Polly's?"

As the wind howled around the old inn, I told him about the box of bullets and the intruder . . . and my trip to the rectory.

"If it was a suicide," he asked, "why would someone bother taking the bullets?"

"Because there was one less than there should have been. Which means it wasn't a suicide."

"But they never found another casing," John said.

"They never looked," I said. "And it's a big bog."

"True."

"What convinces me more than anything is that I told McLaughlin about the bullets, and then someone came to the house less than an hour later and got rid of them."

"Do you think it was McLaughlin?"

"I thought so, at first . . . but McLaughlin is dead. Which kind of takes him off the hook for Polly's murder. Assuming it's the same killer, that is."

John sighed. "We need to tell someone about the bullets." He glanced at me doubtfully. "I don't know if it will do any good . . ."

I smiled ruefully. "Not with Grimes on the case, no."

John turned his bowl around slowly. "Do you think someone might have killed McLaughlin because of something Polly told him?"

"I don't know," I said. "It just seems kind of weird. He said something about the 'sordid details' of Polly's life."

"But Polly's dead, so why would someone kill McLaughlin to keep him quiet?"

"That's the thing. It doesn't make sense." I shivered. "The murderer must have gotten there right after I left."

John's eyes focused on me. "Or was waiting for you to leave."

A chill passed through me. "You mean he . . . or she . . . knew I was there?"

"That's exactly what I'm worried about. If McLaughlin knew something he shouldn't have, and the murderer knew you had talked with him . . ."

"And if McLaughlin told him I was going to count the bullets . . ."

John leaned over and gripped my arm. "I think you need to be very, very careful, Natalie."

I sighed. "And to think I came to Cranberry Island for a quiet life."

He chuckled and sat back. "Unfortunately, Nat, trouble seems to follow you around."

I thought of poor Polly, and McLaughlin, and the "ghost" upstairs, and Candy wanting to buy Cliffside, and Benjamin's proposal . . . "I think I need a vacation."

"Maybe someday, when all this is over, we'll have to plan one." He reached out again and squeezed my hand.

"Maybe," I said, letting the warmth seep up my arm and settle somewhere in the vicinity of my heart.

All too soon, he pushed back his chair and stood up. "You should probably check on Charlene," he said. "And I need to head home."

"Thanks for coming over."

He pulled on his raincoat. "And thank you for dinner. I'll let you know what I hear from Grimes. But don't expect much."

"I don't. Besides, I'll probably have a chance to talk to him myself, when he comes to inspect my knife collection."

"Are they all accounted for?"

My eyes darted to the knife block. "You know, I never checked."

John shrugged with resignation. "To be honest, I doubt it will make a difference." He paused with his hand on the door, staring at me hard. "Good night, Natalie."

"Good night, John." My voice was husky. I stood at the window and watched him until he disappeared into the carriage house. Then I locked the door and walked over to my knife block. Everything was accounted for, except for the French chef's knife; the handle had broken a few months ago, and I hadn't gotten around to replacing it. Besides, I figured, a French chef's knife was for chopping vegetables, not meat. I shivered. *Or people.*

———

It was almost midnight before Charlene finally fell asleep. I had stayed with her for hours, just listening, comforting her, trying to keep her from falling apart. After arranging the quilt over Charlene and Pepper and turning off the light, I headed blearily back to the kitchen to get things ready for the morning. Fortunately, I had a few extra loaves of cranberry walnut bread in the freezer from last week; I pulled them out to thaw, then put some sausage in the pan and grated cheese for the strata I planned to put together the next morning. I had sliced the top off a pineapple for a fruit salad when a click sounded behind me.

FIFTEEN

I WHIRLED AROUND IN time to see the doorknob jiggle, and a flash of movement through the door's dark windowpane. I slid a butcher's knife from the block and sidled over to the light switches. My hand was shaking as it flipped the kitchen light off and the porch light on.

There was no one there.

I crept over to the door to the porch and peered outside. In the watery light, the rain looked like falling silver, but the porch was empty. Then my eyes dropped to the boards outside the door. No one was there now.

But somebody had been.

Muddy footprints, already half washed away by the rain, marred the white paint.

I whirled around toward the swinging door and ran to the front of the house. The door was locked. After checking every window on the first floor, I returned to the kitchen and laid the carving knife on the counter beside me. I quickly chopped the pineapple, the knife slipping in my shaking hands, nicking my finger. Despite the warm, cozy kitchen around me—usually my haven from the world—I felt exposed, vulnerable. If someone had a gun, I realized, I was a sitting duck. I couldn't see anyone outside. But anyone outside could see me.

I dumped the pineapple into a bowl and turned the burner off under the sausage. A moment later, I thrust the sausage and the chopped pineapple into the refrigerator, then turned off the kitchen light before heading upstairs, knife in hand. I laid the blade on the bedside table and changed into a nightshirt, my ears alert for the slightest sound. Who had been outside the kitchen door, I wondered? Polly's murderer? It certainly wasn't a ghost. Ghosts, after all, don't leave muddy footprints.

And why were they trying to get in?

Adrenaline was still pulsing through me as I arranged the covers around me and picked up one of Michele Scott's wine lover's mysteries. I had locked the door to my room. So had Gwen—I checked. And the downstairs was secure. If anyone other than a guest came in, they'd have to break a window to do it, and I'd be sure to hear it. Besides, John was fifty feet and a phone call away.

I tried to lose myself in the California wine country, but tonight it wasn't working. Finally, I turned off the light, and almost had a cardiac arrest when Biscuit jumped up into the bed beside me. She nestled into my shoulder, and after a long while staring at the darkened ceiling and straining my ears for the sound of breaking glass, I drifted off to sleep.

———

It was still dark when the alarm went off a few hours later. I jabbed the button with a finger and turned on the light. As Biscuit burrowed under the covers, I pulled on a bathrobe and headed downstairs to make coffee.

The rain had stopped, but windows still shone cold and black when I flipped the light on and walked to the sink. I pulled the bathrobe tighter around me, once again feeling exposed. Whoever was out there last night must surely have gone by now, I told myself as I measured out coffee. They couldn't possibly have stayed out in the storm all night.

My eyes still strayed to the door as I assembled the strata, stirring the eggs and pouring them over layers of bread, sausage, and cheese. My plan had been to assemble it the night before—the recipe called for the strata to rest in the refrigerator for several hours—but the quickie version would have to do.

When the sky outside turned pearly gray, I breathed a sigh of relief. I arranged the pineapple in a bowl with some strawberries and kiwi slices, popped the strata into the oven, and headed upstairs to change. Only this time I had a cup of coffee in my hand instead of a carving knife.

By the time 8:30 rolled around, the strata was bubbling nicely, I had laid out slices of moist cranberry walnut bread on a silver platter, and the red, green, and yellow fruit glowed in the sunlight streaming through the windows.

Benjamin was the first one down, looking trim and attractive in tan corduroys and a dark red shirt that reminded me with a pang of the one McLaughlin had worn yesterday. Cowboy boots peeked out from below the hem of his slacks. You can take the boy out of Texas . . .

His eyes swept over me. "You look particularly beautiful this morning, Nat."

"Thanks." I straightened my shirt self-consciously; I had picked one of my nicer blouses this morning, a pale blue-gray that matched my eyes. "Can I get you some coffee?"

"Sure," he said, sitting at a table near the window. "I hear there was a murder yesterday. The rector, or something."

"Yes. It was my best friend's boyfriend, actually."

Benjamin shook his head. "I'm sorry to hear that. You wouldn't think an island this small would be a hotbed of crime, but people seem to be dropping like flies." He leaned forward in his chair. "Austin doesn't sound so bad after all, does it?"

"Did Candy ever find you last night?" I asked. He fixed me with those mesmerizing blue eyes as I filled his mug with coffee, and my insides twisted up. When Benjamin wasn't around, I could swear off him forever. But the moment he stepped into the room, all bets were off.

He sidestepped my question and grabbed my free hand, stroking my palm.

Heat shot through me, and I put the coffeepot down hastily, before I spilled it all over my shoes.

"Did you think anymore about my proposition?" His voice was low, urgent.

My body was saying *yes, yes, yes*, but my brain, for the moment at least, was still in control. *Think of John*, I told myself sternly, forcing my eyes from Benjamin's blue ones and focusing on the lighthouse in the distance. I struggled to conjure his sandy hair, his long, lean face . . .

I took a deep breath. "You mean the inn in Austin?"

He gripped my hand. "I mean my proposal."

I swallowed hard. "The marriage thing."

"Yes."

I meant to say no, but what came out was, "I'm still thinking about it."

"Good." He traced the skin of my palm. "Should I call the real estate agent, then?"

I pulled my hand away like it was burned, and grabbed the coffeepot. "No, no . . . not yet."

"I'm not going to bite, Nat. I just want to make sure you explore all your options."

Fortunately, at that moment Russell Lidell walked in, dressed once again in the too-tight charcoal suit. He sat down near the window, and I rushed over to his table. "Coffee?" My voice sounded strangled.

"Sure." He gave me a funny look. "Something wrong?"

My eyes flicked to Benjamin, who was staring at me with a wounded expression. "No, no. Nothing at all," I babbled. "We've got strata this morning, and fruit salad, and cranberry bread . . . in fact, I'd better go check on the strata. I'll have it out in a minute!" Two pairs of eyes followed me as I hustled back to the swinging door and the safety of my kitchen.

I grabbed the potholders and pulled the strata out of the oven, but the aroma of melted cheese and sausage was wasted on me. I slapped the pan down on a trivet. Why had I said I was thinking about it, when I knew the answer should be no? My eyes drifted to the window, and John's carriage house. John, with the pine shavings in his sun-streaked hair, his easy smile, the solidness I felt when he was with me . . . Would I really want to give everything up—the Gray Whale Inn, Cranberry Island . . . John—to chase after a second chance with Benjamin? An image of Zhang's long black hair, Benjamin's hand on her back, floated into my mind, and the pain of betrayal stirred again. It occurred to me suddenly that he had dodged my question about Candy. Benjamin and Candy had been kayaking together, over to the mainland . . . he'd been spending his days with her, even while he was trying to convince me to marry him.

He had been unfaithful once.

I wasn't willing to risk it again.

I gripped the strata pan, steeling myself to go out into the dining room and tell Benjamin it wasn't going to work out. I had almost reached the swinging door when the phone rang.

I put down the pan and grabbed the receiver. "Good morning, Gray Whale Inn."

"Miss Barnes?"

"Speaking."

"This is Gus Fruhstuck from Allstart Insurance. I'm calling about your recent claim on the Gray Whale Inn."

"Yes? Are the repair people coming out this week?"

"Well, not quite yet."

"What do you mean, not quite yet? I thought you said you were sending someone out immediately. I live in Maine, and it's almost winter. The weather's going to get bad soon. We don't have much time."

He cleared his throat. "I'm afraid your case is under investigation, ma'am. It seems there's, um . . ." He paused for a moment. "Well, there's some question as to whether the damage was intentional."

"Intentional? You think I trashed two of my rooms and the hallway *intentionally*?"

"All I'm saying is that the case is under investigation. We'll let you know what the decision is when the department completes their evaluation of the circumstances."

I closed my eyes and tried to stem my rising panic. "How long does that take? I've got a business to run here, and it's going to be hard to sell 'luxury accommodations' with warped floorboards in half the inn."

"Ma'am . . ."

"Can I talk with your supervisor?"

"I'm sorry, ma'am . . ."

"This is my livelihood we're talking about here! This is why I have insurance!"

"As soon as the investigators are finished . . ."

I opened my eyes and glanced at the clock. "Look, Gus. I've got guests to feed right now, but I'm going to call you back in an hour, and when I do, I want your supervisor to explain to me why your company is withholding what it promised to provide . . ."

"Ma'am . . ."

"I have to go. I'll talk to you in an hour." I slammed down the phone, caught my breath, and picked up the strata again.

When I pushed through the swinging door, Candy stood behind Benjamin, rubbing his shoulders with manicured hands. Benjamin shrugged slightly and gave me a rueful grin as I laid the strata on the buffet.

It took two more trips to get the fruit salad and the cranberry bread on the buffet. By the second trip, Candy was leaning against Benjamin, pressing her chest into the back of his head. I headed back into the kitchen a last time and returned with a pot of coffee.

"Good morning, Candy," I said, filling the cup across from Benjamin's. She sidled out from behind Benjamin, slid into the seat next to his, and pulled the cup toward her.

"Good morning," she said. "Anything low-carb for me this morning?"

"I hear you were out at Cliffside yesterday," I said.

She blinked her mascaraed lashes. "Oh, yes. Just doing a little bit of research."

"Someone told me you were talking about making an offer on it. To open an inn."

She looked down and rearranged her yellow scoop-necked T-shirt. "I'm looking into it, of course . . ."

"I thought you were going to open an inn on the mainland."

She darted a glance at Benjamin and pursed her pink lips. "I was, I was . . . I still may be. But when the agent called and told me about it, I thought it wouldn't hurt to look . . ."

"Of course," I said frostily. I glanced at Benjamin, who looked dazed, and turned toward the kitchen. "Breakfast is on the buffet. If you need anything else, let me know."

———

Two hours later, I was still stewing about my ex-fiancé, Candy's offer on Cliffside, and the jerks at Allstart Insurance. After calling Gus back three times, I had only gotten his voice mail, and my frustration was mounting. What would happen if the insurance company refused to cover the damages? Would I be able to afford the repairs myself?

I forced myself to focus on the tasks that needed to get done. On the plus side, at least Candy wasn't haunting the kitchen this morning. I had cleaned up most of the breakfast dishes and was about to wipe down the buffet table when Charlene appeared at the swinging door in a baggy T-shirt and jeans. Her hair was flat on one side, and her makeup was still smeared under her eyes, accentuating dark circles I'd never seen before.

I put the rag back down and headed for the coffeepot, my mind suddenly swept clear of everything but Charlene. "Did you get any sleep?" I asked, scooping fresh beans into the grinder.

"Yeah. Thanks." She slumped into one of the kitchen chairs.

"I've got fruit salad, strata, and cranberry walnut bread for breakfast. Want me to heat some up for you?"

She shook her head. "No. Not yet."

"Whenever you're ready," I said.

She looked up at me with blue eyes that were tired, but determined. "I want to go to the rectory today."

I sighed. "I know. I just don't know if the police have cleared out yet."

"Maybe tonight, when everyone's back on the mainland."

After the coffee grinder finished whirring, I nodded. "Maybe." I poured the coffee into a fresh filter, filled the coffeemaker with water, and sat down next to her. "In the meantime, there are a few things we might be able to do."

"You mean calling Boston?"

I nodded. "Do you know the name of the church he was at?"

"Saint something, I think."

I shook my head and grinned. "Well, that narrows it down."

A faint smile echoed on my friend's face. "I guess that isn't very specific, is it? Maybe we should call the bishop."

"Good idea." The coffeepot gurgled as I reached over and grabbed a pen and paper. "Okay. We'll call Boston and see what we can find out about his life there. Anyone here who didn't like him?"

Charlene pursed her lips. "No one that I know of."

"Anyone he was spending a lot of time with?" I was thinking of Polly . . . and Murray.

"Nothing out of the ordinary. He and Murray were working on something together, though, I think."

My antennae went up. "Do you know what?"

"I know Murray was getting very involved with the church. I think he funded some of the renovations for the rectory."

For what in return, I wondered? "Did they have some kind of an arrangement?"

She shrugged. "Not that I know of."

I thought of McLaughlin's strong support of the development. Was the money for the rectory a payment for McLaughlin's pushing Cranberry Estates to his congregation? Or did McLaughlin have enough put aside from his time as a plumbing salesman to cover the renovations? *Murray Selfridge*, I wrote. "Maybe we can talk to him, see what we can find out." I chewed on the pencil for a moment. "Anyone else?"

She shook her head. "Just the parishioners, really. I know he was counseling a few people, but he never told me who."

I added *rectory* to the list. Maybe we'd find McLaughlin's notes, I thought. If the police hadn't already taken them.

The coffeepot stopped gurgling. I grabbed a mug from the cabinet, poured Charlene a cup, and handed it to her. "Cream and sugar?"

She sighed. "I guess there's no point in dieting now. Yes and yes."

"Why don't I fix you a plate?"

"I'm really not hungry."

"You haven't eaten a thing since yesterday. And you barely touched your dinner last night."

She shrugged. "I guess so."

I heated up a mound of strata, then heaped fruit and quick bread next to it and slid the plate across the table to her. She picked at the fruit a little, but her eyes widened when she tasted the strata. "This is good."

I smiled, relieved to see Charlene eating, and was about to sit down next to her with a cup of coffee of my own when the doorbell rang.

"I'll be right back," I said, and headed for the front door.

My heart sank as I opened it. It was Grimes.

SIXTEEN

"CAN I HELP YOU?"

Grimes dropped his cigarette on the front stoop and ground it out with his boot. "Need to see your knives. And talk with your friend, if she's here."

"We're in the kitchen," I said.

He smoothed his hair back with nicotine-yellowed fingers and followed me through the parlor and the dining room to the kitchen. Charlene looked up as we entered through the swinging door.

"Good morning, Sergeant Grimes." Her voice was flat.

"Good morning, Miz Kean." He turned to me. "Where are your knives?"

I pointed toward the block next to the sink. "Help yourself."

Charlene raised her eyebrows at me as Grimes walked over to the counter.

"Looks like one or two are missing," he said.

"The paring knife is in the dish drainer. The French Chef's knife broke a while ago; I haven't replaced it yet."

"Are you sure it was a French . . . whatever it is?"

I nodded.

"Anyone seen it other than you?"

I shook my head. "It broke several months ago."

"Mmm hmmm." Grimes pulled out his notebook and scrawled something. "Miz Barnes, let's go over this again. where were you on the day Richard McLaughlin died?"

Charlene's eyes widened. I glanced at her and shook my head a fraction. "I was here in the morning, of course. When I finished cleaning up I visited Rev. McLaughlin at the rectory."

Grimes narrowed his eyes at me. "That's what I figured. What time?"

"I already told you. Around eleven thirty."

"Anyone see you there?"

"Not that I know of."

"Where did you go next?"

I sighed. "I left at about twelve, and stopped by Emmeline Hoyle's. She wasn't home, so I went to Polly's house to check on the cats." I cleared my throat. If I was coming clean, I might as well tell him everything. "Someone else went into Polly's house while I was there."

Grimes' head snapped up. "Who?"

"I don't know," I said. "I was hiding in the closet."

"Hiding in the closet?" He scratched his greasy hair with one finger. "I thought you were checking on the cats."

"I was," I said. "I just went upstairs to make sure I hadn't missed anyone. Someone came through the door, and . . ." I shrugged. "After Polly's death, I guess I was scared."

"But she offed herself. I know you keep saying it was murder, but..."

I took a deep breath. "Whoever came into the house took a box of bullets," I said.

"How do you know that?"

"Because they were in her top dresser drawer before I hid in the closet," I said. "When I came out, they were gone."

Grimes shrugged. "So?"

"One of the bullets was missing."

"What do you mean?"

"I counted them. She only shot herself once, but two bullets are missing."

He leaned back in his chair and tapped his pen on the table. "How do you know one was missing? Maybe she shot off a round or two to scare off a stray dog or something. Besides, what were you doing snooping around the place?"

"I wasn't really snooping. The drawer was open, and I thought a cat might have snuck in." I shrugged. "And I guess I was curious."

Grimes peered at me with close-set eyes. "What I want to know is, why were you visiting McLaughlin?"

I straightened my back and stared Grimes in the eye. "I thought he might know something about Polly's death."

"Like I said, that was a suicide."

"I'm still not convinced," I said.

Grimes glanced at Charlene, who was now rigid in her chair. "You two seem pretty friendly now that your boyfriend's gone."

"Natalie is my friend," Charlene hissed. "What's your point?"

Grimes swaggered over to the kitchen table and leaned over one of the chair backs. His paunch swayed as he spoke. "My point,

Miz Kean, is that you and your friend Miz Barnes are my two best suspects in this case."

Charlene blanched. "You think . . . you think I killed Richard?"

"Maybe you found out there was a little hanky panky going on. Maybe you got mad." He nodded at me. "Or maybe your friend here got a little jealous of all the time you and McLaughlin were spending up at the rectory."

"Hanky panky?" Charlene asked. "What are you talking about?"

He stood up and jotted something down in his little book. "Why don't you tell me, Miz Kean?"

Charlene stood up and straightened her back. Her eyes were no longer flat; instead, they were burning with barely suppressed anger. "I don't have the slightest idea what you're talking about, Sergeant Grimes. And if you know something I don't, I would appreciate you telling me instead of using crude innuendos."

Grimes shrugged. "Just a few things I've heard around the island . . ." He studied Charlene's face, which was white with rage. "The way I hear it, you weren't the only filly in the stable."

Charlene gripped the chair back. "What? Who told you that?" Her voice was strained. "Who was it?"

A slow smile spread across Grimes' face. "I don't know yet. But I intend to find out."

———

My old friend came back to life almost as soon as Grimes left. As I sprayed the kitchen with lavender mist to dispel the odor of stale smoke and Grimes' cheap aftershave, Charlene paced the kitchen.

"That *bastard*!" she said. "How *dare* he . . ." She turned to me. "Do you think it's true?"

I shook my head. "I don't know, Charlene. But if it is, I can't think why we haven't heard about it already."

"You're right. It can't be true. It *can't* be." She stopped her pacing and looked at me. "We have to go to the rectory."

"Hold on, Charlene. The cops are there."

"Tonight, then. We'll go tonight."

I sighed. "Fine." There was no way to convince her otherwise. Besides, maybe we would find something—notes, or a diary, or an unsent letter—that would help explain Polly's death. "In the meantime, why don't you let me get some of this laundry started, and then we'll make a few phone calls?"

"You mean to see what everyone is talking about?"

"I mean to find out about what happened while Richard was in Boston."

"Oh," she said. "Okay." Her eyes strayed to the phone. "I need to call the store first, see how Tania's doing."

"Sure," I said. "While you're doing that, I'll throw in a load of towels and check on Gwen."

As Charlene picked up the phone and dialed, I tossed a bunch of towels into the washer and ran upstairs to talk to Gwen, who was finishing cleaning Candy's room. As usual, Gwen was dressed in the kind of clothes I reserved for a date. Even when she was scrubbing toilets, my niece did it in style.

"How's Charlene?" she asked, tugging her turquoise cashmere sweater down as she bent to scrub the toilet.

"She's doing better, now that Grimes has her all fired up."

"What do you mean?"

"Well, he's told us we're the primary suspects . . . and he suggested to Charlene that maybe she wasn't the only woman in McLaughlin's life."

Gwen dropped the toilet brush. "No!"

"That's what he says. Have you heard anything?"

Her curls bounced as she shook her head. "No, but I'll see if anyone else has heard anything."

"How's Adam doing, by the way?"

Gwen's face lit up like it always did when I asked about her lobsterman boyfriend. "He's great. Things are going really well for him this fall . . ." Her face clouded. "But O'Leary's getting the co-op in trouble."

"Marge's husband? What's going on?"

"He's cutting trap lines. I talked with Adam this morning; someone went out and cut fifty or sixty of the mainlanders' traps last night. I'm betting it was O'Leary and some of his cronies."

I winced. Someone further down the coast had been killed over lobstering territories just last year. "What does Adam think of it all?"

"He's just trying to keep his nose clean," Gwen said. I was glad to hear it. That hadn't always been Adam's approach to territory wars.

"Well," I said, "let me know what you find out. I can't help you out this morning, but maybe tomorrow I can give you a hand and you can head out to Fernand's early."

"Thanks, Aunt Nat. But you've got your hands full with Charlene . . ." She glanced around the room. ". . . and Candy."

"That's not all I've got to worry about, unfortunately." I told her about my conversation with the insurance company—and about Benjamin's marriage proposal.

She drew in her breath. "Oh my God. What are you going to do?"

"I'm going to turn him down."

"Are you sure?"

"I should be," I sighed. "But I'm not a hundred percent. And that's the trouble."

"What about John?" she asked.

"Don't remind me."

"I'm glad I'm not in your shoes," she said.

I groaned and headed for the door. "Don't I know it."

Just as I got back to the kitchen, Charlene hung up the phone. She turned to me, hands on her hips. "O'Leary's starting that damned territory war," she said.

"That's what Gwen said. How's Tania holding up?"

"The store's fine. The island is humming with rumors, though; Tania didn't want to tell me, but I wrung it out of her. Apparently the word is that Polly and Richard were planning to buy a yacht and head south, but that an old girlfriend came and put a stop to things." Despite Charlene's light tone, her face was drawn, and I knew she was hurting.

"An old girlfriend?" I said. "That's ridiculous! Nobody new has been on the island!"

"I don't know who comes up with these things. There's a whole cult theory, too, but I'm not clear on the specifics." She shook her head. "Probably Marge O'Leary."

"The O'Learys again. They're a pair of bad apples, aren't they?

She nodded. "So, what do we do first?" She pointed to the short list I had left on the table.

I picked it up. "So far, we've got Murray and the rectory. I forgot to add Boston." I scrawled the name at the bottom of the list. "Which one do you want to tackle first?"

"If it were up to me," I said, "I'd call Boston. I have a feeling there's a reason McLaughlin . . . I mean Richard . . . ended up here." I glanced at Charlene, whose chin jutted out slightly, and decided not to carry that thought any further.

Charlene reached up and touched her hair. "I want to talk to Murray. Maybe Richard said something to him . . ." She sighed. "But if you want to call Boston first, go ahead. I'll go change into something presentable while you figure out who we should call."

As Charlene disappeared through the swinging door, I put the last couple of dishes into the dishwasher and grabbed the phone book. It was times like this that I wished I had an Internet connection. Maybe I would have to head over to the Somesville library on the mainland later in the day.

I looked up the area code for Boston in the front of the book, then called information and got the number for the diocese office. After a moment's pause, during which I constructed a cover story, my fingers picked out the number. A woman's voice answered on the third ring.

"Hi," I said, clearing my throat. "I'm a reporter for the *Daily Mail*, up in Maine, and I was hoping you could help me."

The woman's voice was guarded. "What can I do for you?"

I put on my best professional voice. "Unfortunately, Rev. Richard McLaughlin, the rector of St. James' Episcopal Church on Cranberry Island, died suddenly yesterday. I'm doing an article for the paper on the reverend's good works throughout his life and career, and someone told me that he used to serve in Boston. I was hoping I could find out a little more about his work in your diocese."

"Rev. McLaughlin? The name doesn't ring a bell, but I've only worked here for a year . . ."

"Is there anyone there who might remember him?"

"Yes, there's one person . . . Hold on a second." The phone clicked, and "Amazing Grace" flooded into the earpiece. I gazed out the window while I waited, watching a lobster boat chug by. I strained my eyes to see if I recognized the buoy strapped to the front of the boat, but it was too far away to see.

"Hello?" The voice jolted me, and it took me a moment to remember why I was calling. And who I'd said I was.

"Hello," I stammered, and my eyes flicked to the Cranberry Rock lighthouse in the distance. "I'm . . . Beatrice Lighthouse, calling from the Mount Desert Island *Daily Mail*."

"What can I do for you, Ms. Lighthouse?"

"I was calling to inquire about Rev. Richard McLaughlin. He died suddenly yesterday, and I wanted to see if you could tell me anything about his life in Boston. For the obituary."

"McLaughlin." The voice was clipped. "Yes, I remember him. I'm sorry to hear he passed away. He was here for a few years, at St. Jude's."

"Yes, so I understand," I said. "I was wondering, what prompted him to move from a city like Boston to a small island like Cranberry Island?"

The man on the end of the line cleared his throat. "I think it was a personal decision," he said.

"Did you know Reverend McLaughlin?"

"Yes. Yes, I did. He was a dedicated priest . . . now, if you don't mind, I have a meeting to attend."

"Did you know McLaughlin was murdered?"

The phone was silent for a beat. "Murdered?"

"Yes," I said. "Do you have any idea who might have wanted the reverend dead?"

"I really have to go, Ms—?"

"Lighthouse," I prompted. "And who am I speaking with?"

"John LeGrange. I'm the bishop. Now, I really must go. Good luck with your article." He hung up.

I replaced the receiver and stood staring out the window. When Charlene came down a few minutes later, looking more like herself in tight-fitting jeans and a V-neck top, I was still leaning against the counter, watching the slow progress of the lobster boat across the water.

"What did you find out?" she asked.

I turned to face her. "I think we need to make a trip to the library."

"Why?"

"I just spoke with the bishop."

Charlene stared at me.

"He didn't want to talk about McLaughlin—was in a real hurry to get off the phone. When I asked him why McLaughlin had moved to Cranberry Island, he said it was for 'personal reasons.'"

"So?"

"When I told him McLaughlin had been murdered, he didn't sound surprised."

SEVENTEEN

CHARLENE'S FACE WAS HARD. "So what are you saying, Natalie?"

"What I'm saying is that we need to look into what happened in Boston. I'd like to go to the library and see if anything turned up in the papers."

"The papers?" She crossed her arms. "What exactly are you looking for?"

I shrugged. "I don't know yet. It could be any number of things. If we can't find anything out, I'll keep calling and see if I can find out who his friends were. He was at St. Jude's; I'm sure some of the congregation members remember him."

"Natalie, I appreciate your help, but I think you're on a witch-hunt here. I know Richard isn't . . . wasn't your favorite person . . ."

"Charlene," I said gently, putting a hand on her shoulder. "How I felt about Richard isn't the issue here . . ."

She thrust her chin out. "He left Boston because he needed a change. You're as bad as the *Daily Mail* . . . just looking for a scandal."

"Maybe I'm wrong. I hope I am. But Grimes has his eye on us. If we do find something, at least we can say there was someone else with a motive."

"But neither of us *has* a motive!"

"That's not what Grimes thinks. And unfortunately, it's his opinion that counts right now."

She rolled her eyes. "Fine, fine. So you want to go to the library. What about Murray?"

I shrugged. "We'll talk to him later. Maybe after we go to the rectory. Do you want to come with me, or would you rather stay here?"

"I probably need to head down to the store for a while, if you don't mind."

"Are you sure? Tania seems to have it under control down there."

"It will be good for me. Take my mind off . . . things."

I was about to try to persuade her to stay, but suddenly our conversation with Grimes echoed in my head. She was probably going down to the store to find out if there was any truth to the rumor that McLaughlin was seeing someone else, I realized. So instead of trying to get her to stay at the inn, I said, "I'll swing by the mainland, then."

Charlene headed for the swinging door, a look of grim determination on her face. "Call me when you get back."

———

After checking with Gwen to make sure she didn't need any help, I let myself out the back door, shivering a little when I remembered the footprints on the back deck last night. Who had it been, I wondered? And what did he—or she—want?

Whoever had been lurking at my door last night was sure to be long gone, but my eyes still darted around nervously as I headed down to the dock. Despite all my worries, it felt good to be outside. The air was fresh and clean from last night's storm, and a few water droplets still glistened on the reddish-orange rose hips as I brushed past them. I was tempted to stop in and visit John, but decided to postpone it until I got back. Then maybe I'd have some new information to share, and he could pass it on to Grimes.

I hopped into the bobbing boat, settled myself on the hard wooden seat, and pulled the engine's starter cord.

Nothing happened.

I tugged again, with the same results. After about fifteen minutes of yanking on the cord, my arm was starting to hurt, so I clambered out of the boat and headed to John's workshop, hoping he could figure out what was wrong.

Unfortunately, John wasn't home. My trip to the library would have to be postponed. I sighed as I passed the rosebushes a second time; it looked like it would be laundry day after all.

When I opened the door to the kitchen, Benjamin stood at the refrigerator door, peering at the contents of the shelves. He turned around and smiled when I closed the door behind me.

"What can I do for you?" I asked, folding my arms over my chest.

"I was in the mood for chocolate, but I didn't feel like walking all the way to the store," he said, closing the fridge and bridging the gap between us. "You look tense."

"Tense? Your friend Candy flooded the inn, the insurance is threatening not to pay, there have been two murders on the island, and now my stupid boat won't start." I sank into the nearest kitchen chair.

Benjamin pulled up a chair behind me and began kneading my shoulders. "Things have been tough lately, haven't they? But there are other options."

"I know, I know. That's what you keep telling me." I took a deep breath. "But I just can't forget what happened last time. And I've worked hard for all of this," I said, waving my arms at the buttery yellow kitchen, the gleaming wood floors. "I just don't think I'm ready to give it up."

"This time will be different," he said soothingly, his warm fingers probing my shoulders. "I didn't know what I wanted before. Now, though, since you've been gone . . ."

I closed my eyes and leaned back in the chair. "And what about Candy?"

His hands paused for a split second, then resumed their kneading. "What about her?"

"You've been spending an awful lot of time with her lately," I said.

"Only because you've been so busy here," he said. "And there's not a whole lot to do on this island." He chuckled. "Maybe that's why the murder rate is so high."

I sat up straight and turned to face him. "Benjamin, I loved you once. And you betrayed me."

He dropped his hands in his lap and looked away.

"Benjamin, I still care for you. But the truth is, I don't think I can take that kind of risk again."

He stared at the floor for a moment. My eyes traced the line of his jaw, the little scar on his chin from when he fell from a bike and gashed himself on the handlebars. He looked so sad, so vulnerable. My heart twisted in my chest.

Finally, he looked up. "What can I do to prove myself to you?"

I shook my head. "I don't know, Benjamin. I'm not sure you can."

———

By the time Charlene got back from the store, it was late afternoon, and the morning's sunshine had been replaced by clouds of metallic gray. The temperature had dropped outside, but inside the kitchen it was warm and cozy, and the mounds of dirty laundry were almost gone; I had folded all the towels and was waiting for the last batch of sheets to come out of the dryer. Between loads, I had cleaned the kitchen and whipped up a batch of Barbara Hahn's Berried Medley Lemon Streusel Muffins, trying hard not to think about Benjamin, whose presence in the inn I could feel, or John, whom I hadn't seen all day. My six phone calls to the insurance company hadn't netted me anything, either.

Charlene slipped through the kitchen door, letting in a gust of cold air, and snagged a muffin before plopping down on a kitchen chair. Things were looking up; her appetite was returning.

"What did you find out?" she asked, shrugging off her windbreaker and taking a bite of the fruit-studded muffin. Barbara was right—the recipe was a winner. Charlene's cheeks were pink from the wind.

"I didn't make it over to the library," I said. "The boat broke."

"Couldn't John fix it?"

"He wasn't here." I pulled up a chair across from her. "Maybe I'll go tomorrow. How about you? Is the store in good shape?"

She nodded as she nibbled on a bit of streusel. "Tania did a good job. Everything's running fine."

I hesitated for a moment. "Anything on the rumor mill?"

"Not a word." The expression on her face was grim and determined. "I knew Grimes was wrong. I just knew it."

I nodded, wishing I could agree with her, but privately I wondered. If he *had* been seeing someone else, only the most heartless gossip would point it out to Charlene now that McLaughlin had been murdered.

Charlene set down her muffin after only one bite. "It helped, you know, going down there. But part of me still can't believe it. I keep expecting to turn around and see him, or wanting to pick up the phone and call him." Her face was bleak. "Sometimes I forget for a few moments, then something happens that reminds me, and it all comes rushing back."

I reached out and squeezed her hand. "I know, Charlene."

She wiped away a tear. "They're postponing the funeral. Because of the autopsy."

"Will it be here, do you know?"

"I just don't know. I need to talk to his parents, but I don't know how to reach them. We hadn't met yet."

"Maybe Grimes has the number," I suggested.

She shook her head shortly. "No way. We'll get it when we hit the rectory." Her blue eyes probed mine. "You're still game, right?"

"My only worry is that the police haven't finished their work . . ."

"We won't disturb anything." She fished in her jacket pocket and pulled out a pair of leather gloves. "I picked these up at the house. Fingerprints, you know."

I stifled a sigh. "Good idea. What time, then?"

"How about eight? It will be dark then."

"But what if someone is out and about?"

Charlene glanced outside at the leaden sky. "In this weather? I don't think so."

"All right," I said grudgingly, glancing at the clock. "It's already coming up on five. If you want to do this cloak-and-dagger stuff, then you need to eat. So what do you want for dinner?"

"How about just a few of these muffins?"

"No dice. It's a cold night; how about stew?"

"Takes too long."

"Two hours. It'll be done by seven. We'll have plenty of time."

"If you insist," she said.

"I do," I said, and pulled a package of stew meat out of the refrigerator.

———

The weather had worsened by the time we clambered into Charlene's pickup truck, our bellies full of Beef Zinfandel, spiced apple cider, and Barbara's delicious muffins. Benjamin had popped through the swinging door just before six. Charlene had invited him to join us, and after a moment's hesitation, I relented, figuring the male company would do Charlene good. It had; she'd perked up like a flower in sunshine.

I rubbed my hands together for warmth after slamming the truck door shut behind me.

"Did you get gloves?" Charlene asked as she turned the key. The engine juddered to life.

"Shoot. I'll be right back." I closed the truck door and hurried back to the house.

Five minutes later, I was back in the cab of the truck, clutching a pair of bright orange rubber gloves.

Charlene raised an eyebrow. "That's the best you could do?"

"I'm from Texas, remember? My glove collection is less than extensive."

"You're in for a fun winter then," Charlene said as the truck lurched into gear.

"I'm just excited that I'll get to see snow."

She chuckled. "Tell me that in May."

"May?"

"Just you wait," she said, as the truck climbed the big hill behind the inn. "You'll be begging to go back to Texas."

An image of the Queen Anne Victorian Benjamin had shown me flashed through my mind.

"Speaking of Texas, your ex is a good-looking guy. What's the story?"

"We were engaged," I said. "But it didn't work out."

"What happened?"

"I found out he was . . . well, involved with another woman. Several of them, in fact."

Charlene drew in her breath. "And now he wants you back?"

I nodded.

"What are you going to do?" she asked.

"Feed him breakfast. Send him home."

"That's it?"

"That's it," I said. But it sure didn't feel like it.

Before long, we were bumping down Black Cove Road, coming up on the rectory. I was thankful for the distraction—even if I wasn't too jazzed about breaking a police seal. "Where do you think we should park?" Charlene asked.

"Why don't you pull up behind the rectory?" I asked. "It's kind of out of the way, and I doubt anyone will see us."

"Good idea," she said. "I'd turn off the headlights, but I'm afraid we'd run into a tree."

I eyed the dark pine trees hugging the edges of the road. "Better keep them on."

A minute later, we crunched down the rectory driveway and pulled in behind the half-finished extension. Charlene cut the engine and sat silent for a moment.

"Are you sure you want to do this?" I asked gently.

"Yes," she said, her voice wobbly.

"You can stay in the truck. I can manage by myself."

"No. I'm coming with you." She pulled the keys from the ignition. "You have your gloves on?"

I pulled the cold rubber over my hands. "I do now. Ready?"

She took a long, shuddery breath. "Yes."

The cold wind tore at us as we followed the weak beam of Charlene's flashlight to the back door. The yellow crime-scene tape had ripped loose, and was fluttering like a streamer. "Well, we don't have to worry about breaking the seal," Charlene called to me over the wind.

I stood hugging myself against the cold as Charlene fumbled with the key. A moment later, the door opened inward with a bang, and we hurried inside.

"At least they didn't change the locks," she said, closing the door behind us. The wind moaned outside as we stood in the dark, and I caught a faint whiff of McLaughlin's cologne, and the scent of cinnamon. I glanced at Charlene's face to see how she was holding up, but the darkness hid her expression.

"Do we dare turn on the lights?" I asked.

She took a shuddery breath. "I guess so. Unless you think it would be better to stick with a flashlight."

"I think either one would be obvious from outside. But the house is pretty hidden in the trees, so we should be okay."

A moment later, the room was flooded with light. We were in the kitchen, I realized, squinting as my eyes adjusted to the sudden brightness.

"Where should we start?" Charlene's voice was businesslike, but her eyes were shiny with tears.

"Wherever you're most comfortable," I said, adjusting my gloves.

"Let's look in the study first," she said, her voice quavering slightly. "I think I can handle that."

"The study, then. Lead the way."

I followed Charlene through the living room where McLaughlin and I had sat just yesterday. The row of commemorative toilets still hung on the wall above the sofa, and the plush new carpet was soft under my feet. It was hard to believe the man who had sat on the leather couch just yesterday was dead. Murdered.

"I can't believe he's gone," Charlene murmured, echoing my thoughts. She paused for a moment, then wiped her eyes on her sleeve. Then she marched across the rug to a heavy wooden door.

"This is it," she said, pushing through it and flipping on the lights.

A big walnut desk stood in front of the window, with two richly upholstered red chairs arranged across from it. "He must have done pretty well for himself before taking up his priestly duties," I remarked.

Charlene shot me a look. "He's gone, okay, Natalie? You can lay off him now."

I held up my hands. "That's not what I meant. It's just that I'm used to seeing more of a secondhand look in priests' offices."

She bristled again. "And I'm sure you've visited them often over the years."

"Point taken," I said, wishing I'd kept my mouth shut. "Now, where do you think he would have kept that diary, or document, or whatever it was he found?"

"I don't know," Charlene said, relaxing a little and pursing her lips. She ran a gloved finger over the desk, disturbing a fine layer of fingerprint powder. "It looks like the cops have been through here already. There may not be anything to find."

"You never know," I said. The house was eerily quiet, except for the wind moaning through the eaves. A particularly powerful gust rattled the windows behind the desk, and I shivered. "Shall we start with the drawers?"

"I'll take the credenza," Charlene said, pointing to the chest of drawers by the door. "Why don't you do the desk?"

"Aye aye, captain." The smell of McLaughlin's cologne was strong as I sat in his leather chair. The back was high, like a throne, and I felt strangely protected from the black window behind me as I pulled out the first drawer.

Fortunately, the police hadn't removed any of the files—at least none that I could see. They were marked neatly—utility bills, insurance, credit card bills. I paused at the bank account file, but decided to peek anyway. For a priest, the balances were impressive.

"Find something?" Charlene asked from her spot at the credenza.

"No, not yet," I said, pushing the papers back into the folder and returning it to its spot. Despite the chill in the air, my fingers were sweating in the rubber gloves. "You?"

"Nothing. Just renovation stuff. Plans, bids, that kind of thing."

I slid the first drawer closed and tried the second. The files in this drawer had names on them: Hoyle, Kean, Sarkes. I grabbed the Sarkes file. Empty. Had the police removed the contents? Or someone else? My hopes rose when I saw the label on the next folder: Selfridge.

The only thing inside was a letter, on heavy linen paper. The handwriting was challenging, but the gist of the letter was clear. In it, Murray pledged an undisclosed amount toward the renovation of the rectory. He also thanked McLaughlin for his support.

What kind of support? I wondered. Was McLaughlin counseling Selfridge? Or did his pledge to renovate the rectory hinge upon McLaughlin's backing Cranberry Estates?

"Anything in that file about who's paying the bills?" I called to Charlene.

"Nothing yet," she said. "But some of these invoices are downright frightening. I had no idea renovation was so expensive."

"Being on an island doesn't help. I don't even want to *think* about how much it will cost to fix the water damage at the inn . . ."

I refolded the letter and slipped it back into the folder. My fingers flipped through to Kean, and after glancing at Charlene, I pulled a short stack of papers out. The first few pages were pledge numbers. Since meeting McLaughlin, Charlene had evidently started taking her tithing commitments a little more seriously. As I replaced the papers and slid the file back into the drawer, I noticed a printer tucked away in a corner of the office.

"Did Richard have a computer?" I asked.

"He has . . . I mean he had . . . a laptop," she said, glancing around the room. "But I don't know where it is. He usually kept it on his desk."

"Maybe the police took it with them." *Or the murderer,* I added silently. I scanned my friend's face for signs of strain. "I know this is hard. Are you doing okay?"

Charlene closed the drawer and stood up. "I'm all right. But that diary isn't here, and I don't know where it could be."

"Maybe in the bedroom?"

She sighed. "It's worth a shot."

As I followed her through the living room to Richard's bedroom, the lights flickered, and went out.

Charlene stumbled over something. "Damn."

Fear tiptoed up my spine as she switched on a flashlight, sending a weak beam shooting through the darkness. Was it a power outage? Or did someone know we were at the rectory? "Do you think the whole island lost power?" I asked.

The flashlight bobbed. "I don't know. Probably."

A chill passed through me. "I'm kind of spooked. Let's do a quick run of the bedroom and get out of here."

"I'm sure the wind just knocked a line down."

"I know. But still. We can always come back."

"I'd rather not have to, if it's all right with you," she said as I followed her into the bedroom.

The flashlight beam bounced around the room, giving me glimpses of a cherry wood dresser, a plush green comforter, a carved headboard. "Where do we start?" Charlene asked.

"I don't know. The bedside tables?"

We did a quick search, but the only book was a well-thumbed Bible. I handed it to Charlene. "Why don't you take this with you?"

She hesitated, then reached out for it. "You think I should?"

"I know how much you cared for him," I said. "It's hardly evidence. And I'm sure he would have wanted you to have it."

She clutched it to her chest, her face shadowed in the reflected glare of the flashlight. "Thanks, Nat."

"You bet. Now, let's do a quick run through the dresser—I'll let you do that—and get out of here."

"Did you look in the bookshelves?"

I glanced over at the dark wood shelves near the doorway. "I didn't see them."

The beam of light glanced over the spines as Charlene walked over to the bookshelf. I joined her as she trained the flashlight on the shelves.

Under the religious textbooks was a row of brightly colored thrillers. "Lots of Ludlum," I said. Then I noticed an older book shoved in among the paperbacks, its leather binding crumbling at the top. "What's this?"

"You think that's it?"

"I don't know." My fingers lifted the cover gingerly. "Let's have some light."

Charlene aimed the flashlight at the page I opened to.

Winters are bitter here on the island, I read. *The ink freezes solid in the inkwell unless I leave it by the stove.*

"It's a diary, all right." I flipped back to the title page. "Rev. Martin. Written in the 1800s."

"Why would someone . . . kill Richard over this?"

"I don't know," I said, flipping through the pages. "And if they did, why would they leave the evidence lying around?" My eyes scanned the yellowing pages. "Whoever wrote this seemed kind of obsessed with the bad weather on the island." A strong gust of wind howled around the corners of the house, and the eerie sound sent a chill up my spine. I slapped the book shut. "Why don't we get out of here?"

"What about the dresser?"

I stifled a sigh. "Let's just make it fast, okay? We can come back when the power's on."

"You sound like you're afraid you'll see a ghost or something."

The wind howled again, and I recalled the noises at the inn with a shiver. I'd been meaning to talk to Charlene about my nocturnal visitor; tonight, I'd have a chance. I slipped the diary into my pocket and followed her to the dresser. "Remind me to tell you about something when we're done here."

———

It was almost nine o'clock when we abandoned the search and headed back to the inn. Despite looking through all the shelves and drawers, and even peeking under the mattress, we'd come out empty-handed.

The Gray Whale Inn's windows glowed yellow as we bumped down the long drive; either the power outage hadn't extended to the whole island, or it had come back on.

We hurried through the rain to the back door and let ourselves into the dark kitchen. I reached to flip on the light, and stood blinking at my kitchen.

Someone—or something—had ripped through the pantry, strewing food all over the hardwood floor.

EIGHTEEN

"Oh my God," Charlene breathed as we surveyed the wreck. Two ten-pound bags of flour had been ripped open and dragged across the floor, leaving a line of powdery drifts in their wake. The dried cherries were scattered over it like holly berries in snow, and several bags of pasta had been ripped open. The plate of muffins lay upside-down on the floor. Biscuit and Pepper were nowhere in sight.

As I stepped forward, a thump sounded from the ceiling. *My bedroom floor*, I realized.

"What was that?" Charlene's voice was sharp.

"I don't know," I said, heart pounding, eyes fixed on the ceiling. "Let's go," I whispered.

"Go where?"

I inclined my head toward the staircase, and started toward them. The steps creaked as we crept up them, and a thump sounded from the wall next to us. I rounded the corner and tiptoed to my bedroom door, then threw it open and clawed at the light switch.

The room was empty.

"What was that?" Charlene whispered behind me.

"I don't know," I said, my voice wavering a little. "But it's making it awfully hard to sleep." As Charlene stood in the doorway, I did a quick check under the bed and in the closet, just to make sure the noise wasn't Biscuit or Pepper.

"Nothing here," I said.

"Weird."

"You're telling me." With a last glance over my shoulder, I headed down the stairs again with Charlene. Back in the kitchen, I stooped to turn over the plate of muffins. "Have you ever heard any stories about the inn?" I asked in a low voice.

"You mean the haunting thing?"

I glanced up at her. "You knew about it?"

Charlene leaned over to pick up a ripped bag of rotini. "Everybody does. Eliezer thinks the smugglers who used to use the cove did some of their business out of here when the place was vacant. Did everything they could to encourage the rumors—strange lights, noises in the night. I guess they figured that way, no one would come too close." She shook her head. "But I don't think that's connected with this."

"Nope." I scooped the muffins back onto the plate and reluctantly dumped them into the trash. What a waste. "I'd like to find out more about what's going on, but I'm afraid it'll be bad for business if the word gets out." I glanced at my friend, who usually couldn't hold a secret if it came in a paper bag. "Please promise me you won't tell a soul about this?"

"Promise."

"Even Tania?"

Charlene put her hand on her chest. "Cross my heart and hope to die."

I sighed. "Thanks. This is really creeping me out. For the last week or two, I've been hearing noises at night."

She glanced at the ceiling. "Like what we just heard?"

"Worse. Footsteps."

She shivered. "Are you sure it's not just the pipes thumping?"

"In the attic?"

Charlene's eyes widened as I told her about dragging footsteps that had woken me up the other night, including Biscuit's weird reaction—and the undisturbed dust on the attic floor. "Emmeline told me her husband once saw the ghost of a woman on the landing," I said. "And according to Matilda down at the museum, there was a murder in the inn, once."

"The cook, right? Annie Oakes, or something?"

"That's the one. Matilda says it was never solved."

"That's the legend. I think one of the Selfridges was under suspicion, but no one ever proved anything."

"Do you think she's coming back because of that?" I asked, opening another garbage bag. "Unresolved business?"

Charlene shook her head. "I just don't know. Maybe we should get one of those Ouija boards or something, and ask."

I shivered involuntarily. I don't know if it was too many B horror movies, but the whole séance thing freaked me out a little bit. "The question is, why now? I've been here since spring, and this is the first I've heard of her."

"Maybe we're getting close to the anniversary of her death. And it *is* almost Halloween. Aren't the souls of the dead supposed to come back around then?"

"Actually, I think the Day of the Dead is November first. And it's only the middle of October now." I remembered the big festivals in the Mexican-American community in Austin. Candy skeletons, marigolds, food, and pillar candles on the graves of the dead . . . my thoughts turned to McLaughlin. If this was the time of year when ghosts walked, had the power outage at the rectory tonight been caused by him? And if so, why? Had there been something in the house he hadn't wanted us to find? I shook myself. Last week, I thought the idea of ghosts was ridiculous; now I was conjuring paranormal explanations for simple power failures.

"I don't know if it's the exact day, or just the season," Charlene said. "Anyway, maybe she couldn't get her hands on a good calendar in the hereafter, or wherever she is." I glanced at my friend. Her eyes looked misty again, and her voice was pensive. "Do you think . . . maybe Richard might send me a sign?"

"I'm sure if he can, he will," I said, smiling at my friend. Then I grimaced at the drifts of flour on the pine floors. "Forget the Ouija board. They could just write out what they're looking for in flour."

"That would be handy."

I glanced at the mess of muffin crumbs. "Speaking of flour, what the heck am I going to do for breakfast now?"

Charlene shrugged. "I'm sure you'll think of something. What about those great breakfast flans? All you need is eggs and milk, right?"

Dumping a torn spaghetti bag into the trash, I said, "Good idea. Let's get this place cleaned up, and I'll make a batch." I tossed a mound of cherries, flour, and pasta in after the spaghetti bag and groaned. "I can't believe I live in a haunted inn. No wonder the place was cheap."

Charlene reached for a handful of pasta and grimaced. "Let's just hope the poltergeist activity limits itself to your pantry."

———

The weather was still gray and cold the next morning. Most people aren't big fans of bleak weather, but after fifteen years of endless summers in Texas, I was enjoying the turn of the seasons—including damp, chilly mornings. It gave me an opportunity to pull on the wool sweaters that had been gathering dust in my closet for years. Today I had chosen a red Aran sweater I had picked up on Inishmore, off the coast of Galway, almost fifteen years ago. I pushed up my sleeves as I poured coffee into the grinder, enjoying the feel of the rough wool against my skin. I thought of Benjamin's offer again. If I went back to Texas, my thick sweaters would have to go back into storage. I shook my head. Was I really relying on wardrobe options to make the case for staying?

At eight o'clock, the kitchen was filled with the heavenly aroma of sizzling sausage, and the sky outside was pearly gray and drizzling. I peered out the window; the Cranberry Rock lighthouse was barely visible through the haze, and the rich autumn colors of the mountains across the water were subdued. The gray palette outside made the soft yellow kitchen, with its antique blue and white tiles, pine floors, and farmhouse table feel especially cozy, and I felt a surge of satisfaction. Pepper was nowhere to be seen—probably with Charlene—and Biscuit had curled up next to the radiator. Candy hadn't been into the kitchen in a few days either, I realized. I wasn't thrilled with the idea of her opening a rival inn down the street, but at least she wasn't haunting my kitchen anymore. *Unlike Annie Oakes . . .*

I sipped at my coffee and turned the sausages, then pulled a bag of corn tortillas out of the freezer for *migas*, a Mexican egg dish I had learned to love in Austin. It would go with the flan, and besides, a little spice was good on a cold morning. As I tossed a few tortillas into the microwave and began grating cheddar cheese, my mind turned to the mess Charlene and I had discovered in the kitchen. Had it been the cook's ghost? And if so, was I just going to have to steel myself for a month of paranormal activity once a year?

On the plus side, the manifestations seemed to be limited to the non-guest portions of the inn. I could only hope whoever—or whatever—had caused the mess in the kitchen last night didn't decide to branch out. And at least there had been no further manifestations after the kitchen debacle of last night; although it had taken me a while to fall asleep, nothing had interrupted me, and I woke feeling refreshed. My eyes drifted to the pantry. I would have to ask Charlene to pick up some more flour at the store. And I needed to call the insurance company again, too.

For the next half hour, I focused on the *migas*, dicing jalapeno peppers, slicing avocado, and creating a cheesy, gooey dish that looked so good I put a little on a plate for myself before delivering the platter to the dining room.

Benjamin was already there, looking crisp and fresh in jeans and a blue wool sweater that brought out the color of his eyes. "Thanks for dinner last night," he said.

"My pleasure." I poured his coffee and backed away quickly.

"Have you thought about things anymore?"

"It's been kind of busy."

"I'm only here for a few more days, you know. I'd love to buy an extra ticket to Austin . . . for you."

"Even if I did . . ."

"You're considering it?"

I sighed. "I'm not saying anything at all. You know, maybe it would be better for you to go . . ."

"Good morning!"

Benjamin and I turned to see Candy, who stood in the doorway in tight jeans and high-heeled shoes. Benjamin stood up to greet her. "Hi, Candy."

"Hi, Ben. Are we still on for Jordan Pond House?"

Benjamin glanced at me sidelong.

I kept my smile pasted on.

"Why don't we eat breakfast first, and then we'll figure it out later," he muttered, then turned to me. "Nat . . ."

"It may not be a good day for sitting out on the lawn, but it's nice inside, too," Candy said brightly. "And I've heard their popovers are to *die* for. I'm going to see if I can get their recipe, for when . . ." She glanced at me and trailed off, then fluttered her long eyelashes and sashayed over to Benjamin's table. Her tight pink hooded sweatshirt didn't quite cover her bulging T-shirt—or the inch and a half of cleavage above it.

I filled both coffee mugs and turned on my heel. "*Migas*, grapefruit, and flan this morning. I'll be out with toast in a moment."

My heart was pounding when the swinging door closed behind me. I leaned up against the wall. I *knew* this about Benjamin. So why was I so agitated? And Candy . . . she really *was* planning on opening up an inn. And the hard reality was, if the insurance didn't cough up for the damage she had done, she would have an excellent chance of running me out of business.

I closed my eyes. The right decision—financially, anyway—would probably be to jump at Benjamin's offer; after all, I was still attracted to him, and life would be less stressful without huge mortgage payments looming every month. But that was a terrible reason to embark on any relationship, and besides, I had built a life for myself here. My eyes drifted to John's carriage house. Did I really want to leave all of this behind?

The truth was, whether I took Benjamin up on his offer or not, I might not have a choice.

I fished a few slices of bread from a bag, thrust them into the toaster and slammed the little glass door shut. Then I marched over to the phone to call the insurance adjustor. A moment later, his voice mail message burbled out of the receiver.

Damn.

I left a message and checked on the toast, then crossed the kitchen to peek into the dining room; if any other guests had come down, they'd want coffee. Just before I pushed through to the dining room, a tap sounded at the outside door.

It was John.

"What's wrong?" he asked as I opened the door. The wind swept John's faint woodsy scent in with him. I loved his smell; there was something primeval and clean about it.

"What do you mean?" I asked as the door closed behind him. Like Benjamin, John wore jeans and a wool sweater; unlike Benjamin, the jeans were thin around the knees and the sweater looked like something you'd see on a fisherman. The patterns, I suddenly remembered, were to help family members identify drowned men when they washed ashore. I shivered; death kept creeping into my thoughts uninvited.

"You look stressed," he said.

"The insurance company isn't answering my calls, Candy is planning to open a rival inn, my best friend's boyfriend got murdered, and Grimes thinks one of us did it."

John's craggy eyebrows rose.

"Do you want a cup of coffee?" I asked, pulling down a mug.

"Sure. Let's get back to this Grimes thing. Who—specifically—is 'us'?"

"Charlene and me." After filling the mug, I handed it to him and dug out a spoon.

He shook his head. "I still don't get it. Why on earth would either of you kill McLaughlin?"

I snorted. "Apparently there's a rumor that McLaughlin was seeing someone else on the side. And I was supposedly so jealous of Charlene's new beau that it drove me to murder."

"That's ridiculous." John shook his head and sipped at his coffee. "And where did he come up with this thing about McLaughlin seeing someone else?"

"I don't know, but he's taking it pretty seriously."

He let out a long, low whistle. "Things aren't going your way lately, are they?" He put down his coffee and moved behind me, rubbing my back with calloused hands. I relaxed into him, and something inside me melted.

"How are your floors, by the way?"

I sighed. "We got the water in the hallway cleaned up fast enough, but the rooms are in pretty bad shape. I've left the windows open in the two rooms, but I'm worried about mold."

"And the insurance company's giving you a hard time?"

I nodded.

"Have you thought about asking the woman who blocked the sink up to talk to the insurance company?"

"Who, Candy? She's looking to open up an inn down the street. Why would she want to help me out? I half think she did it just to take out the competition."

His hands kneaded my shoulders. "It's worth a shot, anyway."

"You're right. I'll ask her."

"All she can say is no," John said. He gave my shoulders a final squeeze and released me. "Is something burning?"

"The toast!" I dashed over and opened the little door, but it was too late. As I deposited the scorched squares into the trash, the phone rang.

"Can you get it for me?"

He grabbed the phone. "Good morning, Gray Whale Inn." He was silent for a moment as I pulled a few more slices of bread out of the bag and popped them into the toaster. "No, it's John." A moment later, his voice dropped. "Is he going to be okay?"

I whirled around toward John. His face was grim. Had there been another murder?

NINETEEN

I STARED AT JOHN, whose lips were a thin line. What was going on?

"I'll tell her," he said. "Keep me posted, okay?"

"What?" My voice was tight as he hung up the phone. "What happened?"

He let out a long, low sigh. "That was Emmeline Hoyle. The gear war is escalating. They found one of the mainlanders adrift on his boat this morning. Had to take him to the hospital. Someone gave him a nasty blow on the back of the head, knocked him out cold."

"Is he going to be okay?"

"He hasn't come to yet. They're running tests."

I sank down into a kitchen chair. At least it wasn't another murder; and at least this time, the motive was obvious. "Who do you think did it?"

"I have my ideas," he said, "but we should probably wait for the evidence."

"I guess so." I shook my head. "All this violence lately . . ."

John walked over to me and put his hands on my shoulders, pulling me toward him. I leaned into him. His arms were strong under the soft flannel as he wrapped them around me, warming me from the inside out.

His voice was low and soft. "I'm worried about you, Nat."

I tilted my head up to look at him. "Why?"

"First Polly, then McLaughlin . . ."

"I thought you said Polly was a suicide."

His arms tightened around me. "I'm not sure of anything right now. All I know is that there's a dangerous person at large on the island, and you and Charlene tend to get your noses into places some people might prefer were left alone."

I thought of our trip to the rectory . . . and the footprints outside my kitchen door the other night. He had a point.

He gave me a last squeeze. "Be careful, okay? We still haven't had our dinner date, and I'd hate to have to cancel it again." He turned me around and gave me a soft kiss on the forehead. "I'll check on you later, okay? Just don't go anywhere by yourself."

"I'll try not to. Are you sure you can't stay for breakfast?"

He grabbed his coffee cup and took a last swig before heading for the door. "I already ate, but thanks." He flashed me a last smile and headed back out into the chilly morning.

I stood staring at the door for a minute, my body remembering the feel of his arms around me. Dinner soon, he'd said . . . I gave myself a mental shake. Guests. Toast. *Toast!* I rescued the bread just in time, slathered on some butter, and put it in the warmer before feeding the toaster four more slices and carrying my coffeepot out to the dining room.

Benjamin and Candy sat where I'd left them, laughing over something, and Russell Lidell had taken a seat at a far table. I ignored the happy couple—honestly, after a few minutes with John, I didn't mind nearly so much—and filled Russell's coffee cup.

"Who was that on the phone?" he asked.

"Just a friend," I said.

"Any calls for me?" Today he wore wrinkled khaki pants and a striped shirt a size too small. His doughy face looked strained.

"Not while I've been here," I said. "I don't think there are any messages on the machine, but I'll check."

"Let me know," he said. "I'm expecting a call."

———

I was cleaning up the last of the breakfast dishes when Gwen rushed down the stairs into the kitchen. She'd pulled her bushy hair into a sloppy ponytail and was tugging a sweatshirt over her arms. "Aunt Nat," she said, breathless. "I overslept . . . I was supposed to be at Fernand's first thing this morning!"

"Why don't you head over now?" I said as she grabbed a banana from the fruit bowl.

"But what about the rooms?"

"I'll take care of it," I said. "Do you have a moment for some strata?"

"No, but I'll take a brownie," she said. "If there are any left."

"On top of the fridge," I said, filling a travel mug as she popped the lid off the Tupperware and assembled a short stack of chocolate cherry brownies. How she stayed so slim, I had no idea.

She gave me a quick kiss on the cheek and hurried to the door. "Thanks a million, Aunt Nat."

"Don't think twice about it," I said as the door shut behind her.

The truth was, I was kind of looking forward to some time by myself. Charlene had headed down to the store, so I didn't have to worry about her this morning, and with everything that had been going on the last week, my head was whirling. The ritual of putting things right sounded soothing . . . meditative, almost. Besides, I wanted to be home in case the insurance company ever got around to calling me back.

After starting the dishwasher, I gathered my cleaning supplies and headed upstairs, figuring I'd start with Candy's room and move down the hallway from there. My toe clipped a warped board as I rounded the corner at the top of the stairs, and I cursed Candy silently. My eyes slid to the door of the room she had "accidentally" flooded. What was I going to do if the insurance company wouldn't cover the damages? And would the Gray Whale Inn be able to survive a competitor right down the street?

So much for meditative. I struggled to clear my mind as I knocked at Candy's door. When no one answered, I used the skeleton key to unlock the door and let myself in.

Whatever Candy was, she wasn't a neat freak. The floor was strewn with discarded jeans and T-shirts; one of the logos sparkled in the gray morning light. The vanity was covered with cosmetics, and a lacy thong hung from the bathroom doorknob. If Candy did open an inn on the island, I reflected grimly, she should probably make room in the budget for housekeeping help.

I set down my cleaning supplies and started with the bed. As I stripped the sheets, I found myself inspecting them for one of Benjamin's dark brown hairs. *Why do you care what he does?*

I chided myself as I tossed the pile of white cotton toward the doorway.

After smoothing the new sheets down, I gingerly removed the thong from the doorknob and piled it on the dresser with the rest of the discarded clothing. Then I turned my attention to the desk. Shooting a glance at the doorway, I sidled over to the pile of papers scattered over the scarred maple desk top.

My stomach twisted as I glanced at the top sheet. A contract for Cliffside. It wasn't new information, but seeing it in print made it starkly real. I shuffled through the papers beneath it, wondering what other properties she had looked at, but the only information was on Cliffside.

Anger burned deep in my chest. For all her talk of starting an inn on the mainland, it looked like Cranberry Island was the only place she'd investigated.

I ran the feather duster around the papers, did a quick run-through of the bathroom, and got out of there before I did something unprofessional. Like take a pair of scissors to her thong underwear, although how I could make it any smaller I didn't know.

Benjamin's room was next. Unlike Candy's, his clothes were neatly folded in their drawers, the bed already made. *Opposites attract?* I shooed the thought from my head and tackled the bed and bathroom, carefully avoiding the stack of papers on the dresser. I knew they were the specs for the inns in Austin, and I didn't need the temptation. No blonde hairs on the pillowcases, I was happy to see. So much for equanimity.

My professionalism lapsed only for a moment, when I picked up the bottle of Calvin Klein's *Obsession* and held it to my nose. Closing my eyes, I let a torrent of memories sweep over me . . .

nights on the crisp blue sheets of his king-sized bed, his skin warm against mine . . .

I set the bottle down with a jolt and backed away from the sink. Then I gathered up my cleaning supplies and hurried toward the door, and away from danger.

Slamming the door shut behind me, I leaned against the wall, trying to slow my heart rate. Why did he have such an effect on me? For God's sake, even his cologne was enough to send me into a tailspin! I felt like a teenager all over again. Clutching the bucket of supplies, I struggled to recall the feeling of John's arms around me. A warm tingle coursed up my spine, but it wasn't enough to exorcise the rush of feelings I'd had in Benjamin's room. I forced myself to recall the humiliating moment in Z Tejas. Benjamin's hand on Zhang's back, her black hair like a curtain of silk. . . .

I opened my eyes and gave myself a mental shake. *Focus on work.* This was supposed to be meditative, after all, not masochistic. And besides, the cleaning was almost done—other than Charlene's room, Russell Lidell's was the last on my list; the Hahns had checked, leaving a glowing recommendation in my guest book despite the flooded hallway.

The smell of unwashed laundry hit me as Russell's door swept open, and my nose wrinkled involuntarily. It was a far cry from Benjamin's cologne. Like Candy's room, Russell's room was liberally decorated with discarded shirts and underwear; unlike Candy, however, his taste in underwear tended toward Fruit of the Loom rather than Victoria's Secret. I found myself wishing for my orange rubber gloves as I deposited the soiled clothes in a heap by the closet and pulled out my feather duster.

Wherever Russell had gone this morning, he hadn't taken his briefcase. My eyes kept swerving toward it as I stripped the sheets and straightened the curtains. How was Cranberry Estates coming? Had Polly's cousin Gary sold her house to Murray? Or to Russell's development company?

After running a brush around the toilet bowl and swishing out the sink, all the while entertaining fantasies involving Candy, her future inn, and overflowing toilets, I returned to Russell's room and contemplated the briefcase for a moment.

Then I closed the door, slid the deadbolt, and set the briefcase on the smooth blue counterpane.

The brown leather case was scuffed on the edges, and I was pleased to note that it didn't sport a lock. I hurriedly lifted the leather flap and riffled through the file folders he had shoved inside.

The fattest one was labeled Cranberry Estates. It slid out easily, and a moment later I flipped it open on the bed. The woman at the church was right; Gary had sold Polly's house, and the demolition date had already been set for March. I sucked in my breath and thought of Polly's cats; I'd have to find homes for them sometime this winter, since Polly's house would be gone . . . *Polly.* I set down the paper and closed my eyes for a moment, remembering her smile, the way her round face lit up when she talked about her cats. My heart still ached for the efficient woman who had always had a friendly word, and who had opened her heart and home to animals with nowhere else to go, spending most of her meager resources to feed them.

I sighed, frustrated that I still hadn't figured out who had killed her. And McLaughlin's death had closed off yet another avenue of inquiry. I flipped past the copy of the contract and blinked at the next sheaf of papers.

It was a preliminary environmental assessment, and the information listed on it made me blink.

Russell had said that Cranberry Estates was a go. But the assessment in front of me listed ten endangered species—and denied Weintroub Development the right to build.

I was flipping through the report when someone slid a key into the lock.

"Just a minute," I called, jamming the files back into the briefcase. I shoved it back onto the floor next to the desk, retrieved my basket of cleaning supplies, and hurried to the door.

Russell eyed me with suspicion as I threw the door open and smiled.

"Why was the door locked?"

I tossed off a light laugh. "Habit, I guess. I always lock doors behind me. Comes from being a single woman, I suppose."

Russell's eyes flicked to the briefcase on the floor, and I took the opportunity to scoop up the dirty sheets and bustle past him. "I'm headed down to get these into the washer. Let me know if you need anything!"

The door clicked behind me as I hurried down the hall to the stairs. Thank God I'd used the deadbolt, or he'd have caught me red-handed. It was probably a good thing Gwen did most of the rooms, I reflected—I was entirely too nosy to be a good housekeeper. Had I gotten the files back in order? The thought made my stomach do a little flip. I was probably safe even if I hadn't—considering the state of his room, odds were good he wasn't too orderly in his filing. The environmental assessment still puzzled me, though. Endangered species meant you couldn't build; the report I had just seen made that crystal clear. Was there some way to get an exception that I didn't know about? Yet another thing to check out at the library . . . once I got the boat fixed. I had forgotten to ask John about the *Little Marian*, I realized. Maybe after I finished cleaning, I'd head down to the carriage house.

After lugging the sheets down to the laundry room, I left another message for the insurance company and headed to Charlene's room. Cleaning hadn't been meditative this morning, but it sure had been informative.

I had just finished straightening Charlene's bedspread when the phone rang. I hurried down the stairs, hoping it would be the insurance company with some good news.

"Hello?" I said breathlessly into the phone.

"Yes, is Mr. Lidell in?" The voice was high, nervous.

My hopes plummeted. "Yes, he is. Or at least he was a few minutes ago. May I say who's calling?"

"Frank Edwards."

"I'll see if he's available."

I set down the receiver and headed for the stairs, curiosity piqued. The name was familiar. I had seen it fifteen minutes ago at the bottom of the environmental evaluation in Russell Lidell's' room.

Russell opened the door immediately when I knocked.

"Phone call for you." I smiled. "Someone named Frank Edwards."

"Thanks," he said curtly, pushing past me toward the stairs.

I followed behind him slowly, passing him as he picked up the receiver. He didn't say a word until the swinging door of the kitchen squeaked behind me.

I pressed my ear to the door; when I could hear the low murmur of Russell's voice, I pushed the door open just enough to slide past it into the dining room.

Russell's voice was barely above a whisper. "I don't know if I can go any higher." He was quiet for a moment, then let out a long sigh. "Fine. Let me see what I can do." More silence. Then, "How about tomorrow. Ten o'clock?"

After a pause, he said, "Fine. See you then." I slipped back through the door to the kitchen as the handset thunked back onto the phone. Thank goodness I hadn't sprung for a cordless phone, I thought as I eased the door closed behind me. Eavesdropping was a lot easier when the phone calling was limited to the front hallway. As I loaded the washer with today's haul of sheets and towels, my thoughts turned to the conversation I had just overheard. Why was Russell meeting the environmental assessor?

And more importantly, what exactly was the assessor asking him to do?

TWENTY

As I STOWED THE cleaning supplies and emptied the contents of the washer into the dryer, my mind turned over the conversation I had just overheard. If I asked Gwen to cover breakfast cleanup tomorrow, could I follow Russell to his meeting? Although if the meeting was on the mainland, I'd have to get on the mail boat right behind him, making it fairly obvious what I was doing. Too bad I couldn't get the skiff over to the main dock. My eyes sought the window, and the *Little Marian* bobbing down by the dock. The truth was, the skiff wasn't going anywhere until I asked John to take a look at the motor.

I tossed a new batch of sheets into the washer and hit the start button. Then I headed to the kitchen to find a jacket, spirits lightening at the prospect of a few minutes with my neighbor—and maybe another back rub. Throwing on a windbreaker, I reminded myself that it was always possible John would have more information on McLaughlin's death. Maybe the cops had found something at the rectory before Charlene and I got there. A breath of wood smoke greeted me as I slipped through the door into the chilly air, and I inhaled deeply.

No back rubs for me this afternoon, alas. I knocked at both the carriage house and the workshop, but John didn't answer. I headed back to the inn, jotted a note on a scrap of paper asking him to take a look at the skiff when he had a chance, and wedged it between the door and its frame.

The sky started spitting icy droplets of rain as I hurried back to the inn, feeling stymied. The insurance company wasn't calling me back, I couldn't find out anything more about Russell until his meeting tomorrow, I was at a dead-end concerning Polly—and until I got to the mainland, I couldn't find out anything else on McLaughlin.

I briefly considered taking the mail boat over to Northeast Harbor and driving to the Somesville library, but a fresh spray of rain against the windowpanes made me reconsider. It was a great afternoon for a cup of tea and a good book. There would be plenty of time to chase down rabbit holes tomorrow . . . maybe even later this afternoon, if John had a chance to look at the *Little Marian*.

Ten minutes later, I retreated upstairs with a cup of Chai, looking forward to an hour or two snuggled up under my comforter with a good mystery. Biscuit followed me, meowing, as I opened the bedroom door, and dashed out of the way just in time to avoid getting doused with hot tea.

The diary we had found at the rectory lay in the middle of the bed. But I'd never taken it out of my jacket pocket.

I set down what was left of my tea on the nightstand and wiped the spill from the floor with a towel before approaching the leatherbound book. A shiver passed through me as my fingers touched the crumbling brown cover, and I glanced toward the ceiling involuntarily.

Maybe there was more to this diary than reports on the weather.

I sat down on the bed and opened the cover, leafing through the yellowed pages. The script was flowery, and some pages were rippled, the words blotched by water damage. Illegible. The pages were dry now, and powdery to the touch. Where in the rectory had it been hidden? And how long had it lain undiscovered?

Biscuit curled up beside me as I leafed through the entries. Lots of talk of the fish industry, new buildings going up—I read the section about the Selfridges with interest. Apparently the town thought he was a bit off-center for building a huge house so far from the center of town. Several pages on, there was some mention of the death of the Oakes girl, the inquest and the funeral. Then the priest's shock at discovering parishioners actually slept with their bread to keep it from freezing. After this revelation, apparently, he was reluctant to accept dinner invitations. I chuckled and turned the page, thinking of McLaughlin's tuna casseroles, when suddenly, there was a change in the graceful, careful hand. Goosebumps rose on my arms as I read.

"Spoke with J.S. today; asked to speak to me under the seal of confession. Although I am not ordained Catholic, and we do not have the confession, I agreed, and the story he recounted is one that will haunt me to the end of my days."

I glanced at the ceiling and continued, with Biscuit kneading the pillow beside me. "The story is a sad one; a tryst between a wayward young girl and a married gentleman ... as such things go, the girl came to discover she was in a delicate condition, and spoke to the gentleman of it."

Was he talking about Annie Oakes?

"He encouraged her to return to her people, but she refused. This went on for some weeks, he told me, until they strove with words one late night—then words failed him, and he acted with the basest urge, killing both mother and unborn child in wanton violence. God rest their souls. My heart aches for the babe; he died unbaptized."

The blood in my veins turned icy. One night in October. This had to be about Annie Oakes. And if the killer was her master . . .

"I will write to the bishop for direction in this matter, as I do not know if it is within my purview to contact the authorities. The wretched man is repentant of his actions, and wishes to make atonement for his mortal sin, but the nature of his crime is far beyond my authority to absolve. I pray God that the bishop will recommend a course of action that will lead to justice and absolution."

I flipped the page eagerly, wondering what the bishop had directed him to do, but only two entries remained, dealing mainly with a squabble over some missing fishing nets. The rest of the diary was blank.

Why had he stopped writing, I wondered. Had he been reassigned? Did he buy a new diary? Or did something worse befall him? A dark thought entered my mind. Was the discovery of an eighteenth-century murderer the driver of another, more recent crime?

Biscuit meowed in protest as I jumped out of bed and headed for the stairs. Matilda Jenkins would know what had happened to the priest. And if she didn't, surely the information would be buried somewhere in the museum.

It was still raining and windy when I shut the kitchen door behind me and headed for the bike shed, zipping my windbreaker up to my chin. The chill wind tore through me as I pedaled uphill, fueled by curiosity and unease. Had Annie's ghost put the diary on the bed for me to find? I didn't believe in ghosts, but the last few weeks were enough to make me reconsider.

The museum's windows were dark, but lights burned in the little yellow house beside it. I leaned the bike against a tree and leapt up the steps to the porch, hammering at the front door. I squeezed the diary, which I had returned to my pocket, as I waited. A moment later, Matilda Jenkins opened the door and peered at me over her glasses.

I must have looked disheveled, because the first thing she asked was, "Is something wrong?"

"I need your help."

"Come in, come in," she said, and I stepped through the door into her tiny entryway. "Are you here for that information on the inn?"

"No, although I'll take what you've got."

"I've got a few documents together, but I haven't had time to copy them yet."

"Whenever you get a chance," I said.

"What can I do for you then?" she asked as I unzipped my windbreaker and rubbed my chapped hands together.

"I need to find out what happened to a priest named Father Martin. He was at St. James in the 1870s."

She pursed her thin lips. "I don't recognize the name. Do you know how long he was in residence here?"

"That was what I was hoping you could help me find out."

"I'm sure it's in the files on St. James. If you'll give me a moment to get my jacket, we can go and have a look."

I stood in her hallway admiring the framed hundred-year-old photographs of Cranberry Island as she disappeared upstairs. Several of the buildings I recognized, but there were a few that evidently hadn't stood the test of time. I wondered about the people who had lived here then, and reflected that in another hundred years' time, chances were my life, too, would be reduced to a footnote in a dusty old file.

"Ready?" Matilda interrupted my melancholy thoughts, and a moment later I followed her back out into the cold, wet afternoon. It was a short walk to the museum, and within a minute she was closing the museum's heavy door behind us and flipping the light on. It was cold inside, too, with the musty smell of disuse, but at least it was dry.

"The files we need are over here," she said, walking past a display of ancient fishing tackle and shoving a few dusty boxes out of the way. "What year did you say, again?"

"Eighteen seventy-five."

"Here it is." She took the lid off a yellowed cardboard file box marked "S.J. 1860–1890," releasing a cloud of dust that made me sneeze.

"Sorry about that. I need to get this place cleaned up."

"There's always something that needs doing, isn't there?" I said as she pulled out a stack of documents.

"I know. Some days I don't know where to begin," she chuckled as she flipped through the documents. "The stuff on top is more recent. What we want is closer to the bottom. St. James wasn't built until 1860, so Father Martin must have been one of the first priests." She dug through and pulled out a manila file folder, shaking off the dust. A few skinny insects tumbled back into the box.

"Gosh. Silverfish, too. We really need to get these documents preserved."

I nodded, impatient to see what was inside. She gave the folder a last shake, then flipped it open and peered at the names and dates. The wind howled outside, and a shiver passed through me. "Father Martin. Looks like he was here from 1871 to 1875." She glanced up at me. "That corresponds with your information, right?"

My hand snaked into my jacket pocket, touching the diary. "Right. Why did he leave?"

She peered closer at the records. "Doesn't say here. Hang on a moment, though." She rifled through the papers and pulled out a slim, leather-bound book, edges crumbling with age. "It might be in the parish register. It's 1875, right?"

I waited as her finger slid down the columns. Finally, her finger stopped. I leaned forward to look.

"Looks like he never left the island," she said.

The script was faded, but clear. Father Martin had died of blood poisoning brought on by an infected cut, only a month after J.S.'s confession.

Matilda shook her head. "It's amazing. So many things that we take for granted these days—antibiotic cream—weren't even imaginable back then." She replaced the papers in the folder. "People died of diseases that are just an inconvenience these days. To think that an infected cut could be enough to kill someone . . ."

I shivered, thinking of the knife that killed McLaughlin. He hadn't been the only priest to die by the blade, I thought . . . although as far as I knew the cut that ultimately killed Rev. Martin hadn't been inflicted with murderous intent.

"Do you have a census of who was on the island at that time?"

She shook her head. "There's the parish register, but it focuses mainly on the priests. I know there's a bigger record somewhere around here—births, deaths, baptisms, marriages—but it's incomplete, and severely damaged. I'll look for it, but you might have better luck in the churchyard. Most of the stones are in pretty good condition; since the families are still here on the island, for the most part, they keep them up."

"I hadn't thought of that."

"I'm going to be doing a bit of digging in here over the next few days," she said, nodding at the stacks of boxes surrounding us. "I'll keep my eyes open. Anything else I can help you with?"

"What do you know about Jonah Selfridge?"

"Jonah Selfridge? Well, he was born in 1840 and died at sea in the late 1880s." Her sharp blue eyes flicked to me. "Which means he was around at the same time as Rev. Martin."

"I know," I said. "Were there any other members of the Selfridge clan on the island at that time?"

"Is this related to your question about the priest?"

I nodded. "I found an old diary the other day that mentioned a J.S."

Matilda's eyes brightened. "A diary! What a wonderful find. Did you bring it with you? Whose was it?"

I hesitated for a moment, and decided to hold off showing it to her. "I think it belonged to Rev. Martin, but I forgot to bring it. It's still back up at the inn."

"Can I make a copy of it?"

"Next time I'm in Somesville, I'll do it at the library. Actually, if you want to give me the stack of stuff you have on the inn, I'd be happy to take care of that at the same time."

She hesitated, too, and I suppressed a smile. I wasn't the only one having difficulty letting go of documents.

"I hate for you to have to go to the trouble," she said. "Besides, I need to make two copies. I'll head over in the next day or two and copy what I've got. If you want to swing by, say, Monday, I'll have it for you."

I smiled. "Can I have a look at them, at least?"

"If you'd like to come down tomorrow, you're welcome to them, but I have an appointment this afternoon."

I crossed my arms, frustrated. I was itching to get my hands on those documents. Was it Jonah Selfridge who had murdered Annie? Or was there another J.S. on the island? I forced a smile. "Great. And I'll get you a copy of the diary, too." Minus the last few pages.

"Wonderful. A new historical document! Isn't it exciting?"

"It sure is," I said, thinking of the ghostly apparition in the inn. "By the way, if you have any more info on the death of the cook, could you include that?"

Matilda's eyes narrowed a fraction, and she nodded shortly. "Of course."

"Thanks."

"Will I see you tomorrow?" she asked, locking the museum door behind her.

I hunched my shoulders against the wind. "If I can make it, I will. How about sometime in the early afternoon?"

"I'll look for you," she said.

"Thanks for everything!" I called after her as she hurried back to the little yellow house. It was still raining, and although it was still early afternoon, I knew the sun would drop behind the horizon sooner than later. Still, there was enough time to take a quick tour of the churchyard. The wind tore at my windbreaker as my fingers fumbled with the zipper. I rubbed my hands together a few times and hopped on my bike, aiming the front wheel toward the rectory—and the Cranberry Island churchyard.

———

St. James looked bleak in the gray afternoon light. Although it was a beautiful little church, framed by red maples that blazed in autumn glory, today the quaint clapboard building looked dreary. The wind had stripped the maples of most of their leaves. The church's mullioned windows, which glowed a cheery yellow on Sunday evenings, were a dull black. I rode past it to the picket-fenced churchyard, which was about a hundred feet down the small lane that led to the rectory, and stopped the bike at the front gate.

A chill passed through me as I closed the gate and surveyed the headstones. The older ones, rough and patchy with lichen, were toward the back, and I passed a number of recent marble stones, carved with names I recognized—Hoyle, Spurrell, Kean—on the way to the thinner stones, pitted with age, near the rear of the small yard.

I paused, drawn to a tall stone with a long list of names—children of Hezekiah and Eleanor Kean. One of Charlene's ancestors, I was sure. The dates on this stone ranged from 1860 to 1883, and my fingers traced the carved names. Hezekiah, Sarah, Grace, Prudence, Muriel, William, each name with birth and death dates carved beside it. Six children, and none of them had made it past the age of seven. I closed my eyes. Those poor parents had stood right here, burying each of their children in small coffins ... Matilda was right. Things we thought nothing of—a nasty case of the flu, a small cut on a finger, even a sinus infection—were death sentences for so many, just a century ago.

I offered up a silent prayer for those long-lost children and their parents and walked on, intent on finding the owners of the initials J.S. The rain had started soaking through my jacket, and I shivered as I tramped through the grass to a line of stones dedicated to the Hoyles, then moved on to the Sarkes, pausing at the tombstone of Jeremiah Sarkes. According to the date on the stone, he was twenty-three at the time of Annie Oakes' death. Beside him lay Elizabeth Mary Sarkes, his "beloved wife." My fingers traced the lines in the wet stone. Had Jeremiah been the J.S. that Rev. Martin referred to? According to the priest, the murderer was married. When did Jeremiah marry Elizabeth? Would Matilda be able to find it in the church records?

The only other J.S. among the Sarkes belonged to a girl named Jenny, who died at the age of nineteen, so I moved on to the Selfridge section.

The stones here were larger, probably reflecting the enhanced financial status of the Selfridges during the mid-1800s. It wasn't hard to find Jonah Selfridge's stone; it was the largest in the vicinity, adorned with winged cherubs and harps. The smaller stone next to him was his wife, Myra, and beyond were the markers for his two children, Jonah Jr. and William. Remembering the picture of the small, sullen family outside the inn, I bent down to examine them, squinting to make out the worn letters. Apparently Jonah's children had lived long lives—William until seventy-nine, the other to his sixties. Their luck had been far better than the poor

Keans', who had lost all six. The wind blew hard, and I hugged myself against the cold and moved on.

Jonah was the only J.S. in the Selfridge section, and I hurried through the Spurrells without finding any more J names. I pulled my windbreaker around me and checked to make sure the diary was staying dry in its zipped pocket; the rain was intensifying, and the sky was darkening. If I waited much longer, I'd be heading back to the inn without light.

I was about to head back to the bike when a broken stone, alone under a gnarled pine tree, caught my eye. Even before it was broken, the stone had been small—hardly a foot high—and I nudged the top half right-side-up with my foot.

A chill ran through me as I read the simple inscription.

Annie Oakes.

I knelt down and placed a hand on the wet, overgrown grass, feeling a pang of pity. Even her body was alone on Cranberry Island. Her own family hadn't claimed her, although evidently someone had paid for a gravestone. Charlene had once told me that many of the poorer families used wooden crosses, which rotted away quickly. After righting the stone as best as I could, I stepped back. Was this the woman whose ghost had appeared to Henry Hoyle in the inn?

The wind whipped at my wet hair as I turned and headed back to the gate, averting my eyes from the fresh mound near the front. Skeletal lilies, their curling petals scattered by the wind, framed the small stone that marked Polly's grave. I shivered. McLaughlin would soon lie underground as well.

After latching the gate behind me, I wiped the bike's seat with my sleeve and climbed on. Before turning for home, I rode the few yards to the rectory, drawn by its darkened windows. The wind had swept dead leaves over the freshly painted porch, and the yellow crime-scene tape jerked and fluttered in the wind.

My mind turned over the question that had been plaguing me since John brought me the news of his death two days ago. Why had someone killed McLaughlin? I dug in my pocket for the diary, sheltering it from the rain as I opened it to one of the last pages, reading Reverend Martin's account of the murder again. McLaughlin had found this diary hidden somewhere in the walls of the old building. Were there other secrets in the rectory?

The wind blew a few droplets onto the page. I dried them quickly and pocketed the book, reaching for the handlebars and turning the bike toward home. As I shifted gears to take on the hill, the pedals started spinning with no resistance, and I heard the clack of a dropped chain. I squeezed the brakes and hunched next to the bike to fix it.

My fingers had just closed around the cold wet chain when footsteps rushed up behind me. I whirled around in time to see a flash of blue plaid before something crashed down on my head and everything went dark.

TWENTY-ONE

I OPENED MY EYES to darkness. My body shivered violently as I sat up. Pain roared in the back of my head, and I reached to touch my hair, fingers probing the source of the pain. The pain sharpened, and I winced, touching my wet hand to my lips. It wasn't just water that wet my hair; there was also the coppery taste of blood.

Wiping my hand on my jeans, I tried to remember how I had gotten here. An icy gust of wind sucked away what little heat my skin retained, and my body shuddered. I had to get out of here—had to get warm.

I staggered to my feet, bringing on a fresh wave of pain, and my body doubled over involuntarily. My head spun, and the darkness around me seemed to explode in purples and reds. What had happened? I fuzzily remembered the dropped chain on the bike. The bike. I crouched down, fumbling through the wet gravel until my hand met cold metal. The ten-speed was still there—although with no light to see by, I was probably better off walking.

I took a step forward, hands stretched out before me. I was near the rectory still—the gravel road, the bike. Why had someone hit me? Blue plaid, I remembered. I had been reading the diary. The diary!

My hand leaped to my jacket pocket.

Empty.

I felt through both pockets, then dropped to my knees, ignoring the blast of pain, and felt the gravel for the little book. Wet leaves, mud, the cold hard bike.

No diary.

A fierce gust of wind made my entire body start to quake. The diary had to wait. I had no idea how long I had been out here—but if I didn't get warm soon, the churchyard might soon have a new permanent resident.

I felt for the handlebars of the bike; since I had been aimed homeward when I was hit, I figured that was my best indicator as to which way to go. My hands closed around the taped bars; they pointed to my right. Staggering to my feet, I started in that direction, reaching out into the empty air. After about twenty steps, the crunch of gravel disappeared. I doubled back and adjusted course, figuring that as long as I stayed on the gravel, it would decrease the risk of smacking into a tree.

It seemed I had been stumbling along for ages when a light glimmered through the thick pine branches. Hunching my shoulders against the wind, I plowed onward, determined to reach the beacon in the darkness. Finally I reached it—a lamp glowing warmly through a curtained window. I staggered up the porch steps and knocked, almost collapsing on the doorstep when the door cracked open and someone peered through the narrow slit.

"Holy Mother of God!" a voice said as I swayed on my feet. The door swung open, releasing a blissful wave of warmth, and a moment later a strong arm propped me up and led me into a dim front hall.

———

A half hour later, I sat on a spindle-backed kitchen chair with a steaming cup of hot chocolate clasped between my hands and two wool blankets draped around me. I took a sip of chocolate and winced as Patrice Connolly dabbed the cut on the back of my head with alcohol.

"So you have no idea who did this to you," she said as she inspected the wound. I had been relieved to recognize Patrice's weathered face, and her warm, cluttered kitchen was a welcome respite from the cold rain outside. Thank goodness I had knocked on Patrice's door, instead of the O'Learys'. Patrice was one of the regulars at Charlene's store, and unlike some of the islanders, had always had a kind word for me.

"I have no idea who brained me," I said, yelping and jerking my hands as the alcohol burned my scalp.

"You might want to put that mug down for a moment, or you're like to burn yourself."

I reluctantly slid the mug onto the table with hands that still shook from cold. The fire crackling in the wood stove was starting to penetrate the ice that had formed in my limbs, but I was far from warm. Patrice dabbed at my wound again, and I hissed involuntarily.

"Don't worry," she said, "I'm almost done here."

"How bad is it?" I asked.

"You'll have a headache for a few days, and you might want to see a doctor, but I think you'll be okay."

"That's good news."

Patrice paused and reached for another cotton ball from the pile on the table. "I don't know what's come over people lately. First Polly, then the reverend, and now this . . ." She clucked her tongue. "All this violence. It's just not normal."

My hand moved automatically to the pocket where the diary had been, but my jacket was gone, hanging by the wood stove in the corner of the little kitchen. The diary was gone too, I remembered. Who had taken it? And why?

"The police think Polly killed herself," I said.

"And I suppose they think the reverend stabbed himself with a knife, too," she snorted. "I have half a mind to call the department and complain. Until now, the island's been a safe place. There's people come here to raise children because of it, you know."

"I know," I said, yelping again as she attacked my cut with renewed vigor.

"Sorry about that," she mumbled, attempting to dab more gently.

"No problem," I said, thinking that what Patrice said was true. After all, I had moved to the island with the idea that it would be a quiet, peaceful life. In the six months since I'd moved here, it had been anything but.

"Do you have any idea who might have killed Polly or Rev. McLaughlin?"

"No, I can't say that I do. But I did hear something . . ."

I sat up straight.

"Someone told me that Polly might be getting mixed up with someone she shouldn't be," Patrice said.

"You mean romantically?"

"Maybe," she said.

"Any idea who?"

She sighed. "I don't like to talk—it's just hearsay—and I'm not sure I want to say, what with Charlene and all."

"You mean . . . with Rev. McLaughlin?"

"I don't know," she said. "But it's pretty well known he was visiting her a lot there . . . near the end. And someone I know was down at the bog one morning early, saw someone leaving her house."

"A man?"

"Ayuh. And it was a bit early for breakfast, if you know what I mean. What I can't figger is, who would have wanted both of 'em dead? Other than . . ."

I stiffened. She hadn't finished her sentence, but it was quite clear she was talking about Charlene.

"It wasn't Charlene," I said sharply.

"I know, I know," she said. "I've known Charlene since she was a tot, and she's not the type to . . . you know. It's just, that's what the police are bound to think, isn't it?"

I sank back down into my chair, thinking of Rev. McLaughlin's handsome face. McLaughlin and Polly. . . . And Grimes, who was so determined to involve Charlene—or me—in the investigation . . .

"Anyway," Patrice said, "don't listen to me. I'm just an old woman babbling. Why don't I get a little gauze on this, and you'll be all set."

"I can't thank you enough," I said.

"Don't think twice about it," Patrice said, examining her handiwork one last time before sitting down across from me, straightening her heavy green wool sweater. Her brown eyes crinkled as she smiled at me. "Now, how do we get you home?"

———

"You're a menace," Charlene said as I pulled the truck door shut behind me, still shivering from the cold rain.

"Hey. I'm the victim here, not the perpetrator." I winced, remembering that I wasn't the only victim this week . . . and that I'd gotten off relatively lightly.

The pickup's engine growled as Charlene threw it into gear, and we lurched forward. "Why's your bike by the rectory, anyway?"

"Actually, it's by the churchyard," I said as she swung onto the road leading to the rectory.

"What on God's green earth made you decide to visit the churchyard?"

"I was looking for something," I said.

Charlene's head swiveled toward me. "Does this have something to do with the mess we found in your kitchen last night?"

"Maybe."

"Maybe? That's all you're going to tell me?"

"Remember that diary we found the other day?"

She nodded.

"There was a confession in it," I said, watching the rows of tall pine trees slide by and melt back into darkness.

"What do you mean, a confession?"

"Someone admitted to a murder, and the priest wrote it down. All he wrote was the person's initials, though—J.S. I was trying to figure out who it could be."

The windshield wipers squeaked, and the reflection of the headlights showed Charlene's features in sharp relief as she shook her head. "That's all very interesting, but I think we've got bigger fish to fry. May I remind you that Richard was . . ." she swallowed hard ". . . was killed this week, and the police seem to think that one of us was responsible for it?"

"I think it might be connected," I said softly.

"What are you talking about?"

"Whoever hit me took the diary."

Charlene sucked in her breath. "So the murders . . ."

"Might be related to what happened a hundred and fifty years ago," I finished for her. Although how that related to Polly's nocturnal visitor, I had no idea.

"Jesus," she breathed.

"Exactly."

———

A half hour later, after I had taken a hot bath and drunk a cup of tea, I slipped into sweatpants and a sweatshirt and opened the door to the hallway. The aroma of cheese and melting butter floated up to me as I took the stairs; I had been planning to make dinner for us, but it smelled like Charlene had beaten me to it.

Sure enough, the table was set and Charlene was just sliding two golden grilled cheese sandwiches off the griddle as I entered the kitchen.

"Smells great," I said, shaking a couple of ibuprofen out of a bottle and washing them down with the rest of my tea. The bath had helped, but my bones still ached from the cold, and my head had started to throb.

"Do you like yours with tomato, or without?"

"With," I said, and she slid a few red slices between the buttered slices of bread before setting the plate down at the table.

"More tea?" she asked.

"Thanks. But aren't I supposed to be taking care of *you*?" I asked.

"I didn't just get whacked over the head and left for dead in the rain," she said, refilling my cup and pushing the cream and sugar toward me. "Speaking of which, we need to call a doctor about your head." She grimaced. "In the meantime, though, I've got more bad news, so you'll need to eat to keep up your strength."

I paused with the sandwich halfway to my mouth, feeling the blood drain from my face. "Oh, God," I said. "Did someone else . . ."

"No, it's not that bad," she said, sitting across from me in a soft gray sweater and form-fitting jeans. She'd even put on eyeliner; she must have been feeling better.

"It's about Cliffside."

I squeezed my eyes shut and groaned. "Don't tell me."

"It's under contract."

I opened one eye. "Candy?"

"You guessed it."

I sighed and took a big bite of sandwich. My stomach growled as I chewed, enjoying the melted cheddar cheese and the buttery toast. "Maybe I should have taken Benjamin up on his offer," I mumbled through a mouthful of sandwich.

Charlene's eyebrow rose. "What offer?"

I swallowed. "He's offering to buy me an inn in Austin."

"A *what*?"

"I'd have my pick, actually. One of them's just gorgeous. Rose bushes all across the front, two stories, wide porches."

"And what does he want from you?"

I pressed my lips together. "Oh, just for me to forget about those women he slept with when we were engaged the last time."

Charlene leaned back in her chair and studied me. "So he wants to marry you."

"Why else would he be up here?"

"And do you want to marry him?"

"No."

She narrowed her eyes.

"Are you sure?"

I took another bite of sandwich, and the cheese formed a gluey lump in my mouth. I swallowed hard. "Sort of," I said.

"Sort of?"

"Look," I said, setting down my sandwich. "Things aren't exactly swell right now. Candy ruined two of my rooms and destroyed the hallway floor, the insurance company is giving me a hard time about covering it, and now she's going to be opening a rival inn down the street."

"So you've got obstacles. Who doesn't?"

"Pretty friggin' big ones, if you ask me."

"Actually, you missed one."

I looked up. "What?"

"Grimes thinks you may be a murderer. Remember?"

"Oh, yeah," I said, waving a hand. "But doesn't he always?"

Charlene chuckled. "Seriously, though, is it really worth giving up everything just so you can have a cheating ex-fiancé buy you an inn?" She took a bite of sandwich. "Granted, he's a pretty cute ex-fiancé," she said through a mouthful of crumbs. "But if you take him back this time, he'll just go back and do it again, because he knows you'll forgive him. Besides, there's John."

I thought about Benjamin and Candy, and their kayak trips, and their visits to Jordan Pond House, and knew she was right. Benjamin had done it once. What would stop him from doing it again?

"Okay. So I shouldn't sell the inn and move back to Texas." My head throbbed insistently. "Can we please talk about something else?"

"Sure." Charlene took a bite of sandwich and chewed pensively. Relieved, I took a bite from mine as well, and for a moment, we sat eating our dinners and trying not to think of unpleasant things.

Then Charlene changed the subject. "So who do you think killed Richard?" she said in a quiet voice.

I sighed. "I wish I knew."

"The same person who killed Polly?" Charlene asked.

"I think so," I said. "The question is, why?"

"And who. Do you think it has something to do with the diary?"

I raised my cup to my lips and sipped at my tea. "It's looking that way. But I can't understand why."

"Who do you think J.S. is?"

"There are two options," I said. "There's a Jeremiah Sarkes, who was twenty-three at the time Annie died. And then there was Jonah Selfridge."

"Murray's ancestor?"

Our eyes met. "Yup."

"Would he kill to cover it up?"

"I don't know," I said. "But what worries me is, if the murderer killed Polly and Richard because they knew something . . ."

Charlene looked at me blankly for a moment, then her eyes widened. "You mean . . . you think the killer might come after *me*?"

I nodded. "The thought crossed my mind."

"But . . . but you were the one with the diary! Why didn't he kill you?"

"Maybe he meant to," I said slowly. "It was a pretty hard whack on the head. Also, someone was outside the kitchen door the other night. He—or she—tried to get in while I was here by myself."

"Oh my God! Who was it?"

"I don't know. He was gone too fast." I sipped my tea. "Have you had anything weird happen?"

"No," she said, shaking her head. "But then again, I've been here the whole time—or at the store, where there are people all over the place." Her eyes widened further. "Maybe whoever was at the door the other night came for both of us."

My eyes flicked to the door. It was locked. "We need to be careful," I said in a low voice. "And I need to go down to the museum again, to find out everything I can about the murder."

"What do we do about Murray?"

"Nothing, now," I said. "We don't even have the diary anymore. We need to find out everything we can before we confront him."

Charlene shivered. "I'm not looking forward to that."

"Me neither."

"Are you sure it's Murray?"

"No, I'm not." I thought again of the late-night visitor Patrice had seen at Polly's—but decided not to mention it to Charlene until I found out who it was. If it *was* McLaughlin, then had someone killed the pair in a jealous rage? And if so, who? *Charlene?* I quickly dismissed the thought. I didn't know a lot of things, but I knew my friend wasn't a killer.

But if it wasn't Charlene, then who was it? "I've got a couple of other ideas," I said vaguely. "And we still need to find out about what happened in Boston."

Charlene shook her head. "I still think you're barking up the wrong tree. Besides, what does that have to do with Polly?"

"I don't know," I said, popping the last of the sandwich into my mouth. As I swallowed, Pepper appeared, winding around Charlene's legs.

"Hello, sweetheart," Charlene said, lifting the little gray kitten to her lap. "You're so sweet, I might just have to take you home with me." She looked at me. "Do we have any idea if she's had her shots?"

"There was a number for the shelter at Polly's house," I said. "They would know, if anyone would. I'll swing by and pick it up." At the thought of Polly's house, I remembered Russell's appointment in the morning and groaned. I'd forgotten to see if Gwen could pick up breakfast duty tomorrow. "Did you see my niece, by any chance?"

"No. Why?"

"I was going to ask her to cover for me tomorrow morning," I said.

"Well, if you don't find her, I'll take care of it," she said.

"Really? I just need someone to cover the second half of breakfast."

"Absolutely," she said. "You need to get to a doctor. And besides, what are friends for?"

I didn't tell her that the doctor wasn't what I had in mind, but thanked her anyway. As I climbed the steps to my room a few minutes later, my head still throbbing dully, I reflected with a twinge of guilt that as awful as McLaughlin's death was, it was wonderful having Charlene as a friend again.

TWENTY-TWO

THE ALARM RANG AT six thirty the next morning, and I headed downstairs in the dark to get breakfast started. My head still hurt, but it was better than yesterday, so I just tossed back a few more ibuprofen with my coffee and started in on breakfast. Fortunately, my hair covered the cut.

Charlene had restocked my flour and sugar supplies, so I was able to whip up a quick batch of muffins. Then I cracked eggs into buttered ramekins for shirred eggs, layered frozen peaches in a baking dish with brown sugar and butter, and filled a pan with frozen sausages.

As I expected, Russell came down at around eight forty-five, dressed in his charcoal suit again, but this time carrying a wool coat. It was a chilly morning; the rosehips were glazed with ice, and the tips of the grass outside were frosted white. Although his meeting wasn't scheduled for an hour, he made quick work of his sausage and shirred eggs, helping himself to a second muffin. By nine fifteen, I started to get nervous. Where was Charlene? I filled

Russell's cup a third time and excused myself, heading down the hall to find her.

We almost collided by the staircase. "Sorry I'm a little late," she said.

"It's no problem," I said. "Everything's in the kitchen. Russell's the only one down so far."

"No Candy?"

I rolled my eyes. "The one good thing about her making an offer on Cliffside is that she's leaving me alone."

"It's not much, but it's something. Did you get an appointment with the doctor?" she asked as Russell appeared in the hallway, a heavy black coat over one arm. We both smiled at him as he passed us and headed out the front door, shrugging the coat over his shoulders as he pulled the door shut.

"Yes. Oops! I think I left something on the stove," I said. "Would you mind checking on it? I'll be back soon!" I said, grabbing a heavy brown cardigan from behind the front desk and hurrying toward the front door.

"Exactly what doctor are you seeing?" Charlene asked suspiciously.

"I'll tell you later," I said, peering through the wavy glass. A moment later, I slipped through the door, leaving Charlene staring after me, hand on her hip.

Easing the door shut behind me, I sidled over to a post, waiting until Russell's heavy frame had disappeared over the top of the hill before hurrying after him. The cold wind bit through the two sweaters, and I wished I'd grabbed a jacket, but at least it wasn't raining. My breath caught in my throat as I hustled up the hill, hoping I hadn't waited too long.

As I crested the hill, I caught sight of Russell's broad back not far ahead of me on the hill. If anything, I hadn't waited long enough.

When he disappeared behind a curve, I trotted after him, trying to keep my footfalls soft and hoping he wasn't going for the mail boat. Besides the fact that it would be viciously cold out on the water, it's hard to stay out of sight when you're sharing a thirty-foot boat.

I was in luck. Instead of turning right toward town, he veered left, down the pitted road that led to Polly's house. Since I was pretty sure where he was going, I fell back a bit, crossing my arms and shivering. The wind made little swirls of leaves as I walked, and my breath frosted in the air, but despite the cold, it was a beautiful morning, the sky blue and crisp, a few clouds scattered like stray bits of wool. The birds were silent; except for the rustle of leaves in the wind, the only sound was the clomp of Russell's boots somewhere in front of me.

Twenty minutes later, the sound of footsteps died. I slowed, and a moment later came within sight of the bog. Sure enough, there in front of Polly's house stood Russell Lidell, picking something off his right pant leg.

I ducked behind a tree just before he stood up and scanned the road behind him. About a hundred yards stood between Russell and me. Unfortunately, that hundred yards consisted of bog and road. There was no way to get to Polly's house from where I stood without Russell seeing me.

Fortunately, the other side of the road was crowded with pines and spruces. I glanced at my watch: it was 9:50. Ten minutes before Russell's meeting was supposed to start. Hopefully whoever it was wouldn't be early.

I retraced my steps until Russell was out of sight, then dashed across the pitted blacktop and dove into the woods. When I was a good way back from the road, I started moving toward Polly's house, trying to avoid the occasional pocket of brown leaves among the needles as I stepped over dead branches. Thank goodness it was predominantly pine forest, not hardwood; the crunch of leaves would have given me away in a second. As I drew level with Russell, my foot hit a hidden branch, and I stumbled. Russell's head jerked toward me. I pressed myself to a tree and peered around the trunk as he took a few hesitant steps in my direction before glancing at his shiny shoes and turning back. I sagged against the tree, relieved. Thank God for wingtips.

A gust of cold wind rattled the branches around me, and I took the opportunity to move a little further from the road. When I had put some distance between Russell and me, I doubled back toward the blacktop. At 9:56, I slipped across the road a second time, just out of sight of Russell, and sidled up behind the empty house, wincing at the sound of the frozen grass crackling beneath my feet. I had just pressed myself up against the house when someone called out from the road.

Flattening myself against the rough wood boards, I poked my head around the corner. I didn't recognize the man—he was hunched in a green jacket and brown gloves. I couldn't tell what color his hair was, since his head was covered in a brown wool cap that was pulled down over his ears.

"Over here!" Russell called. Good. That meant they were planning on meeting by the house.

"I hope you've got it with you," the unfamiliar man said as he crunched up to Russell. "I had to get up at the crack of dawn to make it over here, and the boat ride was a nightmare. Couldn't we do this on the mainland?"

"I wanted it to be private," Russell said. "Besides, you're supposed to come out here, so it doesn't look suspicious." I heard a rustling, and peered around the side of the house in time to see the man in the green jacket slip something into his pocket.

Russell was beaming. "Are you sure we're clear?"

"I submitted the report yesterday, so you've got the green light."

"And the one who was giving you a hard time?"

"There was a big shake-up at the department last week, so she just got four or five new cases to deal with." The man chuckled. "No worries there."

Something rubbed against my legs. I jerked my head back and stifled a yelp. It was a gray tabby cat. I reached down to pet her. She sniffed my fingers, which smelled like the breakfast I had just prepared, and meowed.

"What's that?" said Russell's visitor.

"One of the damned cats this woman had," Russell said. "They're everywhere."

The cat meowed again, and another gray tabby and a chunky white cat trotted up beside her to find out what was so fascinating. I jammed my sausage-scented fingers into my sweater pocket, but it was too late; now all three of them were meowing. They must have been out of food.

"What are they meowing at? Is there someone back there?"

I cast around for a hiding place. There was a big gap under the back porch; I dropped to my stomach and wiggled under it as heavy footsteps rounded the house. The cats followed me, joined by a few more of their whiskered friends, and now stood gathered beside the porch, meowing at me. I held my breath and braced myself for discovery.

"No one here," Russell said. "Weird."

"Yeah, but there's something under that porch."

I leaned away from the opening under the porch and winced as the man leaned over and peered into my hiding spot.

"See anything?" Russell asked.

"Nope. Probably a skunk or something, staying out of the cold."

I sagged against the cold, wet ground as the voices retreated. How had they missed me? I glanced up at the morning light leaking through the narrow gaps in the porch boards. It must not have been enough to show my dark sweater and jeans. Thank goodness I hadn't worn white.

When I was sure they were gone, I wriggled back out again, grimacing at the mud on my clothes. I peered around the side of the house, but the two men had headed back up the road.

Swiping at the mud on the knees of my jeans, I climbed the back porch steps and refilled the cats' food. "Next time, just stand by the food bowl, guys," I grumbled, and went inside to fill their bowls with water and rinse my hands. It was almost as cold inside as it was outside; someone would have to winterize the house soon—although with demolition scheduled for March, it wasn't really necessary. But I would have to find homes for Polly's rescued cats, I thought with a pang as a furry body wove itself around my legs.

When the bowls were full, I ducked inside one last time and jotted down the shelter number. The shelter would know whether Pepper was up to date on her shots—and perhaps be able to help find homes for the cats that weren't claimed.

A wave of sadness washed over me as I stood on the worn linoleum of Polly's kitchen, using a paper towel to get the bigger chunks of mud off my clothes. Poor Polly. I remembered her sweet, broad face, the brown hair that poofed up around it "like a dandelion gone to seed," she'd said once. Soon, her cats, and even her house, would be gone. She would be nothing more than a memory—and a name in a dusty old file. I reached down to stroke a Siamese mix that was sniffing my shoes, admiring the blue of the big cat's eyes. Then I closed Polly's kitchen door behind me, casting one last look at the bleak little kitchen, and headed back up the road toward home.

I clutched my now-damp sweater around me and hunched down, walking fast. A sudden gust of wind sent shivers through me as I passed Emmeline's garden gnomes. Glancing at her cheery kitchen window, I decided to drop by and see if she was home. She kept promising to show me those paths, and something told me they might help me figure out what happened to Polly. Besides, I could also do with a cup of tea and a little more of that banana bread. I hurried up the front path, through a forest of gnomes, and rang the bell. Emmeline answered a moment later, dressed this morning in a blue floral housedress and a pink and white apron.

"Natalie! So nice of you to drop in." Her eyes took in the mud stains on my clothes. "Whatever have you been doing?"

"Oh, I tripped on a rock and went flying."

Her left eyebrow twitched, and I got the feeling she didn't quite believe me. But all she said was "Come in, come in," stepping aside and letting me into her cluttered front hall. The little house smelled enticingly of apples and cinnamon, and I sniffed appreciatively.

"Henry went out fishing with the fellows this morning, so it's just you and me. I've got a brown betty in the oven. If you can wait a few minutes, I'll get you a piece," she said.

The warmth of the house started seeping into me, and I relaxed. I couldn't think of anything more appealing than hot apple brown betty and Emmeline's cozy kitchen right now. "It smells great; I think I'll take you up on it. Afterwards, though, I was wondering if you could take a minute to show me those paths you were talking about."

"Oh, yes," she said, brown eyes sparkling. "But first, let me show you that sampler you wanted. And I copied my recipes down, too—for the banana bread, and the cookies you liked so much."

"Thanks, Emmeline," I said, following her into her little kitchen and settling myself into a kitchen chair as she retrieved a small stack of papers from the counter and handed them to me. I scanned the banana bread recipe—cardamom was the secret spice, it seemed. Beneath them was her design for the sampler. It was simple—and beautiful. The words Gray Whale Inn were drawn in a rich blue, with a cavorting whale beneath it, a few beach roses along the side, and a rendering of the inn at the top.

"This is beautiful," I said, touching the little plume issuing from the whale's blowhole.

"Thank you, dear," Emmeline said, smiling.

"I want you to do it. But let me know how much I owe you."

Emmeline blushed. "Oh, it's nothing. I enjoy the work."

"No, really," I said. "This would be beautiful in my front hall, but I want to pay you for your time."

"No need," she said. "I don't like to take money from friends."

Friends. A warm feeling rose from my stomach. I watched Emmeline's short, round figure as she fished a teabag out of the canister beside the stove, and said, "I'm honored, Emmeline."

She glanced over her shoulder at me, eyes glinting. "I may be asking you for your brownie recipe, though. I've had a few, down to the store, and Henry likes 'em, too."

"I'll copy it out and drop it off tomorrow," I said.

A moment later, as Emmeline lit the burner under the teakettle, she said casually, "I noticed you headed down to Polly's this morning."

"Oh?"

She nodded. "I was going to head down there this afternoon." As she spoke, a large brown tabby appeared, pawing at Emmeline's leg. "Are you out of food already?" she asked the big furry cat, reaching down and chucking her chin. At least one of the cats appeared to have found new digs, I thought, smiling.

Emmeline shot me a glance. "Looks like you weren't the only one down at Polly's."

"Oh no?" I said, trying to look innocent.

Her mouth twitched into a smile as she grabbed a pair of crocheted potholders and pulled the apple brown betty out of the oven.

"You didn't happen to notice that developer of yours? The one staying at the inn?"

I didn't respond.

"He was there with another man, right outside the house," she continued. "I don't know how you could have missed it. Your hearing must be worse than mine."

It was no use denying it. I grinned. "You caught me."

"And you weren't muddy on the way over there, either."

"I had to duck under the porch for a moment."

"They heard you, then?"

"The cats gave me away."

She cut two steaming pieces of betty and laid them on green plates, handing one to me. "I'll get you a fork. What were they on about, then? Did you hear anything?"

"I'll tell you, but please don't say anything to anyone. I don't have proof yet."

She handed me a fork, then settled down across from me and nodded. "That bad, eh?"

I picked up my fork and stabbed a golden slice of apple. The topping was thick, glistening with brown sugar and butter. Emmeline really was a first-class cook.

I looked at Emmeline, whose brown eyes were fixed on me, waiting. "I don't have all the details yet," I said, "but I think Russell may be buying off the environmental assessor."

Emmeline leaned forward over her brown betty, her aproned bosom perilously close to the gooey apples. "What do you mean?"

"Paying him money to write a report saying that there are no endangered species in the bog."

She pressed her lips together. Her round cheeks wobbled as she shook her head. "Now, that's just not right."

"I know it's not right. What I have to figure out now is, what do I do about it?"

Emmeline was silent for a moment, staring out the kitchen window toward the little house in the distance. "Do you think that business might have something to do with poor Polly?" she said slowly.

"You mean did Russell kill her?"

Emmeline's eyes darted to me. "To get her to sell her land. If he's paying good money to the environment man, do you think maybe he decided to clear her out of the way, too?"

"I thought about that. The thing is, though, why kill McLaughlin?"

"Maybe somebody else did in the Reverend."

I looked up at her, and suddenly had the feeling she knew more than she was telling me.

"Why, Emmeline?"

She picked up her fork and examined it, avoiding my eyes. "I didn't want to say anything before, seeing as you're good friends with Miss Charlene down there at the store, but there are some rumors floating about."

"What kind of rumors?"

"Rumors like, maybe he was a little too cozy with someone he shouldn't have been."

I swallowed hard, thinking of Charlene. "Who was it?"

She shrugged. "That's the thing," she said. "Nobody knows."

That was the second time I'd heard that rumor. My mind sorted through the women I knew on Cranberry Island, trying to come up with a likely paramour for the handsome reverend. Other than Charlene, I couldn't think of one. "Ingrid Sorenson?" I said tentatively, thinking of the elegantly dressed, but snooty, selectwoman. She was in her late fifties, and significantly older than McLaughlin, but still attractive.

Emmeline's eyebrows shot up. "Oh, that old blowhard? I hope the reverend had better taste than *that*."

I laughed, despite the twist in my stomach. How would I keep this from Charlene? And should I? After all, it was only a rumor . . .

"The problem," I said to Emmeline, "is that I can't think who it would be. There's no one to hold a candle to Charlene."

"I know. It's a puzzler." The teakettle whistled, and she got up to fill the teapot. As she brought the pot to the table along with two carroty mugs, she glanced at my untouched plate. "How's the betty?"

I looked down at the forgotten dessert on my plate. "I don't know yet, but I'm about to find out." I dug my fork into the apples and raised a cinnamon-crusted bite to my mouth, and for the next ten minutes, the kitchen was silent except for the sound of chewing.

When I had scraped the last bit of apple filling from my plate, I looked up at Emmeline again. "That was fabulous," I said. And she hadn't even mentioned my burgeoning waistline. "When you get a chance, could you copy that recipe down for me, too?"

"Of course," Emmeline said, beaming proudly. "I've also got a terrific pumpkin pie recipe—with caramel on top. I'll give you that one too, if you'd like."

"If I ever need a cook, I know who to ask." I took a last sip of tea and helped her clear the table. When we had put the last dish into the dish drainer, she took off her apron and hung it on a hook next to the door. "And now let's go out and have a look at those paths."

I followed her into the front hall, where she exchanged her house shoes for a pair of galoshes. "It's kind of muddy out there," she explained.

"I know," I said, with a rueful glance at my stained clothes.

She laughed. "I guess you do."

A moment later, she closed the door behind her, and the two of us traipsed back down the road. The wind had picked up, and I was shivering again by the time we reached Polly's house. Although Emmeline had donned a thick jacket, I wore only two thin sweaters—now damp—I had picked up before leaving the house, and was beginning to think this wasn't the day for an outdoor jaunt.

"There are two of them," Emmeline said. "One's over there by that stand of trees." She pointed over to the far side of the bog. "The other's not too far behind the house, over there." She turned toward Polly's house and waved a little to the left of it, then glanced back at me. "Although you're going to be frozen solid if we head down either of them today. I didn't realize you went out without a jacket. And you being from Texas, too." She shook her head. "Why don't you head home and get some clean clothes? You know where to look now, and if you can't find them, you can just stop by again."

I nodded, shoving my hands into my jeans pockets. "Maybe you're right," I said, teeth chattering slightly. The thought of a warm bath and dry clothes was appealing.

"I know I'm right," she said, taking my elbow and steering me back toward her house. "You're welcome to wait until Henry gets back with the truck."

"No, no," I said. "I need to go back and take care of things at the inn. But thank you very much," I added. "For the brown betty, for the recipes"—I patted my pocket, where I had tucked them before leaving the house—"and for showing me where to look."

"Anytime, dear. Now, why don't you head on home? They'll still be there tomorrow."

"Thanks, Emmeline."

"Come on, now. I'll walk you back at least as far as the house."

As we headed back toward Emmeline's together, I felt strangely relieved to be leaving Polly's house behind. I was curious where the paths in the bog led—but for now, I was happy to leave it for another day.

TWENTY-THREE

CHARLENE WAS ALREADY GONE by the time I got home, but she'd done a great job on the kitchen; the surfaces sparkled, and the kitchen smelled of lemon soap. Pepper and Biscuit greeted me warmly, but ignored each other—which was progress, I decided. At least the fur wasn't flying.

After checking on Gwen, who was still working her way through the rooms, I peeled my sweater off and threw it into the laundry room, then headed upstairs to take a shower. Twenty minutes later, I emerged from the bathroom scrubbed and warm, slipping into a pair of black fleece sweatpants and matching sweatshirt Charlene had picked up for me on the mainland a few weeks ago, before we'd had a falling out over Cranberry Estates—and McLaughlin.

As I slipped on wool socks and padded down to the kitchen, I wondered what to do with the new information Emmeline had given me. Grimes wasn't the only one who had heard McLaughlin was seeing someone on the side. But who? Could it be someone from off-island? Maybe even someone from McLaughlin's past?

I glanced out the window at the *Little Marian*, bobbing by herself at the dock below. Maybe I'd have to break down and take the mail boat over to the mainland, so I could get to the library and find out what the papers had to say about McLaughlin's tenure in Boston. I hadn't had a chance to ask John to fix the skiff—in fact, since McLaughlin's death, I hadn't seen much of him at all. And since *Mooncatcher* was gone, it was a good bet John wasn't home, either. Police business, probably. I made a mental note to grill him when he got back—and ask him to help me fix my boat. Maybe I could bribe him with brownies.

My eyes strayed to the *Little Marian* again, and it occurred to me that Eliezer White could probably figure out what was wrong with it. He was the island's boatwright—in fact, he had gotten me the skiff in the first place. I hadn't seen Eliezer in a while, anyway; it would be a good excuse to catch up—and maybe pick up a little bit of island gossip. When I dialed his house, he picked up immediately, and promised he'd be over shortly.

After putting on a pot of coffee and pulling a loaf of cranberry walnut bread out of the freezer—it was Eliezer's favorite since, unlike his wife, I made it with sugar—I turned my attention to the small stack of papers I had pulled from my sweater pocket. Recipes for Emmeline's banana bread and chocolate chip cookies—and the number to the shelter. The recipes went into my "try soon" file. Then I smoothed out the slip of paper with the phone number, glanced at Pepper, and dialed.

As the phone rang, I watched the little cat. She seemed to have recovered from the trauma of her mistress's death, and now that she and Biscuit were no longer fighting openly, I was considering adopting her myself. As Pepper yawned and stretched, someone picked up the other end of the line.

"Battered Women's Shelter hotline. Can I help you?"

I stood speechless, clutching the phone.

"Hello. Can I help you?"

"No," I said. "No, I'm sorry. I must have gotten the wrong number." I replaced the receiver and stared at Pepper. Why did Polly have the number for the Battered Women's Shelter on her fridge? I remembered the open suitcase, clothes spilling over the sides, only half-packed. Had Polly been leaving the island to escape someone? I shuddered; if so, she hadn't made it out in time. I scooped up the kitten, wishing cats could talk. Pepper, I was sure, knew what had happened; the frustrating thing was, I couldn't ask her.

As I scratched under her pointy chin, Pepper vibrated in my arms, purring. Had McLaughlin been reassigned because he was violent, I wondered? Had he abused Polly—and maybe someone else, too—and paid the price with his life?

Stroking Pepper's delicate ears, I looked out the window at the *Little Marian* again. I needed to get to that library. If Eliezer couldn't fix the boat, that would mean taking the mail boat over to Northeast Harbor and driving to Somesville. At least a few of the answers lay in that library, I was positive.

The phone rang a moment later, and I reached for it immediately.

"Hello, Natalie?"

It was Matilda.

"Hi, Matilda. How are you?"

"I did a little research on other people with the initials J.S.," she said.

"I found two at the churchyard."

"Good. We can compare notes, then. I've got a Jeremiah Sarkes and a Jonah Selfridge."

"Those are the two I found." I thought for a moment. "I know Jeremiah married an Elizabeth Mary, but could you find out when?"

"I have it right here, in fact. Let me see." I could hear the rustling of pages over the phone line. "They were married in 1876. Kind of late for the times, actually."

"So in 1875, Jeremiah was single?"

"Unless he married earlier . . . but there's no record of it."

"And you're sure there wasn't another J.S. on the island?"

"No one who was recorded, anyway. I've cross-checked it with the census for that year."

Jonah Selfridge. I took a deep breath and looked at the ceiling. Unless the priest's diary was wrong, Murray Selfridge's ancestor had committed murder right over my head.

Goosebumps rose on my arms as I gripped the phone. "Thanks, Matilda. That helps . . . a lot."

"By the way, did you get a chance to copy that diary for me?"

"Um . . . I'm afraid it disappeared."

"Disappeared? You mean you *lost* it?"

"It's a long story. And believe me, it wasn't my fault."

"How could you misplace a historical document . . ."

I cut her off. "Thanks again, Matilda. I'll be down to see you in a few days, and I'll tell you all about it."

"But . . ."

"You've been a big help. I'll talk with you soon!"

She was still sputtering when I hung up.

A shiver passed through me as I leaned against the counter, staring out the window at the leaden water, trying to assimilate what Matilda had told me. Murray Selfridge's great-great-grandfather was a murderer. I glanced at the ceiling again, trying not to imagine what the room above—my bedroom—must have looked like when she was found. Was the discovery of the diary what made Annie restless? Assuming, of course, that a ghost was the source of the nocturnal noises. And the pantry episode.

My eyes returned to the scene outside—the same view Annie must have seen as she went about her daily chores. I knew who had killed her. But the diary with the proof was gone. I touched the lump on the back of my head. Someone else thought that the diary was valuable enough to crack me over the head and steal it. The question was, was that knowledge also enough to have sparked a second—and maybe even a third—murder?

A knock on the kitchen door jolted me out of my thoughts. Eliezer stood on the kitchen porch, a lopsided smile on his weathered face.

A cold wind blew through the door as I let the little man in. He doffed his battered cap, grinning up at me as the door closed behind him. "Chilly day for a skiff ride."

"I know," I said, "but I need to get over to the mainland." I gestured toward the quick bread on the counter. "Can I get you a cup of tea and some cranberry bread?"

He glanced out the window. "Let me just see what we can do about your boat. Then I'll gladly take you up on it," he said.

I grabbed my jacket from the hook next to the door and followed him down to the dock, where his skiff bobbed beside my own. A cold gust off the water tore through my jacket as I hunched on the little dock.

"What's the trouble?" he asked.

"She just won't start."

He grunted and clambered into the boat. "How's the fuel level?"

"Fuel?"

He unscrewed the fuel cap and peered in. "Looks pretty empty to me."

"I called you all the way over here and I'm out of gas?"

Eliezer laughed at me and winked. "Better than tearing your prop off again."

I blushed, remembering the disaster I had made of the skiff one of the first times I took it out. I was amazed he'd gotten her to float again. "I'll be right back. I've got a fuel can in the shed."

A few minutes later, he pulled the cord, and the engine throbbed to life.

"Well, that's it then," Eliezer said. "You goin' now?"

"Let's go up and get warm for a few minutes," I said. "Somes-ville can wait."

He cut the engine and followed me up the hill and into the warmth of the kitchen.

When the door closed behind us, I pulled off my jacket and put on a kettle for tea. "Don't tell Claudette I gave you this," I said as I cut a thick slice of cranberry bread and slid it onto a plate. She did a lot of baking, but almost never used sugar, and gave Eliezer a hard time when he indulged in sweets.

"My lips are sealed," Eliezer said, winking and demonstrating just the opposite as he crammed a hunk of bread into his mouth.

"How's Claudette doing these days?"

He swallowed and wiped his mouth. "Much better, now that she's a granny."

"She's a granny? What do you mean?" A few months ago, Claudette had confessed to me that before she and Eliezer married, she had had a child—her only child—out of wedlock. Her mother had forced her to give him up for adoption at birth, and although she had spent her life keeping tabs on her son and longing to meet him, she had never contacted him. Nobody on the island knew—not even Eliezer. When we talked, I had encouraged her to consider getting in touch with her son, but she had waved my suggestion away.

"She finally told me about the boy," Eliezer said.

"The boy?" I said cautiously.

He nodded. "Her son in Bangor."

I sat down in surprise as Eliezer continued.

"After you talked with her, she pulled me aside, said there was something I needed to know. Then she told me about him." He shook his head. "Poor Claudie, to have to live through all of that and never tell a soul, and then us never having a babe of our own!"

Eliezer took another bite of cranberry bread before continuing, a light shower of crumbs punctuating his words. "Well, I told her she should write him a letter, and would you believe it, she did. After all those years. As it turned out, he called a week later, happy to hear from her, and she's been down there twice since. She's got photos all over the house now. Liam and Sarah, the grandkids' names are." He took another bite of cranberry bread. "They're planning on coming up for a week in the summer."

"That's marvelous!" I said. Sugarless cranberry bread or not, Claudette was a warm woman, with a big heart. "And she's getting along with her son?"

"Brad? It was a bit touchy at first, but when she explained how it was, he came around."

"I'm so glad to hear that." And I was. After the last few weeks of death and disruption, it was nice hearing that Claudette was reunited with her long-lost child. There was something good happening on the island.

"It's a shame about Charlene, though," Eliezer said, popping the last bit of cranberry bread into his mouth.

"I know," I said, cutting him another slice. "She's really torn up about what happened to McLaughlin."

He nodded as I put the slice on his plate. "I just don't understand why that sergeant arrested her."

I froze. "What?"

"You didn't know?"

The knife slipped from my hand and clattered to the floor. "They *arrested* Charlene?"

"You didn't know?"

"I had no idea," I said, steadying myself against the kitchen counter. "How did it happen? When?"

"It was right around noon," he said. "They marched down to the store and took her out in cuffs. In front of the whole island. Apparently it was her knife what did the good reverend in."

The knife. I knew it.

He shook his head. "Terrible thing."

"Jesus. Why didn't you tell me?"

"I thought you knew. I figured that was why you wanted the skiff."

Charlene was in jail. No wonder John had been gone all morning. Trying to get her out, probably. My thoughts reeled, touched on the diary. And the shelter number.

I jerked the chair back and ran to the door, hooking my jacket and grabbing the knob. "I've got to run, Eliezer. Let yourself out when you're done!" The door slammed behind me before he could answer.

Trying to marshal my thoughts, I stumbled down the steps to the dock. They had arrested Charlene. I knew they had the wrong person; but how was I going to prove it? The diary with Jonah Selfridge's confession was gone, and I knew Polly had a number for the battered women's shelter, but that was hardly proof of anything. Besides, I didn't know who—if anyone—had been abusing her.

Now that Eliezer had diagnosed the fuel problem, the engine started on the first try, and I untied the ropes and turned toward the mainland. The wind gusted as I nosed the boat into the swells; the water was choppy, and foam tipped the leaden waves. As Cranberry Island receded behind me, the water got even rougher. Normally I would have turned back—but not today.

Although the engine was at full throttle, it was almost a half an hour before I turned into the sheltered waters of Somes Sound, my hands numb from cold, chin burrowed into the collar of my jacket. Where was Charlene now, I wondered? At the station still? Or had they moved her somewhere else? I shivered, thinking of it. After what felt like hours, the little dock at Somesville came into view. There were fewer yachts tied up in the harbor this time of year, and many of the grand houses that lined the water looked dark and vacant.

Pulling up to the dock, I hopped out and tied up the skiff, then jammed my hands into my pockets and hurried the few short blocks to the library.

The warm, dusty smell of books was a welcome respite from the cold wind howling down Somesville's main street, but did nothing to soothe the anger that was boiling in my stomach. The computer stations were full; I waited impatiently as an older woman examined a pecan pie recipe, resisting the urge to shove her off the chair. Finally, she got up and toddled toward the printer, murmuring "It's all yours" as she passed me.

I slid into the seat and pulled up Lexis Nexis, my fingers fumbling as I typed in Boston and Richard McLaughlin. A long list of articles popped up immediately. He *had* been successful; several articles in business journals popped up, chronicling his progress through the ranks of a New York-based plumbing company. I scrolled down—there was even an article about his decision to give it all up and enter the seminary. "I was looking for something more in life—a way to give back," he'd told the interviewer. Although McLaughlin's motives had always seemed a bit suspect to me, I felt a pang for his lost optimism.

I paged through the articles, feeling my frustration mount. Lots of nicey-nice articles—but no useful dirt. I quickly became acquainted with McLaughlin's history, and was not surprised at what I saw. The diocese obviously viewed him as a priest with great promise—after ordination, he had been assigned to St. Jude's, a large church in downtown Boston. His charisma had transferred well from plumbing sales to church work—I found several articles quoting him on churchly subjects such as donations and interfaith charities.

I scanned an article featuring McLaughlin and his St. Jude's flock, looking for some clue to his reassignment, but found nothing; according to the *Globe*, the church's attendance had gone up dramatically after he took the pulpit, and everything was coming up roses. After scrolling through two pages of articles, there was still nothing to indicate why he had been reassigned—and from the glowing reports I was reading, it would have had to be a pretty big transgression. Maybe the church had managed to keep it out of the papers.

As I was about to try a different search engine, an article heading caught my eye. I clicked on it and sucked in my breath.

No wonder McLaughlin had been reassigned to a small island. Just before he left Boston, the priest had been under investigation for improper sexual conduct—with a thirteen-year-old girl.

TWENTY-FOUR

Fifteen minutes later I was revving the *Little Marian's* engine and heading back to Cranberry Island. The printout of the article crackled in my jacket pocket as I huddled down in the back of the boat, wondering what to do with my new information. It was possible that the parents of the child in Boston took out their vengeance on the priest—but it didn't explain Polly's death. And I still didn't know why she had called the shelter.

Although McLaughlin had been acquitted of the molestation charges, the Church obviously thought there was enough evidence to reassign him. Was it true in this case that where there's smoke, there's fire? And was it at all related to McLaughlin's murder?

As I turned out of Somes Sound onto the open water, something clicked. McLaughlin was rumored to be seeing someone. Polly didn't seem like his type . . . but I remembered the tear-streaked face of a young girl outside the rectory on the day McLaughlin died. My stomach lurched. Had he done it again?

And had her parents discovered it—perhaps killing the man who had violated their child?

My mind switched into high gear. Maybe Polly had found out—maybe McLaughlin had visited her repeatedly, trying to talk her out of telling the girl's parents. He had certainly tried to shut me down every time I asked about Polly. And the shelter number—could it have been for the girl? Maybe Polly was going to accompany her to a safe place where she could get counseling, and McLaughlin found out and killed her before she could do anything more.

But how did that explain McLaughlin's death?

The engine whined as I urged the little skiff to go faster. Maybe he killed Polly too late. Or maybe the girl told her parents.

One thing was sure. I needed to find out who I had seen that day outside the rectory.

Tania would know.

Instead of heading back to the Gray Whale Inn, I veered off toward the Cranberry Island dock. The *Island Princess* was just pulling in as I tied up the skiff; I waved at George McLeod and hurried past the row of little shops, their windows darkened for the winter, on my way to the store.

The familiar smell of dried spices and coffee made me ache for my friend as I threw open the door to the store.

Tania sat behind the cash register, tears streaking down her pale face. "Natalie!" She snuffled and wiped her nose on a tissue. "They've taken Aunt Charlene! They came in and told me while I was in school . . ."

"I know," I said. "But I think we may be able to get her out."

She looked up from her tissue. "How?"

"I need your help." I described the girl I'd seen outside the rectory the day McLaughlin died. "Do you know who it is?"

"Why? What does that have to do with Aunt Charlene?"

"I can't tell you yet. Just trust me."

She nodded. "It's one of two people. Hang on—I think Aunt Char has the back-to-school-night photos here somewhere." She rummaged around in the drawer beneath the cash register and pulled out a pack of pictures.

I found her halfway through the pack. "Tiffany Jeans," Tania said.

"Do you know where she lives?"

"She's over down by the light house. On Seal Point Road." Tania looked at her watch. "She'll be in school for another half hour, though."

"Thanks," I said, heading for the door.

"Will you come back?" Tania called after me.

"As soon as I can," I said. The bells above the door jingled as I pulled the door open and headed back out into the cold.

———

My hands were almost frozen when the battered green door of the Cranberry Island School opened and a dozen kids tumbled through the door. Tiffany was last, along with another girl. I recognized her at once—it was her face I'd seen that day at the rectory.

She was obviously willowy, even in her thick winter coat, and her pink cheeks and bright blue eyes radiated youth and innocence. A wave of tenderness rose in me as she bent down to retie her left shoe, her long limbs gawky, jeans a little too short, exposing a few inches of grayish sock. I hoped McLaughlin had done nothing to destroy that innocence.

After exchanging a few words, the girls separated. I walked behind the thin blonde girl; as she turned to head toward Seal Point Road, I caught up with her.

"Tiffany?"

She whirled around, startled.

"I'm Natalie Barnes," I said, proffering an icy hand. She stared at it, then back at my face. "I run the Gray Whale Inn."

Her eyes were guarded. "What do you want?"

"I just want to talk to you."

She shifted her backpack from one shoulder to the other. "About what?"

"Can I walk with you for a few minutes?"

"If you want," she said, and continued trudging along, eyes fastened to her worn sneakers.

As we walked past the apple trees, I wondered for the hundredth time how to broach the subject of McLaughlin. I wasn't comfortable talking to her without her parents—but I was afraid that if I didn't, she wouldn't tell me anything.

"I saw you outside the rectory the other day."

Her head whipped around. "What?"

"The day Rev. McLaughlin died," I said softly. She was staring at the ground again, walking with purpose, as if she wanted to run away from me. Some of the pink receded from her cheeks.

"Did you know him well?" I asked.

She shrugged. "He was nice," she said. "My parents fight sometimes. He was the only one who listened . . ." She trailed off, and we walked in silence for a moment. "And now he's gone."

We walked in silence for a moment longer. "I'm sorry," I said finally. "It's hard to lose someone who cares for you."

Tiffany nodded abruptly, wiping her nose with a worn blue glove.

"How long had you been friends?"

"Only for a month or two," she said, sniffling. "Once or twice a week. I used to sneak out, after my parents thought I was asleep. I have to go home right after school—my mom needs me to help with my little brother, Charlie. And Mom and Dad . . . well, sometimes they don't get along at night, and I just need somewhere to go . . ." She snuffled. "He was so nice. He always listened, told me it wasn't my fault. He gave me hot chocolate, then told me I shouldn't sneak out."

My throat constricted. Hot chocolate. Sneaking out at night. What had McLaughlin done?

I swallowed hard. "You felt comfortable talking with him?"

"Rev. McLaughlin was the best. He was going to talk to my parents, see if he could help." She sniffed again. "When he died, it was just . . . just so *awful*. Who could have done such a horrible thing?"

"I don't know," I said. "That's what I'm trying to find out."

"They took Tania's aunt," she said fiercely, staring straight ahead now. "They said she did it. But I don't believe them. I saw him, and Miss Charlene loved him. She would never do that!"

"I know she didn't," I said. "I'm trying to figure out who did. Do you know if anyone was angry with him?"

She shook her head. "He was nice to everyone."

I took a deep breath. "He never . . . never made you feel uncomfortable, did he?"

She glanced up at me, eyebrows high with surprise. "Who? Reverend McLaughlin?" She shook her head decisively. "Never."

There was no hesitation.

Thank God.

The breath I hadn't realized I was holding shuddered out of my chest. Then I had another thought. A bad thought. "It sounds like you had a special relationship with him," I said, straining to keep my voice casual.

She nodded. "Yeah."

"Did he ever help any of your other friends out?"

"I don't think so. Why?"

I thanked God again. Maybe for once the jury got it right, and McLaughlin wasn't a loose cannon. I put my hand on Tiffany's thin shoulder and squeezed it gently. "No reason." The wind sent a flurry of leaves skittering by us as we walked past a stand of dark green pine trees. "You know," I said slowly, "if you need someone to talk to, you can always come by the inn."

She lowered her head and kept walking, eyes glued to her scruffy sneakers.

"I know it's hard, when your parents fight. Mine did, sometimes."

Tiffany glanced up at me through a curtain of hair. "Really?"

"Really. I know how hard it is, especially when you have no one to talk to."

She sighed, eyes back to her sneakers again. "I try to talk with Ginny about it, but she doesn't get it. I mean, her family's so happy-happy all the time."

"Come by sometime," I said. "I'd love to talk. Besides, I make a mean hot chocolate."

"But my mom . . ."

"Maybe I can talk to her. Tell her I'm teaching you to cook."

She pushed her hair behind her ears and smiled shyly at me. "That would be fun. Aren't you the one who makes those cool cookies and brownies they sell at the store?"

"That's me."

"I don't know if she'll say it's okay, but I'll ask," she said. "Can she call you if she says okay?"

"Of course," I said. "And if you want, I can always call her. Just tell Tania—she'll let me know."

"Cool."

As another flurry of leaves shot past us, a shiver passed through me. My arms and legs had gone numb, and I wondered if I'd ever get warm again. "I should probably head back now before I freeze to death," I said with chattering teeth, "but it's been nice to meet you, Tiffany." I proffered an icy hand.

She took it this time, giving it a surprisingly firm shake. "You too, Miss Barnes."

"Call me Natalie."

"Okay." She kicked at a stray leaf. "Natalie."

"Will you stop by soon?"

"If my mother says it's okay."

"I hope she does. I'd love to have you over sometime soon. And don't worry about Charlene—we'll get her out of there."

"Good," she said, a smile tugging at her pale lips. "Tania was pretty upset. I guess I would be, too."

"Why don't you hurry home and ask your mom when you can come up?"

"I will. Thanks, Miss . . . I mean, Natalie!" Another shy smile glanced over me before Tiffany's eyes returned to her sneakers.

Then she burrowed her hands into her pockets, adjusted her backpack, and turned toward home.

Despite the icy wind prying at my inadequate jacket, I watched her until she disappeared around a bend in the road. I had done nothing to help Charlene, and all my theories were blown to bits.

But as I watched the thin girl in the puffy coat disappear behind a stand of scraggly spruce trees, I was glad.

———

I turned the problem over again and again in my head as I hurried down the road toward the dock. Whoever had killed Polly had killed McLaughlin. I was almost sure of it. Polly had a number for the battered women's shelter on her fridge, and was packing to take a trip. McLaughlin knew something was wrong there, but wouldn't tell me what.

And now Charlene was in jail, and I didn't even have a list of good suspects.

An icy gust pressed against me as I pulled my jacket closer around me and tried to think. Who had a motive? Russell Lidell was paying off an environmental inspector to let his development go through. Polly refused to sell to him. Had he killed Polly—and then killed McLaughlin because he knew too much? But how did Russell end up with Polly's gun? Unless she was using it to defend herself, and he turned it against her . . .

And what about Murray Selfridge? Someone had taken that diary from me as I stood outside the rectory. Did McLaughlin figure out who J.S. must have been and confront him about the diary? Is that why Selfridge was funding the rectory renovations—

to keep McLaughlin quiet? But that still didn't explain who had killed Polly.

It also didn't explain who had tried to get into my kitchen the other night, or taken the bullets from Polly's dresser after I talked with McLaughlin. It could, of course, have been McLaughlin . . . but why? Unless he told someone else about it . . .

As I hurried past the darkened storefronts on the pier, I thought once again of the paths behind Polly's house. Whoever had rifled Polly's dresser hadn't come by the road—I was sure of it. The paths could lead anywhere—including just a road, which would get me no closer to pinpointing the murderer. On the other hand . . .

I clambered into the *Little Marian*, untied the ropes from the cleats and started the motor. The cold had seeped into my bones, and my fingers felt numb on the rudder. But instead of heading back to the inn, I turned the *Little Marian* toward Cranberry Point—and the bog that lay on the other side of the island.

———

It was only as Polly's little house came into view that I realized the flaw in my plan. I was only a few yards away from land—but there was nowhere to tie up the boat.

I puttered past the bog, then turned around and went by again, searching for an old cleat or something that would let me tie up. Surely on an island like this, there would be plenty of places to tie up—after all, most people used to travel by boat, didn't they?

A cluster of rocks caught my eye, and after maneuvering past it a few times, I decided it was my best bet. I shouldered the *Little Marian* up alongside, wincing when the rocks grazed the white-painted side. Eliezer would kill me.

I tossed the rope out with numb fingers, managing to lasso a rock on the third try. After an awkward couple of minutes during which I almost pitched face-first into the frigid water twice, I had managed to get the boat somewhat secured to a group of granite boulders. I clambered out of the boat and edged around the rocks toward the bog, trying to ignore the sound of grating wood behind me and wondering why I didn't just go home, get a better coat, and walk down.

Despite the near-freezing temperatures, the bog was mushy, and my feet sank into the spongy earth as I made my way toward Polly's house. I tried to ignore the icy water seeping into my shoes, but couldn't help questioning my sanity. Why exactly was I out here? I already knew the answer. Desperation.

I was soaked halfway up my shins by the time I got to the lonely little house. The cats were smarter than I was, evidently—since none of them trotted over to meet me, I figured they were probably tucked up inside. I made my way past the back porch to the space between the spruce trees that marked the beginning of the nearest trail. Jamming my hands deeper into my pockets, I lowered my head and forged forward, away from the lonely little house that used to be Polly's.

The path closest to the house was narrow, but someone used—or had used—it regularly. A few saplings that had attempted to take a foothold had been trampled, and the wet ground was muddled with footprints. I could make out a man's heavy boot, and a smaller print, a woman's, probably. Did many people use this trail? It was a reasonable assumption, I supposed. It *was* cranberry season, after all.

A few times, side trails broke off from the main path, but they were all overgrown, so I kept to the main track. After about twenty minutes winding through the trees, I spotted a break in the dark branches in front of me, and the glint of metal.

I slowed, trying not to crunch leaves, and peered through the branches as I drew closer. The path didn't lead to a road—it led to a house.

Not a house, exactly. It was a run-down trailer, ringed with old appliances, lobster traps, and stacks of rotted cardboard. I had no idea where on the island I was—I'd never seen the place before. The cold forgotten, I crouched down in the undergrowth and crept closer. The windows were dark. The place looked deserted.

I edged up toward the trailer and peered through one of the windows. A saggy couch littered with piles of clothes, dirty TV dinner trays on the small table in front of it, dozens of empty Miller beer cans. The curtains hung sideways, as if they'd been ripped off, and the paneled walls were pocked here and there with odd holes—indentations, almost.

I sidled up to the next window, peeking in cautiously. The bedroom—a stained mattress, no sheets, and clothes heaped around the room's perimeter. My eyes were drawn to a blue plaid shirt jumbled in the middle of the floor, and I shivered. Was it the same one my attacker had worn?

More Miller High Life cans, an overflowing amber glass ashtray. My nose wrinkled in disgust. I stepped past a discarded mattress and tramped around to the side of the trailer. The place seemed to be empty. But something didn't feel right.

As I rounded the trailer, I noticed a small shed crouching in the undergrowth. A few old tires leaned up against the side of it, next to a rusting hulk that looked like it might once have been a refrigerator. The tiny derelict building looked forgotten—except for the muddy track leading from the trailer to the shed's metal door. Whoever lived in the trailer made frequent trips to the shed. But why? My wet shoes squelched in the mud as I followed the path to the small metal building.

There was one small window; unfortunately, it was situated above a tangle of raspberry brambles. I checked the door—it was padlocked. It would have to be the window, then.

The thorns raked my hands as I pushed the leafless branches aside and stepped up to the window. Dozens of them caught at my jeans like sharp teeth, but every time I tried to dislodge one, three more took hold, so I hurriedly wiped some of the grime from the glass with my sleeve and peered in. The sooner I got out of here, the better.

A jumble of tools and discarded junk littered the tiny interior, and a pile of clothes had been tossed into a corner. Nothing of any real value, from what I could see. So why the well-used track?

As I surveyed the dim interior again, something moved in the pile of the clothes. I stepped back involuntarily, and a new batch of thorns nestled into my jeans. I quickly moved forward again, wincing. Probably a rat. I peered through the window again.

It wasn't a rat.

It was a person.

I pounded on the window. Whoever was locked in there must have been freezing—the temperature was in the forties, and there was no heat. "Hello! Hello in there!"

The bundle of clothes twitched, and something like a face emerged from the huddle. The skin was mottled with livid bruises, and the eyes were so swollen only two narrow slits were visible.

"Oh my God," I breathed, my stomach heaving. "We've got to get you out of here."

But how? I ran through my options. Unless I could somehow destroy the lock, the door was out—it was metal. The window would be big enough—but I needed something to break it, and it didn't look like the person inside the shed was in any condition to climb up and out.

I needed help.

"I'll be right back," I called. "I'm going to get you out of here. I'm going to try to find a phone."

The figure nodded feebly as I pushed away from the window and headed back toward the trailer. There was a working phone in there somewhere, I hoped. I also hoped whoever lived there took his or her time coming back.

Although the shed was locked, the trailer door opened with no resistance, and the reek inside billowed out. The smell of rotted food and old beer was overpowering; I pressed the collar of my shirt to my nose and made my way through the trailer, searching for a phone. I found it next to a pile of moldy dishes in the kitchen sink.

No dial tone.

I slammed the receiver down. I'd have to traipse all the way back to Polly's. I hated to leave the shed, but it was impossible to do anything without help. John probably had some bolt cutters that would deal with the padlock . . .

But as I turned to leave the kitchen, the trailer door creaked open.

TWENTY-FIVE

MY EYES DARTED AROUND the room, searching for a place to squeeze into. No pantry, no kitchen table, no nook—nothing. Only a small partition separated me from whoever was in the living room.

There was nowhere to hide.

Weapon. I scanned the pile of filthy dishes in the sink. Heavy footsteps approached from the living room. Suddenly I saw it—a steak knife, coated with grease. I grabbed it just as the footsteps approached.

I turned around and braced myself against the sink as they rounded the corner.

It was Eddie O'Leary.

"What are you doing here?"

He was dressed in a dirty flannel shirt and holey jeans. His small eyes were flat and mean.

I swallowed hard and tried to sound nonchalant. "I was down at the bog, picking cranberries. I got turned around and ended up here. I'm sorry I just came in—the door was unlocked, and I was trying to call the inn to tell them I'd be back late."

His eyes narrowed. Even over the reek of the kitchen I could smell him—body odor, dead fish, and something else—something rotten.

"Where are the berries?"

"Pardon me?"

"You said you were picking berries."

My hand started shaking. "I must have left them outside."

"Show me."

I swallowed again. "Okay. Fine." I edged past him toward the door, still clutching the knife. Could I outrun him? I'd better—it was my only hope of getting out of here. I thought of the poor creature in the shed—probably Marge, I realized now. What had he done to her? My hands started to shake. *What would he do to me?*

He followed close behind me as I walked through the door and out into the fresh air.

"They're over here," I said, taking a few quick steps toward the trail.

And then I ran.

The branches tore at my face as I plunged into the trees. O'Leary's footsteps thundered behind me somewhere, but I didn't look back. I could make it. I had to make it. *Please God*, I thought, *give me the strength to make it to Polly's*. If I could lock the door and keep him out long enough to call the police, then maybe . . .

I leaped over a tree branch. As I landed, my foot squirted sideways in the mud. I grabbed a tree for balance and then heaved my body forward again, the air like fire in my lungs.

"You'll never make it!" he called behind me, his voice ragged with fury. "I should have taken care of you yesterday!" Yesterday. By the rectory. He had been the one.

His footsteps pounded behind me.

Too close.

Run, Natalie. Run hard.

Finally, I caught a glimpse of painted wood. Polly's house. I was almost there. I put on a last burst of speed—I needed to widen the gap enough to give me time to get in and lock the door—and tripped. My body hurtled forward, slamming into the muddy ground. I scrambled to my feet and staggered forward again.

But it was too late.

A meaty hand grabbed my left arm, jerking me back like a rag doll. I swung my right arm around. The knife sliced through the air; then there was a crash and everything went black.

———

It was the cold that woke me. My eyes opened to darkness, and the smell of gasoline and unwashed body—and something fouler—made my stomach heave. I swallowed back the saliva that filled my mouth and tried to prop myself up on my hands. They wouldn't move. I was tied up.

"Hello?" I croaked, teeth chattering with cold. I tested the cords wrapped around my wrist. They were so tight they cut into my skin. My head was throbbing, a deep purple spike above my left ear. Someone moaned, and a fresh wave of fear washed over me. Dark as it was, I knew exactly where I was. In the storage shed next to Eddie O'Leary's wife.

"Marge?" My voice quavered.

"Who is it?" she whispered.

"Natalie."

She stifled a sob. "Oh, no. He got you too." The sobs gave way to a ragged cough. Her voice was weak. "But why? Why are you here?"

"I don't know," I said, shifting to find a more comfortable position on the cold wood floor. Although I was pretty sure I did know. It was because Eddie O'Leary was a murderer.

My feet were numb with cold; I didn't have Marge's pile of filthy blankets. "What happened?" I asked her. "How long have you been here?"

"I don't know." Her voice was faint. "It's been two nights, I think."

"How did it happen?"

"I . . ." she choked back a sob. "He caught me."

"Caught you?"

"He found out I . . . I knew about Polly."

"He killed Polly?"

Her voice was thick. "They were sleeping . . ."

I blinked in the darkness. Suddenly it all clicked into place. "He was seeing Polly, wasn't he?" I said slowly. "And she was going to leave the island." I remembered the half-packed suitcase, the number for the battered women's shelter. The razor in the bathroom, gummy with black whiskers. The gun—she must have been running away, shot at him and missed. And then . . .

Marge snuffled. "Whore," she hissed. I was shocked at the venom in her voice. Her husband had beaten her, then tied her up and left her in a shed for two nights. And she was still jealous of his mistress—the mistress he had killed.

An unpleasant thought tugged at the edges of my mind. If he killed his mistress to keep her from leaving the island, what did he have in mind for us?

"When did all this start?" I asked.

"A couple of months ago. All of a sudden, he started coming home late. Sometimes, he never came home at all."

"How did you find out?"

"I followed him," she whispered.

"Did he know?"

"Not until the day before yesterday. I don't know when . . . he accused me of making eyes at Tom Lockhart, and I let it slip. About Polly. And then . . ." She trailed off, but I could imagine what had happened next.

"Did he ever talk with McLaughlin?"

"The preacher? I don't know." She snorted bitterly. "I can't think why he would."

I stared into the darkness. Marge couldn't, but I could. O'Leary must have known McLaughlin was visiting Polly—in fact, it was probably his visits down to the little house that started tongues wagging about his seeing another woman. I was guessing that the real reason for his visits was to counsel a troubled—and abused—woman. That would explain his comment about the "sordid details" of Polly's life.

And McLaughlin had died just a few hours after I told him my theory about the number of bullets in the gun. Even though he hadn't shown it, my conversation must have rattled him enough to call O'Leary and start asking pointed questions; O'Leary must have panicked, and killed him to silence him. It had been O'Leary in the house with me that day, stealing the bullets from Polly's dresser. I was sure of it.

I remembered the face at the kitchen window of the inn, the muddy footprints on the deck. I must have been asking too many questions about Polly's death. Icy fingers stole down my spine. He had attacked me yesterday—stolen the diary. But why?

A deep shiver passed through my body from the cold. I knew who the murderer was; but unless we figured out how to get out of here, it wasn't going to matter. "Mind if I scoot a little closer?" I asked Marge. "To stay warm?"

"Sure," she said. "I've got some blankets, too." I inched over toward her, and soon our bodies were pressed back to back. I wiggled until I managed to hitch some of the dirty blankets over me.

We passed a few minutes in silence, listening to the cold wind moan around the corners of the shed. Then I said softly, "How long has he been abusing you, Marge?"

Her large body shuddered next to mine. "Since the beginning."

"Why did you stay?"

"What choice did I have?" Her voice was soft, resigned. "This is where my whole life is. My family, my people. I have nowhere else to go."

My mind clicked into gear. "He attacked the other lobsterman, too, didn't he?" I said. "The one in the hospital. Eddie was starting the gear war, wasn't he?"

"Ayuh," she said. "And it's not the first time, either. He's got a bad temper, does Eddie."

My heart ached for the woman pressed up against me. I had never liked her—her venomous tongue, her accusing eyes—but now I understood. She was living a life of imprisonment.

"What do you think he'll do next?" I asked.

I could feel her body tense. "I don't know." She was quiet for a moment, and the wind howled outside. Then she whispered, "I'm afraid he'll kill us."

My body shuddered with fear. We lay motionless for a few minutes, and my mind started wandering in terrifying directions. Would I spend the last hours of my life in this dirty shed? Only to be murdered by a man who abused his wife, then killed his mistress?

"Marge. We have to get out of here."

"It's no use, Natalie." The resignation in her voice turned my spine to ice. "We can't escape."

"No. You're wrong, Marge." I squirmed into a sitting position. The blood roared in my head as I sat up. I'd been cracked over the head twice in two days, and my nerve endings screamed in protest. I sat quiet for a moment, until the pain receded enough to speak.

"I'm going to see if I can get your hands free." I twisted around and felt for her wrists, my fingers exploring the cords that bound them. It felt like some kind of cable, a phone cord or something. "Maybe I can untie this. If one of us can get loose . . ."

"The door's padlocked."

"There's a window. If I can get out . . ."

"It's no use, Natalie."

"We have to try," I said. "Once I get your hands untied, you can do mine. I can get out the window and go for help."

"I guess so," she said as my half-frozen fingers struggled to unknot the cords that bit into Marge's fleshy wrists. My fingertips kept slipping on the slick cords, and the knots wouldn't budge.

"We need something sharp. Are there any tools in this shed?" I asked.

"Up on the back wall. Only I can't get up—I think my ribs are broken."

"I'll do it." The pain in my head hammered at me as I lurched to my feet. The shed was pitch black—I couldn't even see where the window was. New moon, probably.

"Which way?"

"Behind me," she said.

O'Leary had tied my hands, but left my legs free. I did my best to step over Marge's large body, moving slowly toward what I hoped was the back of the shed, until my right shoulder hit something hard. "I think I found the wall. Do you remember exactly what was here?"

She sighed. "Not really. It's a big jumble."

"I guess I'll just have to see what I can find then." Turning my back to the wall, I extended my arms behind me, searching with bound hands for something sharp enough to cut the cords.

After a minute of groping, my fingertips grazed something rough and sharp. A saw. The handle was too high to reach, so I closed my hand around the blade and tried to lift it up and off of the wall. The teeth bit into my skin. I winced, hoping I was up to date on my tetanus shots. Although with what Eddie O'Leary probably had planned, chances were it wouldn't matter much.

"I found a saw," I said.

"Great." For the first time, there was a flicker of hope in Marge's voice.

"It's big, but maybe if I hold it, you can saw back and forth on it, get through the cord."

"I'll see if I can do it."

I groped the saw until I was holding the handle instead of the blade, then blundered back toward Marge. A minute or two later, we were back-to-back again. I gripped the handle of the saw as Marge positioned her wrists against the blade.

She yelped suddenly.

"What's wrong?" I asked.

"I cut myself."

"Me too," I said. "But at least it's sharp."

She chuckled, and I gripped the saw handle harder as she pushed against it.

"I can't tell if it's working," she said.

"Just keep going."

My fingers were beginning to cramp when Marge gasped, "They're looser! I think it worked!"

I released my grip on the handle. "Can you get them off?"

"I think . . ."

We froze as heavy footsteps clumped outside, and a flash of light illuminated the cobwebbed ceiling. I dropped the saw. Marge whimpered. Then a cold blast of wind hit us as the door banged open. The flashlight bored into my face, then moved away. I lay frozen, heart pounding. I could hear him breathing above us. Then something slammed into my stomach.

"Bitch," he hissed.

I doubled over, gasping for air.

He kicked me again, and pain exploded in my midsection again. I couldn't breathe.

His voice was like gravel. "Couldn't leave it alone, could you? Well, you'll pay for it now."

Marge whimpered beside me. "Eddie ... no ... it's all a mistake ..."

"Shut up!" he barked. I heard a sickening thud, and Marge yelped. "When will you learn to keep your big trap shut?"

"I'm sorry ... so sorry ..."

He kicked her again. "I said, SHUT UP!"

I took a ragged breath, struggling to talk through the pain. "Why did you come to my house that night? And why did you steal the diary?"

"You were nosing into things that wasn't your business."

"Why ..." I gasped for air. "Why the diary?"

"I didn't know what it was. Had to be sure Reverend Pansy hadn't written anything down, didn't I? But it was all just garbage. Old stuff."

Keep him talking, Nat. "And the lobsterman in the hospital?"

"Got what he deserved," he said shortly. "Enough jabbering, now. We've got things to do."

"One more question ... where did you get the knife?"

"The knife?" He laughed, a sick, wheezy sound. "Oh, good old Margie stole it for me. Wasn't that nice of her? She just picked it up from your pal's little store. Five-finger discount, you know? And I knew if I used it ..." He coughed, a wet, mucousy sound. "Some people call me stupid. But I'm smarter than they think. A lot smarter."

I was trying to come up with something else to say when he grabbed my shoulder. "Get up."

My legs convulsed beneath me as I tried to stand. My knees buckled, and I sank to the ground.

"NOW!" He belted me across the face, sending me reeling into Marge, who was curled up under the blankets.

"Both of you! Up!"

I staggered to my feet, wheezing, as Marge squirmed, trying to rise.

"Fat bitch. Can't even get yourself up, can you?"

"Eddie . . ."

"I said keep your mouth shut," he said. He put the flashlight down on a broken-backed chair near the door, then grabbed her roughly, hoisting her to a standing position. The light from the flashlight lit his face, and Marge's. O'Leary's eyes were flat in their dark hollows, Marge's barely visible in her swollen face.

He was going to kill us.

Marge tottered to her feet, and he stepped away. "That's better," he said, retrieving the flashlight. Marge swayed. I lurched toward her, catching her just before she fell.

"Now walk," he said, pointing the beam at the door. Marge leaned on me as we shuffled toward the door. I was still struggling to breathe, and fighting the urge to throw up. We were out of the shed. But going where? And had Marge managed to cut through her bonds? I should have had her hold the saw, I thought. If I were free, I could. . . . *Could what, Natalie?*

Could get us out of here. Somehow. Maybe I still could.

"Where are we going?" I rasped.

"To your boat."

"The *Little Marian*?"

"Enough questions." He shoved me hard. I reeled forward, catching myself just in time, but Marge, who had been leaning on me, stumbled and fell.

"Stupid cow. Get up!" She grunted in pain as he kicked her again.

"She can't," I said. "She's hurt too badly."

"She's a lazy bitch, that's what. Always has been."

"Eddie . . ." Marge moaned.

"Shut up! I don't want to hear your whining voice again. I've been listening to it for ten years. Now, get up!"

I hurried toward her, trying to help her as she staggered to her feet. "Are your hands free?" I whispered.

"Not quite."

O'Leary cuffed me on the neck. "Keep your pie holes shut and get moving."

We trudged forward with O'Leary walking behind us, pointing the way with the flashlight. "That way," he muttered, and we followed the light into the forest.

Except for the crunch of leaves and the occasional hoot of an owl, we marched in silence, trying not to trip over the tree roots that jutted up at our feet. Marge stumbled and fell more than once. O'Leary hauled her to her feet every time, cursing at her. Once he slapped her across the face so hard that blood leaked from her mouth.

I forced myself to focus on the path in front of me. The pain still throbbed in my head and my stomach, but my mind raced to find a way to escape.

O'Leary hadn't lied; we were headed back to where I had tied up the *Little Marian* hours earlier. It felt more like days, now. But why? Where was he taking us? And was there any way I could run to Emmeline's house, get help? A cold breeze wafted O'Leary's stale smell toward me again. I was hurt, and my hands were tied. And he was faster.

There had to be another way.

But what?

No matter how hard I tried, I couldn't come up with another solution. And if I couldn't come up with something, then Marge and I were dead.

The ground softened beneath our feet—we were back at the bog. I turned and strained to see Polly's house, but it was too dark. The stars shone bright and cold and hard above us, and the waves slapped somewhere nearby. Occasionally I heard the clunk of wood against the rocks—the *Little Marian*. We were getting close.

I couldn't stay quiet anymore. "Where are you taking us?"

He guffawed behind us, a sound that froze the blood in my veins. "We're goin' on a one-way trip, lady."

"What do you mean?"

"You're goin' down to meet Davey Jones."

"No . . ." Marge whimpered. "You can't."

"Don't tell me what I can or can't do, woman." I heard another thump, the sound of flesh hitting flesh, and Marge's stifled cry.

Then O'Leary spoke again. "Get moving. It's cold out here, and I want to get home."

Davey Jones. I wasn't sure what that meant, but I didn't think I wanted to know.

What I did know was that time was running out. I strained to loosen the bonds at my wrists. If I could just get free, then maybe I could hit him with the anchor, knock him out or something. As we marched across the spongy bog, I tugged at my wrists with all my strength, trying to loosen the tight cords.

All too soon, we were at the *Little Marian*.

"Get in," he said. When Marge didn't listen, he pushed her, and she fell into the little skiff with a thud. I stepped in hurriedly to avoid being pushed, and almost fell down as I tripped over something unfamiliar. I caught my balance just in time and sat down hard on the wooden bench.

"What's that?" I asked.

"Lobster pots."

"Lobster pots?"

He laughed again. A cold laugh. "Thought we might do a little lobstering." He shone the beam on the two pots at my feet, and my stomach turned over. Now I knew what he meant when he said it was a one-way trip.

The two traps were loaded with bricks.

TWENTY-SIX

PANIC ROARED THROUGH ME as O'Leary stepped into the boat and fumbled with the engine. He was going to tie us to the traps and drown us. No bodies this time. My boat would be found, floating empty. And Marge? He could just say she disappeared.

Who would know better?

Maybe the motor won't start this time, I thought, squeezing my eyes shut and praying. *Please, God, let it not start.*

No luck. The engine roared to life on the first try. I closed my eyes and felt the cold wind on my face, gulping air. Death by drowning. I could already feel the icy water, the bursting lungs, the burn of water in my chest when I finally gave up . . .

No.

My hands were tied, but my feet weren't. He hadn't tied us to the traps yet. And I could swim.

But could Marge?

The engine thrummed behind me; we were headed out to sea. Marge was right next to me in the middle of the boat; I could feel her thigh pressed against mine. "Marge," I whispered.

She didn't answer.

"Marge!"

She grunted.

"Can you swim?" I hissed.

She was silent for a moment. Then she whispered back so quietly it was almost swallowed by the wind. "No."

Damn. How could I leave her here? I scanned the black water for a light, for signs of another boat. Nothing.

O'Leary gunned the engine harder, and the nose tipped up a bit more. The little skiff was low in the water, not built for the weight of three people and a load of bricks. On the plus side, I thought grimly, it would be lighter on the way home.

Stop it, Nat.

I needed to think. Marge couldn't swim, but if one of us didn't try to escape, we were both sure to die. If only there were another boat . . .

I strained my eyes, looking ahead into the blackness. Nothing. I kept waiting, dreading the moment when O'Leary would cut the engine, but the boat kept moving further from the island. Suddenly I caught a glimmer of something. It disappeared, then sparked again.

Another boat?

O'Leary hadn't seen it—we kept moving toward it. Soon, it was more visible—a blotch of white and a pinprick of red. Another boat, headed right into our path.

Only now I wasn't the only one that had seen it. O'Leary slowed the engine and shifted course, away from the light.

It was now or never.

"I'm going to get help," I whispered to Marge. Then I lurched to the side and flopped headfirst into the icy water.

The cold took my breath away. I struggled to push my head above the water. The boat was turning around now. I searched the horizon for the light—there it was, a glimpse of it, not far off. The thrum of the skiff's engine roared behind me, and a bright light skimmed over me, then doubled back, focusing on my head. He was using the flashlight to search for me.

I gulped for air and dove down, feeling the bottom of the boat slam against my foot as I plunged into the inky water. When I couldn't hold my breath anymore, I pushed back up, my clothes dragging me down in the water. *Better than a lobster trap.* But how long could I survive?

My head burst through the water's surface again. My foot was injured, but I could still kick. My head was throbbing, the cold was already numbing my legs, and my lungs were struggling, weakened by the kicks O'Leary had dealt me earlier. I didn't know how long I could hold on.

As I treaded water, panting, the flashlight found me again. The skiff was turning around for another run. I sucked in as much air as possible and dove down again, kicking with as much force as I could muster.

The boat roared overhead again, but this time I was deep enough to avoid being hit. When I struggled to the surface for the third time, I heard another sound—a lower thrum than the *Little Marian.* The other boat.

"Help!" I cried, choking as a wave cut off the word. I sputtered, then yelled again. "Help! Over here!"

The flashlight beam swung toward me, and the skiff turned again. I glanced in the direction of the low thrum—there it was, a red light. And a green one. Coming toward me.

Then the *Little Marian* roared up behind me. I dove, my body numb with cold, but O'Leary was faster. A loud crack exploded in my head.

And then I drifted away.

———

"Natalie?"

I struggled up through the depths, seaweed clawing at my feet. Light, up above me . . . had to get to it . . .

"She moved!"

It was Charlene's voice.

Charlene? Where was I? I opened my eyes to a square of bluish light. And Charlene, bending over me.

"Where am I? Am I in jail with you?" Marge. What happened to Marge? I struggled to sit up. "Marge. He's got Marge."

"Marge is fine," she said. "And neither of us is in jail. Now settle down, or they're going to shoo me out of here."

A moment later, a flurry of nurses burst through the door.

"She's out of the coma," Charlene said.

"That's great news! I'll tell the doctor," a woman's voice said. Charlene squeezed my hand, and I squeezed back.

As the nurses bustled about the machines flanking the bed, I closed my eyes and sank back into the pillows, letting it all sink in. Marge was okay. "It was him," I told Charlene. "O'Leary. He killed them. Polly and Richard. And he was the one who went after the lobsterman, too. The one in the hospital."

"We know. The police have him in custody."

"This isn't the time for this," said a reproving voice. "She just came out of a coma."

"Sorry," Charlene mumbled.

I opened my eyes again. My right temple throbbed, and Charlene swam in and out of focus under the glare of the lights. I closed my eyes again. "How . . . what happened?"

"I'll tell you the whole story later—you need to rest now. The coast guard found you. They were out looking for whoever was cutting the lines. They saw the flashlight and went over to investigate. Nearly ran over you."

"And Marge?"

"She was still in the boat. With those awful traps." A shudder passed through me as I remembered the brick-filled lobster pots on the bottom of the boat. If I hadn't dived into the water, I'd be at the bottom of the ocean right now—tied to one of them. And no one would ever know.

"But Marge is fine," Charlene said, squeezing my hand again. "You rest now. I'll be here. When you're up to it, we'll talk some more."

"Okay," I said, allowing my focus to drift. Marge was okay. And O'Leary was in custody. I could sleep now.

I was safe.

———

I don't know how long I slept, but the next time I woke up, John was sitting next to the bed.

I smiled weakly at him. "Hi."

His green eyes were soft with concern. "How are you doing?"

"Much better now, thanks. How's the inn?"

He laughed. "You almost end up at the bottom of the ocean, get hit by a boat, end up in a coma . . . and you want to know how the inn is?"

I laughed, then stopped when it hurt.

"Shouldn't do that," he said. "Ribs cracked."

"O'Leary," I said. "He kicked me. Marge, too."

He nodded curtly, his face suddenly hard. "I wish you'd told me where you were going. Taken me with you."

"I didn't know," I said. He gripped my hand and squeezed it tightly. I tried to make my voice light. "Now, how about the inn?"

"Well, I found your ghost."

"Annie?"

His sandy eyebrows rose. "I guess you could name her Annie. She looks more like a masked bandit to me, though. Maybe Bonnie—you know, for Bonnie and Clyde?"

"A masked bandit?"

He grinned at me. "It was a raccoon. Got into the space between the attic and the ceiling of your bedroom. Even got into the heating system, and figured out how to get into the kitchen."

"The pantry . . ."

"Exactly."

I started to giggle again, until a lance of pain in my ribs stopped me. "So all that time, when I was convinced there was a ghost, it was actually a raccoon."

He nodded.

"But the diary . . ."

"What diary?"

I shifted against the pillows, trying to make myself more comfortable. "The diary I found at the rectory. There was a murder in the inn. Jonah Selfridge did it." I tried to prop myself up a bit. John reached out and pressed the button to make the head of the bed rise. "Didn't they find it at O'Leary's house?"

He shook his head. "Not that I know of. And even if they did, they probably wouldn't think anything of it. They know who killed Polly—and McLaughlin." His mouth was a grim line. "The Selfridges had nothing to do with it."

An alarm bell went off somewhere in my head. Selfridge. Cranberry bog. Polly's house. "John. I need to tell the police something else."

"There will be plenty of time for that when you're better. Marge has given the police enough information . . ."

"It's not about that. It's about the development. Russell Lidell paid off the environmental assessor."

To my surprise, John just nodded. "No need to worry. Emmeline already sounded the alarm. The deal is dead. They fired the environmental guy, and are going to press charges."

"Emmeline blew the whistle?"

"Seems she didn't want a new subdivision right down the road. Speaking of new subdivisions, I've been doing a little investigating of my own."

"What do you mean?"

"Those rectory renovations? They seemed a little steep to me. I've been asking around . . . since McLaughlin was so buddy-buddy with Selfridge, I wondered if there might not be something there."

"You were investigating, too?"

"On the quiet," he said. "Anyway, what I found out is that Murray Selfridge was kicking in for the repairs . . . in exchange for McLaughlin supporting the development."

"I figured as much," I said. "How much?"

"A hundred grand," he said.

"Wow. He really wanted that development, didn't he?"

"By the way, Emmeline told me to tell you she's got a new cranberry bread recipe for you to try. Once you're well again, that is."

"Speaking of that, how long are they planning on keeping me here?"

"I was wondering when you'd get to that question." He stood up. "Why don't I go get the nurse?"

"Wait just a moment," I said.

"What?" He turned to face me, looking totally out of place and completely irresistible.

"Come here."

As he approached the bed, I reached out and grabbed his arm, pulling him toward me.

He paused. "But what about your ribs?"

"As long as you don't make me laugh, I think they'll be just fine."

———

It was four days before they let me go back to the inn. As Charlene and John helped me up the steps to the front door, I realized I hadn't heard anything about my ex-fiancé. Or Candy and Cliffside, for that matter. Or, it occurred to me suddenly, the insurance company.

"Did Allstart ever call about the damage?"

As Charlene swung open the door, the smell of fresh-cut wood greeted me, and two workers smiled at us over a pile of boards. "They authorized the work the day you went into the hospital. I talked Candy into calling the insurance company, and she convinced them it was an accident. They're paying for everything."

"What about the guests?"

"They all checked out."

"Candy?" I swallowed. "And Benjamin?"

"There's a letter in the kitchen for you," Charlene said, laying a hand on my shoulder.

They led me to the kitchen and settled me into a chair. Then Charlene glanced at John. "Why don't we check out the upstairs?" she said.

"Good idea," he answered. With a last glance at me, he followed her out of the kitchen, leaving me alone with my letter.

My name was on the front of it, in Benjamin's bold script. I opened it carefully and unfolded it.

Dearest Natalie,

I'm sorry to have barged into your life again, and I hope you will forgive me for causing any further upheaval. You have created a wonderful place up here, and it was wrong of me to ask you to change your life just to suit me. I've asked too much of you. It is time for me to bow out and let you live your own life.

If you're ever in Austin, please look me up. I'd love to have dinner with you, just for old times' sake . . .

Love always,

Benjamin

Tears welled up as I folded the letter and returned it to the envelope. I was sad, but at the same time a feeling of peace, of resolution, flooded through me. I knew it wasn't right with Benjamin. We weren't meant for each other.

But what had prompted him to leave?

Someone knocked lightly at the kitchen door.

I wiped my tears away quickly and said, "Come in!"

It was Charlene. "What did the letter say?"

I pushed it across the table toward her. "Go ahead and read it."

She gave me a lopsided smile. "I already did," she admitted. "Are you okay?"

"I'm sad, of course . . . things weren't good between us, but I did love him . . . but happy, too. It was the right thing." I wiped at my eyes again. "The thing is, why did he change his mind?"

"I'm not sure you're going to like this . . ."

In a flash, I understood. "It was Candy, right?"

She nodded. "They're opening up an inn together in Austin. I'm not sure if they're engaged, but they're headed in that direction."

"So she's not opening a rival inn down the street?"

"Nope. She's decided to move to Texas."

I let out a long sigh. "Thank God."

Charlene blinked. "What?"

"It's a perfect solution! My two problem guests have moved to Austin together, and now I'll have the island to myself. Besides, they deserve each other. He can't cook, and she doesn't eat."

Charlene stared at me for a long moment. Then she began to laugh. A giggle bubbled up in me, too, but the pain in my rib twinged in protest.

"Don't make me laugh," I said.

"Sorry," she gasped. "But I can't help it."

I couldn't either. And that's how John found us when he walked into the kitchen a few minutes later—doubled over, sobbing with laughter—and pain.

———

Richard McLaughlin's memorial service was on a Tuesday evening. Although his family had claimed his body and buried him in his hometown in Pennsylvania, Charlene insisted on a memorial service on the island.

The little church was fragrant with lilies and carnations, and the reedy voice of the skinny young minister couldn't have been any further from the dulcet tones of Reverend McLaughlin. John sat to my left, an arm around my shoulder. Charlene was on my right; I squeezed her hand as islander after islander stood to give testament to the reverend's good deeds. Gary Sarkes, thankfully, was not among the speakers.

I had run into Eliezer just before the service, and he'd passed on some good news. Now that the development had been scuttled, the development company had agreed to sell the house to Claudette's long-lost son so that the family could come up and visit more often. I was glad Polly's house would stand where it always had—and perhaps play a new role in helping a family grow closer together. But what about the cats? I still needed to find homes for them—except for Pepper, who had been adopted by Charlene, and the big tabby Emmeline had taken under her wing—but I knew the islanders would find a way.

I nodded as Tiffany Jeans walked up and stood behind the pulpit, her young voice trembling as she spoke. Richard McLaughlin hadn't been here long, but he had made a difference in people's lives. I leaned back in my pew and closed my eyes, saddened by the island's loss—two good people, gone because of one evil man—and praying this would be the last memorial service I'd attend for a long, long while.

As we filed out of the church into the gusty darkness, I offered to stay with Charlene. She smiled sadly and shook her head. "I need some time. Alone."

"I understand," I said.

She dropped John, Gwen, and me off at the inn a few minutes later. John gave me a last hug and headed for the carriage house, and Gwen and I hurried inside, closing the door tight against the chill wind. Another storm was coming.

Gwen headed up to take a bath while I put the kettle on for a cup of chamomile tea. As I pulled a tea bag out of the box, a strong smell of roses swept over me, and a prickle rose up my back. I dropped the tea bag and turned around.

There, at the base of the stairs, stood a pale young woman in a long dress, her hair streaming over her shoulders.

"Annie," I whispered, feeling a pang of loss. The diary with the proof—I'd had it, but now it was gone. And now only I knew the story of what had really happened.

As if hearing my thoughts, she looked at me and smiled, raising her right hand in a gesture of—was it thanks?

And then she disappeared.

THE END

RECIPES

PEACH SUNRISE COFFEE CAKE

2 cups all-purpose flour

1 Tbsp baking powder

½ tsp salt

2 Tbsp sugar

⅓ cup butter

1 egg

1 cup milk

½ cup melted butter

¼ cup brown sugar, packed

½ tsp cinnamon

2 cups peaches, thinly sliced

⅓ cup sour cream

½ cup raspberry preserves

In a large bowl, stir together flour, baking powder, salt, and sugar with a fork. Cut in butter. In a separate bowl, beat together egg and milk; add to the flour mixture, stirring until just mixed. Set aside.

Combine melted butter, brown sugar and cinnamon; spread over the bottom of a greased 9-inch square baking pan. Arrange peach slices in four rows. Spoon half of the batter over the peaches, smooth. Combine sour cream and raspberry preserves, and pour over batter. Drop spoonfuls of remaining batter over preserves mixture and smooth.

Bake at 350° for 50 minutes. Cool for 15 minutes on a wire rack; then invert over serving plate.

TO-DIE-FOR CHOCOLATE CHERRY BROWNIES

2 eggs

1 tsp vanilla extract

1 cup sugar

½ pound good quality dark chocolate, chopped

½ cup butter

½ cup flour

¼ cup unsweetened cocoa powder

½ cup dried sweet cherries

½ cup dark chocolate, chopped

Whisk together the eggs, vanilla, and sugar until smooth. Melt the ½ pound of chocolate and butter in double boiler; add to egg mixture and whisk in. In a separate bowl, mix flour and cocoa powder with a fork; fold into the mixture. Fold in cherries and the dark chocolate pieces. Spread into a greased or parchment-lined 8-inch square pan and bake at 350° degrees for 20–25 minutes.

These brownies are so chocolatey that they're delicious even without frosting, but if you're a true chocoholic, go ahead and frost with Cherry Chocolate Frosting, and serve with Bluebell Homemade Vanilla ice cream, if you can get it!

Cherry Chocolate Frosting

4 oz. dark chocolate, chopped

½ cup cream

1–2 tsp cherry liqueur (optional)

Bring cream to a full boil over medium-high heat. Add chocolate; remove from heat and allow to stand a few minutes. Stir gently until chocolate is completely melted; add liqueur, and spread over cooled brownies.

SMOOTH VANILLA FLAN

Nonstick spray
4 eggs
⅛ tsp salt
2 cups milk
1½ tsp vanilla extract
10 Tbsp light corn syrup
6 Tbsp brown sugar

Half-fill a 9x13-inch pan with water; place on a rack in center of oven, and preheat oven to 350°. Spray 6 ramekins with nonstick spray. Break eggs into medium-sized bowl, add salt, and beat lightly with a whisk until yolks are broken. Slowly pour in milk and vanilla; keep beating. Spray a tablespoon with cooking spray; use it to measure out corn syrup. Drizzle corn syrup in as you whisk, mixing until all 10 tablespoons are blended in. Press 1 tablespoon brown sugar into bottom of each ramekin, then pour custard over the ramekins, dividing it equally. Gently place ramekins into pan of hot water; bake for 35–40 minutes, or until a knife inserted all the way into the flan (halfway between edge and center) comes out clean. Remove pan from oven and take out ramekins, cooling them on a wire rack. (I use a potholder to grab the edges of the ramekins; they're hot!) Cool to room temperature; run a knife around the edges, then invert onto a small plate, making sure all the syrup comes with them! Serve cold or at room temperature. (Nice with a few fresh raspberries around the edge of the plate.)

This is a great accompaniment to breakfast, but is also a fantastic finish to a good Tex-Mex meal.

EMMELINE'S CARDAMOM BANANA BREAD

2 cups all-purpose flour
¾ tsp baking soda
½ tsp salt
½ cup sugar
½ cup brown sugar, packed
¼ cup softened butter
2 eggs
3 bananas, mashed
⅓ cup sour cream
1 tsp cardamom
⅔ cup walnuts

In a large bowl, cream sugars and butter. Add eggs one at a time, beating after each addition. Add banana, sour cream, and cardamom; beat until blended. In a separate bowl, combine flour, baking soda, and salt, stirring with a fork. Add flour mixture to banana mixture, mixing just until moist. Stir in walnuts and spoon batter into 9x5 loaf pan coated (bottom only) with cooking spray. Bake at 350° for one hour or until center springs back to touch. Cool ten minutes on wire rack, then remove from pan.

GRAY WHALE INN BREAKFAST STRATA

½ pound sausage

8 slices bread, cut into cubes (crusts removed)

¾ pound Monterey Jack cheese, grated

4 eggs

1½ cups milk

½ tsp salt

1 tsp Dijon mustard

Pinch of cayenne powder

½ tsp Worcestershire sauce

3 Tbsp butter, melted

Brown sausage in skillet, breaking it up with a fork. Drain on paper towels. Grease a 1-quart soufflé dish; arrange ⅓ of bread cubes in bottom of dish and sprinkle with ⅓ of cheese. Top cheese with all of sausage; top sausage with half of remaining bread. Sprinkle half of remaining cheese over bread, then top strata with remaining bread and press layers together slightly.

In a bowl, whisk together eggs, milk, salt, mustard, cayenne, and Worcestershire sauce. Pour over strata and sprinkle the top with remaining cheese. Drizzle with melted butter and chill, covered, one hour or overnight.

Remove from refrigerator; let stand at room temperature for 30 minutes. Put dish in a baking pan, adding enough hot water to reach halfway up sides of dish. Bake at 350° for 1 to 1½ hours, or until golden brown and set.

BARBARA HAHN'S
BERRIED MEDLEY LEMON STREUSEL MUFFINS

Streusel Topping

¼ cup melted butter

½ cup flour

2 Tbsp sugar

1½ tsp finely shredded lemon peel

Muffins

2½ cups flour

2 tsp baking powder

1 tsp baking soda

1⅓ cups sugar

1 Tbsp finely shredded lemon peel

1 egg

1 cup buttermilk

½ cup melted butter

1 Tbsp lemon juice

1½ cups (about 6 ounces) frozen berry medley (strawberries, blackberries, blueberries, and red raspberries) slightly thawed

1 Tbsp flour

Preheat oven to 400 degrees.

Stir all streusel ingredients together in a small bowl to form, soft crumbly dough. Set aside.

Whisk dry muffin ingredients and lemon peel together in medium size bowl. In a separate medium bowl, combine all liquid ingredients. Add in dry ingredients and stir until almost fully incorporated.

Cut slightly thawed large berries in pieces. Leave small berries whole. Toss berries with 1 tablespoon flour to coat, then gently fold into dough, handling only enough to incorporate berries.

Line large muffin tin with paper muffin liners. Fill each muffin tin ¼ inch from top. You will only use 9 out of 12 muffin holders. Fill empty muffin holders with water to ½ inch full.

Crumble streusel topping over each. Bake for 15 minutes, then reduce heat to 350 degrees and bake for another 10 minutes, or until lightly browned and muffin springs back when pressed lightly with fingertips. Cool for 5 minutes in muffin tin and then serve on platter.

Makes 9 large muffins.

ABOUT THE AUTHOR

Although she currently lives in Texas with her husband and two children, Karen MacInerney was born and bred in the Northeast, and she escapes there as often as possible. When she isn't in Maine eating lobster, she spends her time in Austin with her cookbooks, her family, her computer, and the local walking trail (not necessarily in that order). In addition to writing the Gray Whale Inn mysteries, Karen teaches several writing workshops and is also the author of a new paranormal romance series, which is scheduled for release in Fall 2007. You can e-mail her at karen@karenmacinerney.com or visit her online at www.karenmacinerney.com.

If you enjoyed *Dead and Berried*, read on for an excerpt from
Susan Goodwill's Kate London Mystery

Brigadoom

COMING MARCH 2007 FROM MIDNIGHT INK

ONE

"You look ridiculous, Kate," my Aunt Kitty said.

This coming from a seventy-four-year-old in a black feathered turban, yellow dance leotard, blue high-tops, and red plaid mini skirt.

I sighed and closed the door behind her. I felt ridiculous. Golf clothing was new to me, pink was not my color, and the socks, with their little pom-poms bouncing around my ankles, made me feel like the rear window of a Chevy low-rider.

Kitty and I stood in the lobby of the London family's dubious legacy, the Egyptian theatre. She handed me a Styrofoam coffee cup.

"The outfit's for Ronnie's golf outing," I said. "He picked it out."

"Well, darling, you can always divorce him," she said, maneuvering her way across the loose floor tiles behind me. "They'll get easier now that you've gone through one. By your third or fourth, you'll slide through like a hot knife through butter."

"Can we at least wait until I marry this guy?" I set my coffee on the glass top of the dusty concession stand. *If. If I marry him.*

"It's for *Brigadoon*—my own version of method acting." Kitty smiled her semi-famous, former-movie-star smile and raised a scrawny arm over her head. Her feathery headgear flapped as she shuffled her high-tops in an abbreviated Highland Fling. "Look out world. The Mudd Lake Players are back to break a few more legs."

She beamed that thousand-watt grin at me, waiting.

"They're ba-ack!" I said, but I sounded like the girl from *Poltergeist*. I tried again. "Look out world!"

Once you threw in The Mudd Lake Players, our dubious legacy became a full-fledged family curse.

A narrow shaft of sunlight flashed through the dust motes in the air between us. I looked up at a jagged opening in the ornate plaster. "I swear to God, this place has a terminal disease. That hole wasn't there yesterday."

Kitty leaned her head back and squinted at the ceiling. "At least it matches all the others," she said. "No worries, luv. The Grand Marquis'll be here at ten. He'll patch us up in plenty of time for next month's show."

The Grand Marquis, A.K.A. Morris Hirschberger, was not royalty; he was Kitty's fourth ex-husband out of seven. He drove a Grand Marquis. She had trouble keeping all their names straight, but she never forgot their cars.

Her last few words hit me, and I felt my eyes go wide. "Did you say next month? We aren't due to open for three months . . . at least."

"I've been meaning to tell you. I've consulted with my astrologer, and Roland swears all the planets and houses and whatnot will be aligned precisely on my birthday. Can you believe it? We've been rehearsing at the Senior Center."

Kitty reached in her tote bag and pulled out the local paper, the *Mudd Lake Eavesdropper*. She held it up so that I could see the back of section one.

"Surprise!" she said.

A full-page ad trumpeted the news:

LERNER AND LOEWE'S

Brigadoon

At the Egyptian Theatre
Grand Re-Opening October 10!

October tenth, Kitty's seventy-fifth birthday, was a month from today. A month? A pounding headache stomped into the space behind my eyeballs.

"Kitty, there's just no way-"

A loud crash, followed by clattering, cut me off. I trotted to the first set of doors that led to the main theatre and squinted through the dim light from the doorway.

Down on the stage the curtain moved. There was no wind in the theatre. And there were supposed to be no people. I froze.

Faint scuffling and then a tearing sound came from behind the curtain. The fabric moved again.

I reached around the corner and pulled a club out of my brand new golf bag. Clutching it, I stepped into the auditorium.

"Hey," I tried to make my voice deep, "who's down there?"

Kitty was right behind me.

"There's somebody in the theatre," I whispered, "probably kids."

She shoved her way up beside me. "Perhaps it's the Naked Bandit. Let me see!"

I kind of wanted to see the Naked Bandit myself. Word had it he snatched women's purses wearing only a ski mask and Adidas. I held Kitty back with one hand.

"Stay here," I told her and jogged down the aisle toward the stage. "You'd better be gone by the time I get there," I yelled. I brandished my seven-iron in the direction of the curtain. "I'm armed."

I stopped midway down the aisle and listened.

"If you're the Naked Bandit," Kitty trilled, "hang on a second. I've got my camera in my bag. Don't leave."

Head feathers flapping, she trotted toward the lobby.

A clatter came from behind the curtain. "Shit!" said a muffled voice. More clattering, then, "Ouch!"

A figure emerged from behind the blue velvet and ran down the stairs at stage left. I let out an involuntary yelp and my heart started doing Tae Bo kicks. I turned to run back up the aisle and almost ran over Kitty.

She held her digital camera up to her face. "Say cheese, darling!" The camera flashed in the dim light.

Nobody breathed for a few seconds, then the emergency door flew open and sunshine glared from outside. The figure wasn't naked. It was clothed from head to toe in a hooded monk's robe. I couldn't be sure, but from the back it looked like Obi-Wan Kenobi.

"Yes, that's Obi-Wan," Kitty said. "I'm certain of it."

We were back at the doorway to the auditorium, examining the digital photo on her camera.

"That outfit's from our costume rack, from the Mudd Lake Players' *The Star Wars Monologues*," Kitty said. "What a stinker that was."

There was no arguing that point.

"There's no way to tell who this is," I said. "It could be anybody."

"And, if he's naked under there, you'd never prove it by me." Kitty peered at the display. "Darn it all."

"Flip on the lights, and I'll go see if there's any damage." I started back inside, grabbing my seven-iron again just in case.

Kitty switched on the houselights and the huge art deco chandelier above the seating area came to life. I looked up. Kitty's father had ordered that chandelier from Vienna in 1926. When I was little she told me it came from an enchanted castle—a part of me still bought it. When I'd come to Kitty a bewildered little five-year-old, shattered and alone, she'd used this theatre, this magical place built by her parents, to put me back together again, to bring me back to life. Now, restoring the Egyptian was my chance to return the favor. The headache marched back with reinforcements. *A month*?

"Would you like me to call the sheriff?" Kitty asked.

My stomach did a somersault. "Nope," I headed for the wide staircase to the balcony.

I checked the seating area, then jogged back downstairs and peeked into the control booth—no signs of damage. I walked down the side aisle to the emergency exit and shoved the push bar. The steel door swung wide and slammed against the brick wall of the building. The lock had been pried apart.

I stuck my head into the narrow alley. Deserted. The wooden stairs that led up to my apartment were empty, and the steel door at the top remained untouched. Ernie was up there, and woe to the Naked Bandit who met up with my little dog.

I grabbed a rope from the wings and used it to tie the exit door shut, then I headed backstage. Aside from a few toppled scenery cutouts, everything looked untouched.

Kitty stood at the back of the theatre while I walked up front and pulled the rope that opened the huge velvet house curtain.

"Good Godfreys!" Kitty said, and under her breath, "Holey tamoley!"

I swiveled to her, saw shock on her face, and turned back. Streaks of red spray paint marred the stage floor. Cans of scenery colors lay on their sides. That must've been the clattering. One of the lids had come off a paint can and thick baby blue Latex formed a puddle across the boards.

It was then that I saw the backdrop: the idyllic Scottish hillsides cloaked in mist that I'd spent every night for the last two weeks painting. I stood for several seconds while my heart snaked its way into my shoes and tightness gripped my throat. Material hung down to the floor from deep gashes. Spray-painted obscenities covered what fabric remained on the frame: mostly references to female body parts, the oldest profession, and non-missionary style sexual positions.

Yikes.

Kitty walked down the main aisle and stood in front of the stage.

"My heavens." She held her hand over her chest, turned her head sideways, and read the obscenities. She pointed to a word. "I don't believe I've tried that one since the sixties."

I turned back to the stage and ran my finger down a slice in the canvas.

This wasn't a kid, and I guessed it wasn't the Naked Bandit either. The angry gashes and choice of words made me think this guy'd do more to women than snatch purses with a pink plastic squirt gun. And he had a knife. Suddenly, I was very glad I'd stopped halfway down the aisle.

TWO

I didn't want Kitty alone in the theatre so we cancelled the Grand Marquis, then I dropped her at the Senior Center for Yoga. I wanted to grab a fried egg sandwich at Mama's Deli but there wasn't time, so I drove toward Bramblewood Hills on the outskirts of town.

To get the Egyptian open in three months would take a minor miracle; a little over four weeks would take downright divine intervention—especially after the damage this morning. Plus, I was hungry, I was crabby, and I didn't have a clue how to play golf.

I drove under the *Buy Rite Real Estate, Where Everybody Goes Home Smiling* banner and parked my car. I slipped off my Puma Speedcats and tied the laces on my brand-new, clunky golf shoes with the little plastic points on the bottom—a gift from Ronnie. I frowned down at my feet. They looked fat and unattractive.

Now, I'm no fashionista, and I admit, I wear a lot of jeans and black sweaters, but I have a thing about my shoes. Life is too short to wear the ugly ones—or to pay full price, for that matter. If I planned to keep golfing, I'd have to go online and shop. Surely I could find a close-out on these things—at Prada, maybe?

My spikes clicked on the pavement as I walked up to the kiosk to register. Lance Beaton, Buy Rite's office manager, stepped to the counter and stood next to me—very much next to me. I took two steps to the side.

The crisp fall sunshine glared and flashed off Lance's synthetic shirt, a shiny Lycra number that featured fifties couples bowling. A carpal tunnel brace surrounded Lance's right wrist. Today's look aimed for Retro Chic, but he'd missed and touched down on Fashion Refugee.

Lance winced as he lifted green flip-up sunglasses. He squinted at me and moved closer. "I –s-s-saw the paper. Wh-wh-when are the t-t-try-outs for *Br-r-rigadoon*?"

I took a step back. "Sorry, Lance. *Brigadoon*'s already cast and in rehearsals. The Mudd Lake Players are doing the whole thing."

"Ohhh, n-n-n-no."

I knew just what he meant.

"M-m-maybe I should j-j-join the Players." He eyed me up and down and began breathing through his mouth.

I folded my arms across my chest and resisted the urge to squirm. He handed me a black Buy Rite hat with its white smiley-faced house logo and shuffled closer.

"Thanks," I said. I sidled further away. "Um, what do I do?"

Lance slid his eyes away from my chest and consulted a clipboard. "Y-y-you're on eighteen," he said and pointed toward the collection of golf carts at the back of the clubhouse.

I could feel him watching as I clacked around the building.

The golf pro strapped my clubs into a golf cart, a silent, electric model.

I hopped in, and using the little map on the back of the scorecard, followed the pro's directions to the eighteenth tee. Maybe golf would cheer me up. My buggy purred along. I was outside and not selling real estate. The birds were chirping; the sky was that crystalline blue that only happens on a sunny Michigan autumn morning. Plus, I was engaged to the perfect man.

I knew he was perfect—knew it, successful, attentive, responsible, charisma up the wazoo. I said a quick prayer to the God of Second Chances, "Please God, help me out. All I have to do is set a date."

I heard a cell phone chirp, and that's when I saw them.

My cart was so quiet, we were almost a ménage a trois before the couple in the bushes even noticed me.

"Ronnie?"

I jammed hard on the brakes and jerked to a stop. My fiancé, Mayor Ronnie Balfours, and his real estate client, Estelle Douglas, rustled around in the shrubs at the edge of the path to the seventeenth hole. At first, I thought the two of them were searching for a lost ball, but upon closer inspection, I realized the only searching they'd been doing was on each other. They looked up, two shifty-eyed deer caught in my headlights.

"Kate! Oh jeez, Kate. We were, uh . . ."

Ronnie shoved and tugged at his clothing, trying to stuff everything back where it belonged.

"Woops!" Estelle's cell phone chirped again. She put it to her ear as she began climbing upward through the shrubs and brambles.

"I was just leaving," she called over her shoulder. "Sorry, Kate."

She acted more like she'd just borrowed my putter, not taken her own personal PGA tour of my betrothed's body. Ronnie climbed down and stood on the blacktopped path directly in front of me.

Big mistake.

His normally neat blonde hair stuck out in random clumps all over his head.

"Kate?"

I glared at him. "Ronnie, I cannot believe this. You rotten . . . you cheating . . . you . . ."

There wasn't a word bad enough for how I felt about him. I banged the steering wheel and growled in frustration.

Ronnie started toward my cart, then he must've caught a good look at my eyes because he stopped dead and began backing away.

"Let's not get emotional here, Kate. I'm Mr. Right. Remember? You said so yourself." He shoved his lavender golf shirt down into his belt; it hung out on one side. "I'm still perfect for you."

Uh-huh. Now I knew why every time I tried to set a date, I felt like I did when I tried on a pair of $100 size 7 shoes marked down to ten bucks. . . . I wear an eight.

I pressed my size 8 toward the floor, and the golf cart nosed forward.

"Kate, wait—This is my golf outing for cripes' sakes. Our clients . . . my voters . . . let's reason this out . . . this is just a little—this doesn't matter." He was backing away faster now.

I thought about how Ronnie had pushed me to set a wedding date. How I'd pushed myself. My stomach rolled itself into a fist-sized knot.

"Hey Ronnie, guess what?" I yelled. "You can't be Mr. Right without fidelity. Fidelity matters. It matters a hell of a lot!" I sped up. I'd never driven a golf cart before. It was easier than I thought.

Ronnie turned and broke into a trot, stuffing again at his shirt.

"Kate, it was a mistake. Anyone can make a mistake." He tossed the words over his shoulder as he picked up speed.

"Mistake? You call that a mistake? Mashing Estelle Douglas is not a mistake, Ronnie. Spectacularly stupid, but not a mistake." I lobbed a golf ball at his head. I missed; maybe if I'd taken lessons. . . .

I finally found a good word for him.

"Ronnie, you bastard!" I yelled. My voice echoed through the valley. Other golfers got out of their carts, men in plaid pants, women in unflattering Buy Rite golf hats. They all peered in our direction.

Ronnie looked desperately from side to side. A steep, brambly hill rose to his right and the ground dropped off to his left. He stayed on the path.

"Sweetie . . . shhh . . . my vote—your clients," he climbed the incline toward the crest of the hill.

"Don't you sweetie me." Those golf carts don't go fast enough. I tried lifting my foot and jamming it down again.

We were almost to the eighteenth green. Ronnie was running now. "Kate, calm down . . . Kate, stop it . . . Help!"

Four port-o-johns were lined up, obedient soldiers at the crest of the hill. The sun peeked out from behind them. It glinted off their shiny metal doorframes and glowed through their green plastic walls.

The hill steepened, and my buggy hesitated a bit from the effort. Ronnie gulped up a second wind and ducked into the end port-o-john.

So. I ask you.

What's a girl to do?

I sat there a second or two while my whole future, my whole new life, slithered down the drain.

Well, to Hell with Mr. Right. To Hell with Buy Rite Real Estate. To Hell with it all.

I jammed my foot to the floor.

The cart jerked forward and I slammed full force into Ronnie's port-o-john. The impact rocked my head forward and there was a resounding "crack" as metal hit plastic. The sound soared through the fall sunshine and sang over the makeshift village of waiting golfers.

I froze. The potty teetered tentatively for a moment. Then, all at once it lurched over on its back like a prom queen in stilettos. A satisfying smack and a small whooshing sound spilled out. The toilet emitted a huge slosh, a gurgle, and a few rumbles. It launched itself and sledded down the grassy hill, gaining momentum as it went. From its bowels spewed a long, loud, and exceptionally flamboyant stream of swear words.

Ronnie'd always had the gift. Words I'd never even think of, he'd put together.

"Uh-oh," I muttered.

Toboggan Alley, we used to call that slope when we were kids. I got out of the cart and looked over at the clusters of people that stood on the surrounding hills. Some held their hands to their mouths in horror; a few started to snicker. Everyone peered into the sun-drenched valley.

Thanks to the natural amphitheater formed by Bramblewood's sloping terrain, there wasn't a bad view in the house. The entire course witnessed Ronnie Balfours, our mayor, my boss and ex-fiancé, climb out of the capsized port-o-potty. He looked a lot like a cosmonaut, emerging from his little green space capsule in the middle of the fairway, or perhaps more like an alien, since he was dripping with slimy blue antiseptic from head to toe.

"Kate, you bitch!" he yelled. "You're fired. Your theatre's history! Somebody call the police."

WWW.MIDNIGHTINKBOOKS.COM

From the gritty streets of New York City to sacred tombs in the Middle East, it's always midnight somewhere. Join us online at any hour for fresh new voices in mystery fiction, book club questions, author information, mystery resources, and more.

Midnight Ink promises a wild ride filled with cunning villains, conflicted heroes, hilarious hazards, mind-bending puzzles, and enough twists and turns to keep readers on the edge of their seats.

MIDNIGHT INK ORDERING INFORMATION

Order by Phone:
- Call toll-free within the U.S. and Canada at
  1-888-NITEINK (1-888-648-3465)
- We accept VISA, MasterCard, and American Express

Order by Mail:
Send the full price of your order (MN residents add 6.5% sales tax) in U.S. funds, plus postage & handling to:

Midnight Ink
2143 Wooddale Drive
Woodbury, MN 55125-2989

Postage & Handling:
Standard (U.S., Mexico, & Canada). If your order is:
$24.99 and under, add $3.00
$25.00 and over, FREE STANDARD SHIPPING

AK, HI, PR: $15.00 for one book plus $1.00 for each additional book.

International Orders (airmail only):
$16.00 for one book plus $3.00 for each additional book

Orders are processed within 2 business days. Please allow for normal shipping time.
Postage and handling rates subject to change.